Caratacus

AAG WHITEHEAD

First published in 2018 by Sharpe Books.

ISBN: 9781724123152

CONTENTS

To all the archaeologists who have worked so hard over the years to preserve the superb historical artefacts and sites across the land.

PREFACE

In the age before the Roman invasion of Britain, Brigantia was the land inhabited by the Brigantes. A British Celtic tribe which occupied the largest territory in ancient Britain, Brigantia was centred in what was later known as Yorkshire, County Durham and some of Northumberland.

Four other Celtic tribes bordered the region: to the south was the Corieltauvi, and the Cornovii, the Carvetii across the Pennines in the north-west, with another Celtic tribe known as the Parisii in the east. To the north were the lands of the Votadini, which occupied the border region of modern day England and Scotland.

The Brigantes were a large tribe, like their neighbours the Votadini; they were made up of a federation of smaller communities. The name means 'upland people' or 'hill dwellers'. This name is very apt as the Pennines formed the heart of their territory.

Some of the Brigantes welcomed the Roman masters but some openly resisted the uninvited occupation, it appears to have taken many decades for the legions to stamp the authority of Rome on the lands. In 51 AD the governor of Britain, Publius Ostorius Scapula defeated resistance leader Caratacus forcing him to seek sanctuary with the Brigante queen, Cartimandua, but she showed her loyalty to the Romans by handing him over in chains.

Following her separation from her husband Venutius, he took up arms against his ex-wife, then her Roman protectors. During the governorship of Aulus Didius Gallus he gathered an army and invaded her kingdom. The Romans sent troops to defend Cartimandua, eventually defeating Venutius's rebellion. Venutius staged another rebellion in 69 AD when great instability haunted Rome during what was called the "year of four emperors". This time the Romans were only able to send auxiliaries, who could only succeed in evacuating Cartimandua but left Venutius and his anti-Roman supporters in control of the kingdom.

The next governor Gnaeus Julius Agricola appears to have been instrumental in regaining the Brigante territory. He won great glory by systematically destroying the forts of the Brigantes, re-establishing Roman rule.

Evidence suggests there was another rebellion in the north sometime in the early reign of Hadrian, but facts are hard to come by to support this theory. One of the risings of the Brigantes has been offered as the reason for the infamous disappearance of the Ninth Legion, stationed at York. It is also suggested by some that one of the purposes of Hadrian's Wall was to keep the Brigantes from making contact and building alliances with the tribes in what is now the lowlands of Scotland, the Scoti and Picts. The Roman emperor defeated them after they began an unprovoked war against Roman allies; this is said by some to be the campaign that led to the building of the Antonine Wall. As with all occupiers the Romans no doubt had to deal with continuous insurrections, there would always be certain elements of the native population who rightly or wrongly wanted rid of the unwelcome guests.

From the 2nd century A.D. onwards Romano-Britain now found itself under attack from barbarians tribes living outside the Roman Empire. Britain having been mainly subdued now relied on the Roman army and navy for defence.

A few hundred years later, even more barbarian tribes were attacking Rome but this time in other parts of the empire. Emperor Honorius decided that the Roman legions in Britain were needed elsewhere. The Roman Empire needed to shrink so it could consolidate its armies so the occupation of Britain ended. The troops were withdrawn, exposing Britain to barbarian raids from the North, East and West. Flavius Stilicho, was the general mainly responsible for overseeing the withdrawal of Roman forces from Britain.

During this period known as Roman Britain, new evidence unearthed by archaeologists, confirm that gladiatorial contests were taking place at the largest amphitheatres in this country. The recent finds during the excavating at the arena in Chester provide conclusive evidence that it played host to the well known gruesome fights to the death for public gratification, that have been long portrayed by popular fiction. Eighty burials unearthed in York in a large cemetery on the outskirts of the Roman town of Eboracum, across the river from the legionary fortress also add to the weight of evidence. The male skeletons displayed extensive trauma, in the form of decapitation, amongst other injuries, suggesting these were in fact a group of gladiators, who lived, fought and died in York during the Roman occupation.

In Rome itself, these fighters were celebrated by both the high and low classes of society, their value as entertainers being commemorated throughout the Roman world. Gladiators became big business for trainers and owners, for politicians wanting to gain in stature and those who had reached the top and wished to stay there. Roman gladiator combatants reflected the sponsor's requirements; whether that was to exaggerate their own part in some great victory or to win support from some senior general through flattery it was as theatrical as it was bloody. Splendidly, exotically armed and armoured barbarians, from across the empire would re-enact events or just simply fight one another; it was even a way to execute criminals. One thing was for sure it would be a spectacle that packed in the crowds. The trade in gladiators was empire-wide with Rome's military success producing a ready supply of soldier-prisoners who were redistributed for use in state mines, amphitheatres and for sale on the open market.

To add something a little more exotic female gladiators or gladiatrix were used for the exceptionally lavish events. It is suspected that these female fighters probably followed the same codes, career paths and training disciplines, although probably slightly less strenuous regimes, as their male counterparts. Very little information as ever has been found about them, other than a few inscriptions and records written by Rome's elite.

If a gladiator distinguished himself bravely in a particular fight or, at some periods during Roman history, had won five fights he could be granted his freedom and where better to distinguish yourself than the Coliseum in front of fifty to eighty thousand adoring spectators.

The Anglo-Saxon settlement of Britain describes the process which saw the withdrawal of the Roman occupiers and the arrival of the Germanic tribes such as the Jutes, Angles and the Saxons. This was by no means a smooth transition as all were motivated by gain and did not particularly relish the prospect of sharing. Add to this the native Britons and one can see why the country was about to enter the "dark ages".

Prior to the arrival of any nations settlers there is a period of tumultuous upheaval as their warriors battle to make a homeland for themselves and it is fair to say that the Romans were having to deal with not only insurrection by the local tribes but by the Scoti and Picts in the north as well as the probing raiders from across the sea. This threat was real enough for the Roman Emperor Constantine I to have the Saxon Shore military command set up. This was a 3rd century series of defensive fortifications on both sides of the English Channel, led by the grandly titled, "Count of the Saxon Shore". Several Saxon Shore forts survive in east and south-east England to this date.

Caratacus.

Caratacus was the son of the local chieftain. His father, Conorus had resisted the Romans from the day he had been born as his father had before him. He had named his son after a great Brigante resistance leader from years earlier. It was no surprise that the young warrior hated the Romans as he did. With every breath he took, every stride he made, Caratacus was trained to fight.

His father had taken the position of chieftain by means of force, killing the previous leader when he showed an inclination to make peace with their mortal enemy. His father had been a giant of a man and it had not been much of a fight as the two had squared off to each other. His unusual height (well over six foot) allowed him to bring his mighty war axe down with ever increasing velocity and backed by his considerable bulk it struck with devastating force. The old chief was out of his depth and the first blow had been met by his shield, offered up against the onslaught but it only withstood the first blow and was split in two. He had tried to counter with his Roman style Gladius, thrusting a straight jab aiming its point into his assailants gut only to have it smashed backwards by a heavy shield that most men would have had trouble holding up, let alone fight with. Caratacus had watched his father build his forward momentum driving the old chief into an ever failing and desperate defence. Even the massive shield, rammed forward with such force became an offensive weapon and used, as his father had been able to do, in conjunction with his wielding of the double edged axe it was almost unstoppable for one man. With his shield broken in two

6

and lying on the floor the falling axe had nothing but a forearm to deflect its path. The clear noise of bone snapping like a dry twig rang out a split second before being drowned by the fatal crack as the skull was sliced open, the axe blade burying itself deep, bringing the end of the chief's reign.

Caratacus instinctively knew what to do, even though he was just a young warrior at the time. He moved forward and stood alongside his father, Conorus's followers did the same as they circled facing the rest of the village, daring anybody to come forward and challenge their new leader. After a few seconds of silence one man, not from the tribe but a Druid from a near extinct race had stepped forward lifting his staff into the air and chanting something in a foreign tongue, followed by a shrill cry and this brought a supportive cheer of the remainder of the village, all except for the dead man's son and wife. She led her young boy back to the largest circular hut in the fortified stockade, home of the village leader and no longer hers, where she awaited her fate.

The evenings celebration had followed the more solemn burning of the defeated mans corpse. A leader killed in battle or dying of natural causes who had led with distinction would get a much more privileged send off. But he had been over thrown and found no such favour, he would be sent to the goddess Brigantia in disgrace and nothing would be left of his legacy. His wife new well enough her future was uncertain and more so that of her son, she had already sent him away to hide until their future was made clear.

After the feast Caratacus had watched his father take his prizes. They had firstly moved into the chieftain's hut. His mother had died of fever several years earlier and had experienced his father's appetite for women as he had regularly listened to him humping many different young girls some not much older than him. When they had both moved

7

into the main hut his father's attention had been drawn to the women who cowered in the shadows.

"Where is the boy?" he questioned in an uncaring manner that did nothing to put her at ease.

"I have sent him away my lord," She trembled in reply.

She had kept the fire well stoked and fed with logs so it gave off plenty of light and heat, hoping that by performing the tasks of the woman of the house she might find a kind reception.

"Come over here into the light so I can look at you," he demanded.

She stood in the centre of the room, next to the flickering flames so she could be examined as if she was a stock animal waiting for a decision on her fate, useful or not; dead or alive. It all hung in the balance at that very moment.

Although the old chief had been well past his best it had not stopped him from taking a new bride just five years earlier when she like most brides had been no older than fourteen when he had married her. This made her approximately the same age as Caratacus.

She was a good looking woman with a firm, rounded figure. Giving birth to just the one child three years ago had not ruined her shape and it was this that Caratacus thought had saved her.

He watched his father stand up and move towards her. She had dropped her fur shroud off her shoulders so as to give the best possible presentation of herself as she also new this was the moment that would define her future. His father had roughly stripped her naked and had walked round her as a farmer might check the condition of a new addition to his herd. He walked up behind her and taking one of her breasts in a great hand he grabbed her sex with the other, probing his giant fingers deep inside her so as to cause her to cry out in what seemed to the young observer as the mixture of shock, pain and relief as she obviously knew that he wanted her. Conorus worked his hands around her bare breasts while he continued to thrust his penetrating attention between her legs. Aengir, as she was called had started to lose some of her fear and inhabitations as she found security and some pleasure in the attention that her husband's killer was bestowing on her. Her cries had become timed to the strokes of his huge hand and grew in ardour as his hand speed increased. Her final and most lustful cry was followed by Conorus spinning her round to face him and forcing her down on to her knees as he started to undo his breeches. He did not need to. Aengir was experienced enough to know what was expected of her so she deftly moved in and opened them up exposing his manhood which she took in her mouth. They disappeared behind a curtain of furs that provided a little privacy. Whether she enjoyed the next hour or so was hard for Caratacus to know but she put a good performance up if she didn't. Either way it secured her place in the hut for the coming few weeks if nothing else.or Caratacus it was the beginning of a new chapter in his life. Not only was this women to become his step mother he was about to gain a younger brother. More importantly for his status as a warrior and future leader he had been notice by the strange Druid who had arrived in their village a few months earlier and had had the inhabitants spell bound by his tales of mysticism and the power of mother earth.

Amergin Gluingel, to give him his full name, was more simply known as Gluingel and moved around wearing a full length robe of dirty grey. It neither looked clean or dirty nor did it ever get any worse or better. A thickly spliced necklace was formed by a series of thin oak vines and mistletoe twisted beneath his long white beard and sometimes it appeared that there were things living amongst the combination of plant and facial hair. On his head he wore a matching wreath which sat on top of limp white hair that blended into the beard below. From within his robes he could bring forth a small leather pouch from which he managed to reveal an unbelievable amount of produce only useful to a man of magic and medicine. But of all the most striking features about Gluingel it was his eyes. They penetrated where or who they fell upon and being of different colours the brown and blue with a thin, silver/white circle around the coloured centres they set most people on edge causing nervous fidgeting when in the stranger's presence.

Immediately after seeing the young Caratacus stand by his victorious father, Gluingel had taken him to his heart as if something was telling him to steer the young man, and that he did. The very day after his father's victory he was out hunting in the nearby dense ancient forest after several hours of sword and spear practice with his father. The old Druid had watched the giant man never spare his son as he time and again reinforced the young man's mistakes by painful rebukes with the flat of the sword. But he liked what he saw; Caratacus got up every time without a word of complaint and went back to the lesson. It was Conorus who called a halt to the proceedings as the young lad had worn the great man down.

Caratacus was stalking something in the dense undergrowth. It was just out of clear sight and every time he drew a little closer to improve his view it moved off maintaining the tantalisingly obscured vision that kept moving him deeper and deeper, hooked and without him realising he was being played like a fish on a line.

Caratacus suddenly felt he was no longer alone, something was circling him; the hunter had become the hunted. The hairs on the back of his neck stood up and he could feel his heart start to ready itself for action as it pumped the blood around his body quicker than normal even though he had seen nothing to raise its rate. Looking around he realised he did not recognise his surroundings. That was strange as he had grown up in this forest and knew almost every tree intimately. But every one of these great oaks that trialled tendrils of mistletoe from every branch was new to him, these mighty arboreal kings had nearly blocked all the daylight so he had to rely on his hearing rather than his eyes to keep up with the beast that prowled in what seemed to be a decreasing circle.

It had stopped directly in front of him, just the other side of a particularly thick cascade of mistletoe that was hanging down from a stand of Alder trees. He still had not been able to get a clear view of his adversary but know knew it was within spear throwing distance. He drew his arm back readying himself, drawing on all his might so as to propel the spear as hard as he could. Suddenly without knowing why, he dropped his arm lowering his only defence against the unseen foe, giving up his chance to strike the very thing that had been stalking him.

"Why do you not strike, Caratacus?" The voice had him almost leap into the lower limp of the nearest oak in fright. It was Gluingel.

When he had regained a little composure he whispered with his heart still leaping in bounds, "I was not sure whether whatever it is wanted to do me harm and I certainly don't know if it is a prey animal that I would want to hunt."

"Wise words, for one so young. You need to know your friends and your enemies before you make any move in this world. See. Look through the veil of green elixir that can clear the mind and prepare the body." The old man was talking in riddles but that wasn't anything new, he was pointing to the drape of mistletoe which screened him from his quarry.

Slowly Caratacus reached forward with his right hand pulling a handful of the vine to one side. He was speechless.

"I am Becuille, I have been watching you," the most beautiful girl he had ever seen was reaching out to him and touched the hand he still held the mistletoe back with. She had a ring that she slid down his first finger and as it moved over his knuckle it seemed to tighten so it fit as if made for him.

Caratacus looked round to get some sort of reassurance from the Druid but he had disappeared as silently and quickly as he appeared. The girl reached out with her other hand taking his free hand that hung loosely by his side still hold the spear which he dropped as she took hold of him. He walked, led by the hands by this vision of magnificence, through the curtain of shrouding mistletoe and once on the other side it was as if he had entered another world. The near darkness was lit by golden sunbeams that projected through the forest canopy catching the glittering tree pollen that was so heady that he felt lightheaded.

He had no idea how far they walked, but she led the way until they came into a small clearing where he saw a pool of iridescent green water fed by a water fall tumbling off a huge granite slab that towered above them. He started to concentrate his mind looking at his captivating host. She was wearing a long flowing gossamer thin white dress that trailed along the ground but had not become dirty unlike the robe of the Druid. A broad black rope was round her narrow waist holding the two sides of the wrap around dress together, their ends hanging down her front swaying as she walked. Her hair was the lightest golden and reflected the sunbeams as they danced in the flowing curls that reach down to the base of her back. A braid of her luscious hair from either side of the her forehead was swept back and tied together by mistletoe which was interwoven through the platted locks and was rich with white berries that matched the colour of her robe. He could now see that she was not a young girl, but a young woman with all the attributes that one would have. Her skin was perfect and pale, her delicate features, having a balance that gave complete symmetry to a face that showed an innocence that needed protecting. Looking down her body from the side, he saw the profile view of her small breasts that were topped by up turned nipples that stood firmly pressing through the thin material that clung, smothering them. From just below these gorgeous orbs there were dark patterns that he could not make out but they hugged her flat stomach and continued down the top of each thigh.

She continued to guide him towards the waterfall, where without faltering she passed through the torrent of plunging water.

"Amergin Gluingel, I have brought your pupil." They had passed under this column of water but neither of them was wet. She looked as pristine as she had seconds earlier, as she spoke for the first time since she had introduced herself she was looking into the depths of a large cave. It glowed orange from a large fire that roared away in the centre of the area that very surprisingly was not filled with smoke. A large halved tree trunk rested on two chunky logs creating a table with more logs placed around serving as seats filled one side of the cave on the other was a mass of tree roots that wove themselves into a huge bowl that were lined with thick matting like moss and a few animal furs. More roots spread across the back wall and had been used as shelving by the old Druid who was working to mix some concoction from heaps of leaves and grasses amongst other things.

Very good Becuille my dear can you sit him down then take this and mix it with mother earth's live giving tears. A speechless, Caratacus was led to one of the large logs and without complaint sat down as the old man had instructed. Becuille glided over to the Druid and took a rough clay fired goblet and moved to fill it with water from the fall.

"And now the tears of the daughter of a goddess, if you please," he said as he watched over the proceedings.

The goblet was brought up to her eyes and without reason from both eyes came a stream of orange glowing liquid, coloured by the flickering flames. With just a hand gesture from the Druid, she presented it to Caratacus who without giving it a second thought drank the potion.

"Now you are prepared internally, we need you ready externally, once again came a hand gesture and as directed she took him by the hand back under the cascading water. He was suddenly shocked as the coolness of the water hit him and the power of the water crashed down on his head. Instead of leading him off to the side where they had entered from, they left straight through the middle of the wall of water. He was immediately knee deep in water but felt warm hands squeeze him giving gentle encouragement to follow her. As they both reappeared on the other side he, like she, was dripping wet, her once gentle curls plastered to her head, but it was not her hair that got his attention. Her robe was now see-through and what his imagination had been working hard to paint in his mind was clearly visible.

She approached him and started to remove his clothes and instinctively he pulled on the rope belt which slid easily untying itself before floating way. They were standing near enough to the tumbling water for stray streams of the effervescing liquid to drive her robe apart and off her shoulders. She was completely unperturbed as she bent down and removed his breeches, having already bared his chest. When she had finished undressing him she stood up and was also as naked as he was.

"Let the cleansing waters of the mother wash away your earthly chains and ready you for the enlightenment of the gods." With cupped hands she started to pour water over him and then wash him using her hair that had increase to twice its original length now it was flattened, wet.

He could not contain himself. He had never experienced anything so erotic before. Sure he had experimented with some of the girls of the village and in doing so had felt his excitement grow but nothing like this. He seemed to be building so much pent up fervour he was getting ready to burst.

She stopped, and then once again taking his hands she formed them into a cup and indicated he was to do the same to her. As he washed her down he now saw that the mysterious dark patterns he had observed through the thin robe were green painted feathery fingers of ferns that grew up her legs and spreading across her stomach coming to a supporting rest under her breasts with just one frond reaching up to touch each red, hard nipple. She guided him to carry on until all traces of the vascular green leaves had been sponged and her body pure of all but her blemish free skin. For all she was a fully developed woman there was no sign of the hair that grew between the legs of other women and it all added to the mystic, sensual anticipation that had not allowed Caratacus's state of excitement to diminish.

She led him back inside the cave the ache from his manhood growing even when he walked under the cooling shower. Fortunately Gluingel had once again disappeared and they made their way to the huge bowl of roots mosses and furs, where she positioned him on his back in the most comfortable bed he had ever laid. Still standing she straddled him positioned so he looked up directly at the mound of her sex with her breasts just visible above. Engulfing his hardness with her warm wetness she rocked back and forth growing into a wild carefree animal from the demure young girl as her movements got ever more demanding.

The young man had never actually had full sex before but even so he knew this was not the normal way of things. He knew that this was no regular woman but he was not complaining.

When Caratacus woke Becuille was laying beside him, a picture of sleeping innocence and naked splendour. The fire still raged and the whole cavern was soaked in a warm orange glow.

"At last the young man is rid of his slumber and has carried out his duty!" It was Gluingel, sitting on the floor cross legged on the far side of the fire.

The Druid stood, "Well come on we have no time to delay, we have only one moon for you to be trained as a warrior and there is much to do. If you think you have learnt anything from your father you are in for a big surprise."

Hopping on one leg, pulling on his breeches and grabbing his shirt he followed the old man outside the cave.

Firstly you are now ready to shed the body of a boy and with hard work it will be replaced by the physique of Taranis himself. He moved over to a fallen tree stump. It was at least the diameter of a full pace whilst being four or five paces long. The Druid position Caratacus at the narrower end of the great lump of timber.

"Well get hold of it and lift it above your head," he commanded.

It was an impossible task. Even his father with his mighty strength could not hope to move such a weight let alone lift it above his head.

"I can't do that. It would take ten men to move that. It is physically impossible."

"Ahh, physically impossible, he says so what if your physical state is enhanced by your inner mental strength?" the Druid had a smile on his face.

"Maybe you are right we need to build up to this," he pointed at the stump and then moved to another similar trunk that was half the size.

"But that's ...."

The Druid had brought his hand up signalling his immediate silence. "You never face an obstacle with a negative thought. Stand!" he pointed to the end of the fallen tree. "Close your eyes and see in your mind, you lifting this unimaginable weight, believe it to be happening and it will."

Caratacus did as he was told and he could actually visualise himself lifting the weight. He bent at the knees and heaved. He felt a momentary reddening of his face and the tension across his shoulders and down his back into his legs. His eyes were tightly shut and he heard Gluingel's words again.

"See it rising from the ground, paint the picture in your head and your heart will make it happen."

He had a vision, it was of himself lifting the huge timber weight to his chest and then repositioning himself before throwing it above his head and standing below it, his arms locked. But the tension had gone from his body; he could no longer feel his face burning in the impossible effort. He opened his eyes the surprise was shocking but also impressive. Caratacus stood underneath the hefty object his arms locked supporting the vast weight.

"Lower it to your chest and press it back into position," came the order.

He spent the next hour heaving the trunk up and down exercising every muscle in his body that he knew of and some he didn't.

"Enough! Time for a short rest and some more of mother earth's nourishment."

Becuille arrived carrying a goblet of the elixir he had drunk before. He downed it in one and she led him to the pond. Once again they went through the same sexually charged cleaning process. As she removed her robe he saw that the fern paintings had returned so he needed no encouragement to wash then away. He was taken back inside the cave and she performed with the same passion as the first time growing wilder as she approached her zenith.

When he woke the old man was there again and took him outside for his combat lessons. From the darkest depths of the wood appeared a cloaked figure. The full length, heavy hooded garment was fastened across the neck down the chest and all the way to the floor. The hood was hanging forward, hiding the wearers face. In fact no actual body part could be seen, the sleeves were longer than its arms so the shield and sword hands dwelled out of sight. His opponent never said a word; he just wielded his sword and hammered at Caratacus's shield, blocking his puny attempts to counter. From sword they went to axe and then to spear. Darkness came and still they continued. Why was he not tired?

Gluingel clapped his hands causing Caratacus to turn and look round, realising he had dropped his guard he instantly turned back to face his foe. He had disappeared.

"That is enough of the heavy work, now it is time for speed and agility."

The bemused young man followed but his seemingly boundless energy although very gratifying was also mystifying, "Gluingel what am I doing here and why am I capable of such feats of strength and stamina?"

The old Druid stopped in his tracks and turned to look at him. "Are you not enjoying yourself?"

"Why yes, but.."

"Well then," the old man cut him off, "don't ask stupid questions. Just when I was growing to like you, you start asking stupid questions and spoil it. This way!" he moved back into the cave.

The table had been moved into the middle of the floor. Becuille stood on top of the table with a light staff in her hands. The old man pushed another staff into his hands; it was three times the size of hers.

"Up you go, this will teach you to ask stupid questions."

When he stood facing her he smiled warmly and the end of her shaft rapped down on his foot. He hopped backwards as she spun the staff round her head with lightning speed, cracking him over the echoing skull. He stopped hopping and shook his head trying to stop it from spinning. He had no wish to hurt his lover but he wanted her to stop before he lost his temper so he pushed his staff forward to keep her at the other end of the table. Before he had even managed to get it in position she had taken off into the air spinning through a full summersault and twist and landed behind him jabbing him in the back of the knee causing the joint to buckle. With an almighty crash he was on the floor.

"You need to look at your opponent and see the slightest twitch of the muscle that will tell you where they will move next. Absorb every fraction of the image that stands before you so you sense the change in their stance, the shifting of the weight before they make their move and thus you can anticipate it and counter." This went on for another hour until the old man clapped his hands once again.

Caratacus was given another drink of the potion and the two young lovers went out to wash in the pond, ending back in bed with Becuille on top of him straddling his manhood. When he tried to change their position so he could ride her, she just clamped down on him screaming like a banshee, riving back and forth only dropping off to one side as she finished her climax and having drawn his last seed.

The next day the entire process was repeated, the only difference was that when he entered the pond with Becuille he could see in his reflection an unbelievable transformation in his physique. She could also, when she straddled him in their sexual bouts she ran her hands across his broadening chest and bulging arms. This went on for so many days he lost count and during the whole time the only nourishment he had was the elixir that contained Becuille's tears. And she still did not allow him on top during the regular and frantic love making.

Caratacus woke; he had managed to grow a beard during his stay, no mean feat for an eighteen year old. He felt the tightness of his skin pulled across the ever growing muscles, he liked how his new body felt and he knew his diminutive lover who slept by his side did by the time she spent stroking and massaging them as they made love.

"Caratacus we need to move fast," it was the Druid and this signalled a departure from the daily training regime he had grown used to. "There are three Picts in the forest watching your village we need to intercept them so they do not take their information back to their tribe."

Abruptly the training made sense and the thought of taking on three warriors brought no fear into his heart. For an old man the Druid could move fast and silent and he guided Caratacus to the edge of the forest not far from his village. He was back in familiar territory and recognised landmarks within the wood. He could not understand why it had taken such a short space of time to get back into these well trodden paths as he had been in a totally alien place for so many days. But now was not time for questions. Gluingel was pointing to a series of boulders that he knew as the "Hurling Stones" as tales told of giants having hurled them into their current place. The three spies were hidden from the village but from his vantage point he had a side on view of the blue painted wildlings.

"Caratacus we need one alive," was all that the old Druid said.

The rocks were just on the tree line. It enabled Caratacus to get behind them and start to close in on his prey. Slowly using one tree at a time he drew nearer, he could sense the placing of each foot fall ensuring he avoided any dry vegetation that would cry out in complaint if he stood on it, all the time his focus fixed on the men ahead. When he was no more than ten paces away he hefted the spear back behind his head, using the full length of his arm and its new found power to propel it with such force that he heard the tip strike to rock that the first enemy warrior was leaning against. Straight between his shoulder blades it hit with such venom it caused his arms and legs to flatted spread-eagling him and sending his weapon sliding along the rock alarming the other two to his presence. He was up and running before the two startled men could really react the drove his battle axe into the second mans chest, simultaneously smashing his shield into the third's face. Two dead and one unconscious in the blink of an eye.

"Good lad you remembered. This one is required to finish your training." Where the old Druid had come from he had no idea, but he had stopped trying to fathom out the mystical powers of Amergin Gluingel. What he meant by required to finish his training he did not both to question as he would only get a tangled web of non-sense that the old man always spun when he asked him anything.

From seemingly nowhere the Druid had produced a good length of twisted ivy and mistletoe vine and bound the Pictish prisoner by his feet and hands. "Right over your shoulder and we will be away to the cave," was the matter of fact order that he gave Caratacus.

"Can I not just run down to the village and let them know I am alright and warn them they are being watched?" he pleaded.

"No time for that, we have only one more day for your training and power building before the new moon. After that we will see if you have made the gods happy. Tonight you must build your body through your cock once again."

They trudged back into the darkest recesses of the forest and just like the first time he had made the trip it seemed to take a long time, far longer than it had taken him to get back to the village. The dead weight on his shoulder hardly felt a burden which was surprising as even for a Pict this one was quite large. As he walked he was trying to fathom all that had happened to him over the last few weeks. Moon beams projected dancing, silver rays through the canopy and in the strange eerie night light he noticed that the arm that was supporting the body over his shoulder was tensed. His muscles were massive, he was aware that he had been undergoing a strange metamorphous but this was staggering. As he walked he felt light on his feet but still the muscles in his legs seemed to flex and become rock solid with his motion, indicating they too matched his arms muscular size.

Caratacus had no idea where he was but suddenly they stood in the opening by the pond, the waterfall bathed in the silver lunar sheen. He looked up to the sky as a brilliant flaring light trailed across the darkness its radiance such that it put the other stars to shame.

He nearly walked into the stationary Druid who had seen where his attention had been. "Impressive, no?"

"What is it?"

"A message from the gods, there will be many more tomorrow night, mark my words."

The prisoner had started to come too. He had been tied to a tree at the edge of the clearing, his arms pulled backwards and lashed round the trunk. His feet and knees were also fixed together but bent backwards so he was kneeling. Caratacus was standing in front of him when he opened his eyes and all that was in them was pure hatred for his captor. That was until he saw Gluingel and even his blue painted face seemed to pale as utter fear flooded his face.

"Here lad you need to drink," he pointed to Becuille who was offering the goblet. He downed it as he had done the hundreds before and was led by this beautiful nymph into the pond where the pre-hump washing took place. He had noticed for the last week the painted ferns on her body seemed to have spread and took a little more time to wash of. But hey, that was a small price to pay for what was to come!

The next day they seemed to pack even more into the day and as he lay next to Becuille after their second bout of coupling where yet again she had refused to allow him on top he heard chanting that penetrated the background noise of the crashing of the waterfall.

It was dark when he walked outside to find the old Druid looking up to the sky standing in front of the prisoner who was now tied to the large tree trunk that he had not tried to lift since his first day. But it was stood up right next to the pond, thus so was the terrified Pictish warrior. The embers of a fire were smouldering to one side.

"I live with the moon." The old man raised his arms.

"I live with the stars," as soon as his words had left his mouth a shower of the night flares raced across the sky.

"I cherish the earth as she cherishes me," his arms swept down, gesturing to the ground.

"I am the trees, I am the waterfall, I am the air that you breathe."

In a flash he had an axe in his hand and had sliced the prisoner from one side of the abdomen to the other. Unbelievably he was still alive while at the same time his guts were on the floor. Gluingel studied the entrails and nodded his approval. He beckoned to Caratacus, immediately Becuille took him by the hand and they approached the gruesome sight. Hand in hand the intestine was wrapped, binding the pair up to the elbow. The old man ripped out the liver and took a bite out of it before offering the same to Becuille. There was no hesitation and it was his turn.

In should have been an abhorrent prospect but for some reason he was drawn to follow suit without any second thought. He felt the soft, warm textured meat melt in his mouth and he greedily took a second and third bite. By the expression on the other two blood soaked faces his actions were well received.

"I am the wolf, I am the bear, I am the eagle," he old man reached up into the chest cavity and tore free the still beating heart and showed it to the sky. Another deluge of glittering flares shot overhead as the fading embers of the fire burst into life. Once again he took the first bite, Becuille the second. It was as though the taste of meat for the first time in weeks had resurfaced a deeply hidden hunger, because as it was passed to Caratacus he devoured it like a wolf would bolt its kill before any rival could take it.

The Pict was still slightly moving as Gluingel took some embers from the re-energised blaze and stuffed it into the empty cavern that had been so recently the torso of the warrior from the north.

"He is your servant, he is the appointed one and he will return to defeat the coming tides." With that final line to his incantation he turned to Caratacus. "You are ready, hurl the trunk into the water," he pointed to the pond. The smaller trunk had become his daily test of strength and he performed countless repetitions of such a move that it had become automatic but this was a different proposition it was far greater in size and it had the remnants of the man attached to it. The ease with which it flew into the water did not surprise him, why he did not know because it should have. Five men could not have performed such a manoeuvre.

"Accept this sacrifice, killed threefold as the ancients would have it. Blade, fire and water. Give your final blessing on this man of the earth."

Becuille was standing by his side with the goblet. After draining it they bathed as usual and entered the cavern. But instead of the usual move towards the bed she climbed the table taking her staff in her hand and throwing his to him. He faced her and watched intently, he could see the rise and fall of that beautiful chest, and he saw a finger twitch on her lower hand, as her shoulder just fractionally dipped as she was preparing to strike. With the speed of a snake strike his staff jabbed forward striking hers between her hands and snapped it. He fainted left and moved right and was behind her before she could react. He dropped his staff and lifted her by the waist and threw her on to the bed. This time there was only going to be one on top and as he ripped her robe off he sank between her legs burying himself in her warmth. As he roughly thrust he felt her legs curl round his back and her arms round his neck pulling him deeper into her.

In the morning when he woke he turned to face the woman he had humped for hours the previous night. He wanted to see if she wore the usual pleased expression he had noted when she had led the sexual dance. She was nowhere to be seen. He was lying next to a smouldering fire in an area of the forest that he knew so very well, just a few hundred paces from the village.

That had been several years ago and his return to the village had been greeted with great celebration. It appeared that all of them, including his father had known he had been chosen by the Druid for the training from the three gods: Tuetates; the tribal protector whose name was carved into the ring he had been given during his first encounter with Becuille. Esus, the deity who gathered the wood of the forest with his war axe to give protecting heat and light to his people. Finally, Taranis, God of Thunder, who gave power and stamina in battle as well as guiding the believer's weapons in battle ensuring they struck true. It was these three that demanded the sacrifice of threefold death.

Even though his father had known of what Gluingel intended he was still amazed in the physical transformation his young son had undergone in just the span of one moon. The chief knew he was no longer the strongest man in the village but his son's loyalty was never in question and it ensured his position as chieftain.

Caratacus had not finished his training with Gluingel. He was to spend many more days walking in the forest listening to the Druid talk, sometimes it seemed to be nothing other than riddles, whereas other times it was very powerful and philosophical explaining about his part in the way of the earth and how he had given his seed to the daughter of the Woodland Goddess Flidais so mother earth could be reborn. They would also talk of war strategies and using stealth as well as natural features to gain advantages. It was clear from what he learnt that there was a greater purpose to his tutorage but all the old man said about that was that he would travel far and wide and be given the sternest tests before he would return to face the scourge of Britannia.

It was following one of these days of enlightenment that they returned to the village to find a commotion at his father's hut. One of his bodyguards came running up to Caratacus and Gluingel when they saw them enter the stockade.

"Conorus has been wounded by a boar tusk while out hunting; he had his leg skewered by the beast but still hung on to it and held it fast before we managed to spear it. I fear it has done him great injury."

They both moved quickly to see the damage. It was not good; the tusk had taken the flesh and muscle off his lower leg from the side baring the bone. Gluingel sent everybody but Caratacus and Aengir outside. His men had bound the wound tightly but it was the old man's knowledge of medicine that had Caratacus tie the rope around the leg above the knee that actually arrested the bleeding. Aengir was put to work fetching herbs from the forest and boiling water while the enchantments of foreign invocations streamed from Gluingel, all Caratacus could do was watch.

"There is a small unit of the Frisiavones from Lavatre (Bowes) moving down towards Vinovia (Binchester) they have no cavalry and number just fifty auxiliaries." The messenger was slightly confused as he was delivering his message to Caratacus and not his chief, Conorus.

Gluingel was at Caratacus's side and advised him, "That is a small number and without cavalry the auxiliary would be a soft target. We should be able to gather at least one hundred warriors without delay."

"Where were they when you set off with this information?" asked Caratacus.

"They were not ready to set off when I left, so should have only travelled a short distance."

"So how do you know they have no cavalry with them?" quizzed the sharp chief's son much to the pleasure of the old

Druid who already saw the seeds of his strategy training paying off.

"All the cavalry with some infantry set out for Luguvaliun (Carlisle) three days ago. There will be just a small garrison left to man the fort after the unit get down to Vinovia."

"Considering how long it took you to ride down to here, how far will they get before we meet them if we set of immediately?" Caratacus continued his shrewd questioning. Again the Druid smiled at his pupil.

"They should have just dropped off the great fell near the Forest of the Gaunless if we move now."

Get the men ready to move immediately we can intercept them before they get near to the fort at Vinovia and after a few hours marching they will have little spring in their step and even less enthusiasm for a fight.

Conorus was barely conscious when his son came to report to him. Caratacus wasn't sure if he actually understood what he was saying but did feel a slight tightening of his grip as he held his hand. He did not look well and Caratacus wondered if he would still be alive by the time he returned.

Every warrior in the village was on the move and a runner had pre-warned the neighbouring village to be ready to join them. Caratacus estimated he should get to the ambush site he had in mind at least one if not two hours before the Roman unit arrived. The few village tribes that Conorus ruled had few horses and they were used by the men stationed at all the major Roman garrisons to bring news of any movement. It had served his people well and had allowed them to disappear many times when their enemy had tried to launch attacks on the strongholds that still refused to acknowledge Rome's authority over them. But just as it had done that day it gave opportunities to pick of small isolated groups that rather stupidly ventured out without the adequate backup. That was the very issue that troubled Caratacus.

"Why would they be moving in such a small group, especially when they have already weakened their garrison strength by sending their cavalry to Luguvaliun?" he asked his mentor.

"I can't think why they should do such a thing. You might want to send your rider back and keep an eye on things, especially watching their rear in case they are trying to lure you out and actually have a larger force in close support?" he answered as he rubbed his dirty white beard which demonstrated his concern. "We must tread carefully and ensure we have a safe route to retreat to if something was to happen."

All the warriors were on foot so it took a few hours at a fast pace to get into position on the upper slopes of the forest which swept down the valley side. As his men rested teacher and pupil examined the ambush site. Gluingel letting the lad talk through how he wanted the trap to unfold.

"We will come down from the high ground and push them down the hillside where we will have the other half of our force waiting. Once they are running they will not have time to react when the second wall of warriors appear in front of them."

"And where do you propose to close the trap?" asked the old man.

"In the centre of the forest, so they have the greatest distance to run to escape."

"I can see the logic in that but would you not consider using the latter part of the forest? After all that means they will have been marching through the darkness of the forest for much further and their nerves will be fraying. Once they start to think they are nearing the end of the danger area they are much more likely to drop their guard and be caught unawares?"

Caratacus nodded his understanding, thankful that if his father wasn't by his side he did have this wily old fox. That was something else he had learnt that day as he seemed to pickup vital snippets of useful tactics constantly; psychology of warfare was as important as the weapons and numbers involved.

The first man through the trap was their own rider and he reported that he had circled round the unit and had not seen any signs of support troops. He was sent back out to continue his watch.

A few men were hidden in the tree line and watched the small Roman column march into the shadows of the forest. Waiting until they were well inside the near impenetrable mass of giant pines they shut off the escape route and trailed their foe at a suitable distance. The old man was right in his prediction, every legionary seemed tense and expecting the worst. Furtive head glances accompanied their forward march as every man seemed to be sensing that the shadows hid a killer behind every tree. Of course it did, but not until they had started to see the beams of sun light increasing through the canopy and by that time their mood seemed lighter, their attention being plainly fixed on the road ahead. The small cohort had been on the go for eight hours by this time and still had a further two hours before they would be safe in the fort at Vinovia. They knew they were approaching the last leg of their journey and when they left the dark arboreal surroundings behind them they would be close to safety. The anticipation of reaching the fort and seeing friendly faces and resting in the bathhouse spurred them all on, it also distracted them, allowing them to drop their guard.

Caratacus was at the front of the column behind a giant pine. He let out a shrill cry of a wounded hare and waited for the riposte. It came threefold, each one mimicking a fox responding to hearing that an injured prey was nearby, telling him the ambush was in place. But it did suddenly snap the troopers back to the impending dangers but only by a fraction of a second. Because the front men witnessed the apparition of the biggest barbarian they had ever seen step out into their path and hurl a spear fifteen paces taking their leader, the only man on horseback, in the middle of his breast plate. A wave of spears crashed down on to the cowering unit who belatedly brought up their shields. Those fast enough to react heard the crack of the iron tips bounce of the central boss of their scutum's or thud, burying deep into the red softer wooden outer which coming down from higher ground knocked them off balance. Before they had time to react, screaming banshees were upon them, appearing from behind every tree to their right. With the high ground assisting their charge they hit their struggling Roman's with force, simply knocking the survivors of the avalanche of spears off their feet and down the descending bank on the other side of the track. It was all the encouragement that the poorly disciplined Frisiavones auxiliaries from Lavatre needed. They took to their heels and headed down hill away from the danger.

As his men crashed into the poorly constructed scutum wall, Caratacus arrived at the officer who had been knocked off his horse. The spear tip had indented a deep hollow in the metal breast plate, knocking the wind out of the man who had subsequently smashed his head as he struck the floor, he was clearly unconscious so Caratacus eased towards the spooked horse, it being a valuable commodity. With the horse reigns in his hand he watched down the hill at the fleeing Romans, chased by his fellow Brigante running straight in the second line of men who timed their appearance so that the scything axes added to the momentum of their flight, hammered them with body and head blows bringing their upper body's to a standstill so that their feet continued with an almost comical result.

"Not one survivor!" he bellowed down to the men below. "Salvage what you can," he added.

"We need one alive so I can question him." Gluingel had appeared in the way only Gluingel could. Caratacus pointed to the officer.

That one will do after I have his armour. It must be good it didn't allow the spear tip to punch through it; he offered the bent iron tip up as evidence at the quality. The old man nodded his appreciation at the quality of the metalwork.

It wasn't until their attention was drawn back to where the column had been ambushed that they saw the unit had been carrying a large chest and they knew they had hit the jackpot.

All the forts and even the great wall in the area had been constructed to protect the expansion of the empire. But the empire only expanded where it was profitable to do so and the lead and silver mines in this area of Britannia was well known. Once gathered it was amassed at different strongly defended garrisons before being transported to the major transport routes such as Dere Street the main road from Eburacum (York) up to Coria (Corbridge). This road connected major fortresses together to allow fast movement of the Roman legions and the proceeds of the land rape that fed the greed of the Imperial Roman Emperor. Caratacus and his men had just intercepted a small but very valuable consignment of silver.

After the bodies had been pillaged the Brigante warriors ghosted back into the very depth of the forest to take stock of their situation and allow Gluingel to question the prisoner.

It wasn't a straight forward sacrifice as Caratacus witnessed in the enchanted forest during the final stages of his passage to become a man of the earth and gods. Firstly the Druid slowly skinned the arms of the officer. Cutting small incisions at the top of his shoulders, he peeled the skin down towards the screaming mans hands. By the time the flaps of skin hung down far enough to touch the blood drenched ground from his tree bound, standing position he had told all he could tell. At that point the same fate despatched the Frisii officer as it had the Pict. With a deft swipe if his razor sharp axe he opened up the gut and exposed the entrails and examined them before ripping out the liver and heart replacing them in the remaining empty cavity with the glowing ashes of a fire. With the heart still beating held high in his hand he cut the corpses free and directed two men to cast it into the nearby stream. The threefold death and the axe had paid its tribute to the gods once again. This time it was Caratacus that was offered the two organs first and as his men looked on incredulously he took mighty bites out of them. When he had finished he handed them back to the old Druid who cast them on the fire and raised his axe in salute at their leader. The rest of the warriors all joined in cheering and screaming as Caratacus held his axe and sword aloft as he beamed with joy through his blood soaked beard. He had and would continue making the Romans pay for their trespass.

The officer's information was of enormous importance:

"So he claims that an entire legion will be marching up to the wall from Eburacum. How many men will that be?" asked Caratacus.

"They will have over five thousand men and he was not talking about the first great wall he was talking about the one to the north in the lands of the Votadini and Picts," answered the Druid.

"Even if we gather all the resistance across the lands of the Brigante we might manage one thousand, no more. We need to find allies and find them fast."

"Our enemies over the wall in the north have the same hatred of the Romans as we do. We might be able to convince them to form an alliance long enough to defeat this Ninth Legion?" The old man had drawn a map of the extended route they would most likely take to get to the Antonine Wall. "Here the road moves through the Forest of Otterburn and it gives a similar opportunity to the one we have just been presented with. My kind gathered in this forest once a year to pay homage to Flidais. I know these woods we could defeat an army twice our size in the right conditions."

"I hate to say it but we will need help from the blue faces. As you say, we might defeat an army twice our size but not five times."

"You need to send a messenger, with an offering of some of this silver," Gluingel pointed down to the chest that stood at their feet.

"I will take it and I will get assistance from those sly blue face bastards that have been watching us all day." Caratacus nodded slightly and moved his eyes to the ridgeline on the opposite side of the valley, where amongst an out crop of rocks he had noticed a small band of Picts observing the day's events.

"Ah, you are getting very aware of your surroundings and when mother earth is out of balance by the presence of foreigners."

We move on the Roman fort at Lavatrae tomorrow and while we are on our way I will pay a little visit to our friends. Make sure the men gather all the uniform of the Frisiavones auxiliaries. I want the fort to allow us to walk right in.

Five Pictish warriors had been watching the small unit of soldiers from distance. They had seen them enter the forest where a couple of hours earlier a large band of Brigante had arrived. They had heard the faint battle noises and the fact that no Roman force left the forest told them all they needed to know. What they did hear far clearer was the screams of agony of one man. So it was true the Brigante had a sorcerer, priest of the earth, known as a Druid. Only a warlock or sorcerer could inflict so much pain and keep a man alive. It must be the band led by the Chieftains son, the one people said was a giant with unbelievable strength who was possessed by the gods. The Picts had spent most of the night huddled round a small fire hidden behind the rocks where they sheltered. They had been discussing what they should do next. Should they keep on watching the unfolding events? Or return north with their new information? After hours of heated debate they had decided to wait until they saw what the Brigante intended to do the next day.

While the men in the rocks traded suggestions as what to do next Caratacus had set off under the cover of darkness to pay them a call. He had taken ten of his most trusted and stealthy warriors moving well to the south of their target and moving over the ridge top into the next valley where they gained the rear of the Picts camp. They knew they were near their targets when they came across their horses. Just like the Brigante only these men rode as it could be vital to deliver messages as rapidly as possible.

The Pictish sentry called the other to look at the scene across the valley. The Roman unit was marching with the Brigante directly behind them. Caratacus could not make out what was being said but understood when their voices and actions became very animated. They had just seen a group of warriors split off from the main force and head directly in their direction. Five blue faces came into view chattering excitedly making towards their horses only to run face to face with ten warriors ready and willing to fight. There was no mistaking their leader; it was the man they had been describing earlier that previous evening. The giant was standing blocking their way with a sword at the throat of one and a spear just a short thrust away from a second, his men had surrounded the stunned warriors from north of the wall before they could even start to think about resisting.

It wasn't often these days that Caratacus was surprised at anything Gluingel did but when he called out to the Picts in their own dialect from behind his shoulder every man in the Brigante war party were just as amazed. They had left the old man back at the camp in the forest hours earlier.

"It is alright Caratacus, they know we mean them no harm and we have a proposal for them to take to their leader."

It was agreed that two of the Pictish warriors would stay and march on the fort while the other three returned to their band which they said was attacking the fort at Luguvaliun with an allied band of Scoti from across the sea to the west. This explained the garrison of Lavatrae needing to be depleted, while at the same time allowing for a meeting with both Pict and Scoti. Maybe the gods were smiling on them.

As usual for the area the fort was shrouded in low lying mist. Everything was grey and visibility was so poor that they were within a few hundred paces before the warning alarm was given to bring what remained of the garrison to readiness. Three men stood on the ramparts of the two towers from which the main gate was suspended. A few more were arranged across the front wall. The two Picts were roped together and were being paraded out in front of the returning unit and the cheers from the wall hinted at the relief the troops felt at the bolstering of their numbers. What they could not see, as they remained out of view behind cover and well into the thick mist was the horde of barbarians waiting for the gates to open.

Caratacus had beaten the large indentation out of the chest plate but his thoughts of having the armour for himself had proved to be wishful thinking, it was far too small. He could only use the front section with the red officer's cape hiding the missing back piece as he rode the fine horse, which he was taking for his own. The gate swung open and the cheer that greeted them was heart warming and played right into their hands. The entire garrison had their attention on the returning force who had managed to catch a couple of barbarians. They would be a welcome boost to the garrison funds as they should fetch a reasonable price at the slave market.

As one of the men approached Caratacus taking his horses reins he saw the riders face for the first time. He never got to call out the warning of his discovery. Caratacus had known it was just a matter of time so had been ready to pull his war axe from under his cape, behind his back. The axe blade was buried deep enough into the top of the skull for the blade to have reached down separating the dead man's eyes. It was the signal all the other Brigante and the two Picts had been waiting for. The others outside were already halfway from the hiding place to the gates and the first of the mock Roman soldiers ensured the gates remained open. There was probably no more than fifty men left to defend the fort, and that would have been insufficient to stave off a concerted attack from outside let alone one from within.

Caratacus jumped down of his horse and threw the breast plate at the first man who attacked him. As he blocked the flying armour the man saw the axe rise high above. He never did see the Gladius that took him in the throat puncturing his windpipe before being twisted and withdrawn. Rotating round the mighty Brigante saw two men were rushing him from across the courtyard, battle. The first was just beginning to angle himself telling Caratacus he was going to assault his left while the other, still two paces further back was using the first attacker to shield himself. After all his training, it was easy for Caratacus to read; the first man was the bolder of the two and the second, slightly less so but he was the sly one, but would be put on the defensive if the first man was dealt with swiftly. The long Pilum was being presented like a lance; the first attacker was totally committed to the charge his body position which was in line with the spear evidenced this. Caratacus was amazed that his training had enabled him to see such tiny detail in the midst of chaos and his brain could process it so rapidly.

As the Pilum tip was shooting forward it was parried by Caratacus's sword, as he spun through a full circle he multiplied his velocity fivefold with his out stretched arm that held his war axe. Through the corner of his eye he noted the different posture of the second man. His lead leg planted and his shoulder beginning to turn; he intended to throw his Pilum, javelin style. So as the axe snapped into the rear of the first mans neck slicing a deep gouge at the base of his skull he continued his spin so as not to give the sly one a stationary target and as he came back round to face the assailant he sent the war axe spinning end over end. It struck the auxiliary Frisii trooper square on his chainmail covered chest. For all the blade was finely honed into a sharp blade over such a broad area the armour prevented the weapon penetrating. But what it did do was knock the wearer on to his backside momentarily winding him and sending his Pilum flying free from his grasp. Even as the axe was still in flight Caratacus transferred the short stabbing sword from his left to his right hand with a slick flick of his hands. Another rotation and two side steps had him pass around the seated adversary with his Gladius blade being dragged across the stunned mans throat opening him up like a slaughtered animal.

Caratacus had come to a halt from his revolving attack and immediately took up a crouching pose, reducing the target he presented. Looking round he saw the men from outside the fort had poured in through the open gates charging past him taking the fight to the retreating Frisiavones auxiliaries. They fought till the last man; they knew what lay in store for any captives and would rather die than what their leaders told of the fate that awaited prisoners.

It was only the few civilians that resided in the fort that did not lay butchered across the courtyard and battlements. The stone flagged floor ran red with blood, it dripping down the walls from some of the scything death blows that had been meted out. But with relatively light casualties the Brigante raiders had taken the fort and it made the perfect meeting place for the allied Picts and Scoti who had withdrawn having failed to take the fort at Luguvaliun. They had little time to discuss their accord as they knew that the main garrison of their newly acquired fort would be returning and there style of fighting was not one that lent itself for fighting off a siege.

Alvor spoke for the Picts. He was a short but muscular man with a mass of red hair flowing from his head joining a tangle of similarly coloured facial hair that made it difficult for Caratacus to read his facial expressions.

The left side of his face was painted the blue so common amongst their tribe with further painting across his bare chest and arms. A sturdy, broad leather belt held his green tartan breeches up while it also supported his scabbard that allowed the sword handle of polished antler to be displayed. The breeches were wrapped at the ankles by several turns of leather braid that spiralled down the top of course leather boots. He carried no shield his other weapon was a Roman cross bow its quiver hung down his back was packed with iron tipped bolts.

It was evident that there was little love lost between Alvor and Pinonii the Scoti leader who was the slightly taller of the two but less muscled. He was also painted similarly but his mop of hair was better controlled by the helmet he wore and he seemed to tend his beard as it was cut to give two points, creating an inverted "V". He was barefoot and his breeches was a dirty red colour while he sported long sword and spear along with a small round shield that Caratacus thought was neither a good defensive or offensive addition to his armoury.

The biggest dispute between the two was that Alvor had the greater number of warriors so he demanded a greater share of the spoils. Neither of the men seemed bothered about having the opportunity to deliver their common foe a decisive blow. But when Gluingel suggested that as a gesture of goodwill that they were given the prisoners from the fort and a little silver both agreed to the temporary alliance and to follow Caratacus as the leader for the battle and the plan that was presented to them.

It was not ideal and when they returned from the meeting both Caratacus and Gluingel agreed that it was a risk trusting these men who clearly did not trust each other and no doubt that mistrust stretched to them also.

The great Caledonian forest spread as far as the eye could see as they moved down the rolling hills that ranged from the Roman wall and across the land of the near extinct Votadini who had been decimated by attacks from the other Picts to the north as well as the Romans and Brigante to the south. Although Alvor had boasted he had nearly fifteen hundred warriors it proved to be an exaggeration to gain more loot in the pre- battle bartering. He brought with him no more than the thousand warriors that had moved north from Brigantia with the Scoti providing a similar number. They totalled what they expected to be just over half the number that the Ninth Legion would be moving north with. Caratacus's spies had kept him informed with the enemy progression and an uneasy truce barely held while the three armies waited a full week as the Ninth resupplied and rested at Coria. They moved over to the large fort at Vindolanda where they left some of their troops to strengthen the garrison so it could be used as a relief column if sent for. This suited the triple alliance as it reduced the enemy numbers, evening up the size of the protagonists.

The tall evergreen timbers of the forest caused a perpetual dark grey, even during the brightest of days. There was a dank, green moss covered appearance to every boulder and rock that hung on to the steeply sloping hill sides. A heavy carpet of pine needles deadened all sound giving an eerie, super natural aura to the superstitious who ventured in to its unknown depths. It would take a man several days to travel through it and during that time you would not hear a living daytime creature. But it would echo to the sounds of the nocturnal spirits, accompanied by the howling of the invisible wolves that prowled looking for the unsuspecting. Even the streams and rivers that cut their path down the valley sides and congregated in the valley bottoms seemed to warn of impending doom in their babbling song.

The Legio IX Hispana was based at Eboracum. Their regular commander had been ill when they had received their orders to march north to try and re-establish a presence back on the Antonine Wall. So it was his second in command, Sextus Octavia who led the Spanish Legion under their gold Eagle mascot. The army set out from Vindolanda, through the great gates, on to the road that the soldiers called the Military Way. Beyond lay the lands north of the empires current boundary.

Every one of the four and a half thousand men felt they were being watched from behind every knoll in the rolling countryside that soon gave way to the great forest of pine. That would take two full days to travel. The road that they marched on was the one made by the troop's predecessors when the empire had pushed beyond the wall that Emperor Hadrian had ordered built.

Constructing that wall had been a major feat of military hardship starting in the west with the fort of Alauna (Maryport) crossing some seventy three miles of the wildest country in the empire to Segedunum (Wallsend) in the east. But at least the local tribes had been partially subdued. When the three legions that had been stationed in the land of the Votadini started their build they were under siege from both north and south. But at least those previous experiences gave them the knowledge of what they were heading into. It allowed their commander a good idea where they were likely to come under attack and he would therefore be sending out scouting parties to check the route.

The Military Way, like all Roman roads took the most direct route between two points. Thus ensuring it passed through the densest section of this arboreal nightmare. The road had passed close to a river where during the earlier and brief occupation a small clearing with a timber walled fort had been constructed for units to take refuge as they traversed through the forest. That was their objective on day one of their march.

The scouting party had been seen giving the vanguard the all clear from the edge of the tree line they had waited for a while encouraging their progress before they had set off into the gloomy interior, eager to make progress. It had been the last that they had seen of them until they got to a point where the road passed under a series of tall rock faces that towered out of the ground immediately beside the road.

A wall of stakes had been driven into the road surface, each sharpen point had a member of the scouting parties head on it. Their ghoulish stares worsened by the blue, hanging tongues and limp hair mattered with dry blood.

The men did not need to be readied, they knew this had all the hallmarks of an ambush, but where would it come from and why did their commander stop and waste time with the dead? He needed to be thoughtful of the living everyone was getting agitated at the delay while Sextus Octavia had the heads gathered into sacks.

The stakes had been thrown to one side and the order had been given to move forward when a heavy rumbling was heard over head. At the front centre and rear of the column a tidal wave of tree trunks fell like torrents off the top of the overhanging cliff taking out hundreds of unsuspecting soldiers who had been expecting an attack from the front or the rear but not from above and certainly not by falling trees. Men and horses were taken out and those nearby shocked and stunned failed the react as hundreds of warriors appeared on the cliff tops hurling spears and boulders raining further death of the beleaguered legion. Sextus knew they were in trouble so sent riders back to bring up the re-enforcements they had left back at the wall. The unit of cavalry tip-toed their mounts round the carnage of dead and fallen trunks before galloping south, out of sight. The barrage had ceased and the attack evidently broken off. Was this due to the size of the attacking force? They had no wish for a direct confrontation they would just keep taking opportunities to pick at the superior force when they could.

"Forward to the fort! We will set up defences there and they will not dare to confront us," cried Sextus encouraging his men, waving his Gladius high in his hand.

Several times over the next two hours a small party of barbarians appeared and shot cross bows at different parts of the column. To Sextus's growing frustration and regardless how often the officers told them, his men gave chase and whoever disappeared out of sight were never seen again until their heads appeared, paraded across the road for all to witness.

When they got to the site where the old fort had stood it was clear where the barbarians had got their timber avalanche from. There was not a single post left of the old palisade, just recent signs of excavations in the earthworks that had housed them. In the years since the Roman occupation the forest had worked hard to reclaim the clearing, thick dark vegetation grew all the way up to where the fort had stood on three sides, the forth being the roadside. The area wasn't big enough for all the troops to set up their camps so some begrudgingly stayed on the road. When they managed to get their campfires started and a head count taken Sextus was shocked. With the Cavalry unit that had gone for help added the legion had lost nearly one thousand men from the mighty column that had left the wall just hours earlier. He was considering turning back, commonsense told him to do so, but the humiliation for Ninth Legion, himself and therefore his family would be too much, he had to push on.

The guards were doubled for the night. It had been a long weary march up Dere Street from Eburacum and even with the short rest at Vindolanda the days march with all its tension had tired the men. Even in their current predicament the camp was silent by the time the moon was high above.

Gluingel stood alongside Caratacus. Alvor and Pinonii flanked them. They looked over the encampment through the coniferous cover. The Druid pointed to the sky as the flare trail sign of an extra-terrestrial body arced high above, that combined with the south westerly wind picking up, was as the old man had foreseen. Both Pict and Scoti saw the power of the man, he who could read the nights sky. They felt uneasy in his presence it was as if he knew what they were thinking, he could read the future. At least it was better to have him on their side for once.

Alvor went right to lead his men, as Pinonii went left. Having given them time to be at the head of their armies Caratacus had a single flaming arrow fired into the sky. It was not the signal for an all out attack rather the start of a slow stealthy move forward. There were now merely a few trees between the sentries behind the earthworks and the front line of the Celts. The signal for the action to commence was to be all together more dramatic and designed to bring despair of the defenders. The flaming heads of the cavalry unit that had supposedly gone for help had been intercepted before they ever neared the edge of the forest and detached from their bodies.

A series of small groups fainting attacks had spurred the horsemen into a head long charge for the freedom of open countryside. So keen to reach the relative safety of the daylight they had failed to spot the vines pulled taught across the road designed to trip the horses or garrotte the riders.

It was these fearsome signals that bounced into camp startling the Spaniards by its gruesomeness that brought on the next part of their plan. The men with their backs to the wind now lit the next and even more terrifying weapons. Piles of the gathered vegetation, rolled into bales the blazing masses were flung down the slopes. The floor was covered with pine needles and therefore burnt ferociously taking all other fuel with it, fanned by the wind that pushed the growing inferno towards the scene of panic. The roaring of the conflagration tearing skywards up each of the colossal Scots Pine forced the legion to withdraw back to the road creating a crushing mass of bodies, just as a swarm of barbarian Celtic warriors engulfed them. The battle raged for hours, the legion had not had the time or space to gather into their customary fighting formation and without that unity and sense of control they were at a disadvantage from the start. It was the Celtic warrior who excelled in this the most chaotic of fighting scenarios. With flames at their back, on their flanks and with hordes of barbarians cutting them down by their hundreds, from the only fire free quarter, it quickly became every man for himself. Most could see that their only escape route was the road itself. As the panic grew either direction became a better option than their current situation and it appeared to be free of the Celtic fiends. A trickle of men fled the bedlam in both directions and as their comrades saw these escape routes the trickle became a stream and finally a torrent.

When panic sets in to a fleeing army they tend to have no interest in anything than speed and to ensure they maximise this they discard anything that might slow them down. Shields, weapons and even helmets were cast aside just before they ran into the final part of the ambush. The ones who took the left route found Alvor and his Picts while those who went right ran into a thousand Scoti led by Pinonii. It was slaughter. An unarmed panicking mob, running blindly, into a hateful enemy that craved blood and death. Their craving was fed that night.

Caratacus had lost count of the men he felled, his war axe moved continuously in a swinging cross motion driving forward, splitting, cleaving, smashing while his Gladius held firmly in his left hand jabbed taking any unfortunate that came in its path. He saw Sextus Octavia surrounded by his guard and the golden eagle perched on top of the pole that also carried the Ninth Legions insignia and colours.

He screamed his challenge that seemed to drown out all the other battle din and roaring of the burning timberland. Sextus recognised the situation and to his credit he turned to face the biggest man he had ever seen. The battleground parted slightly as both sides saw that their leaders were to face each other. Caratacus continued to wield the great axe, the Gladius now stationary but poised. Sextus did his best impersonation of the barbarian's war cry and started to run towards his foe, hoping that momentum might assist overcoming this substantial warrior. As he took his second step forward he saw a Pilum on the floor.

Caratacus steadied himself watching the charge; he noticed a slight glance of the head and the spear on the floor. His opponent was about to forego his momentum for this extra weapon. His move was lightning fast, so fast that Sextus was still in the process of bringing the Pilum up off the floor when the Gladius slapped it back down and the looping arc of the double edged axe came round driven by the twisting motion of Caratacus's attack. The axe blade struck exactly where he had seen it in the image he had painted in his mind before he even made the move. It took Sextus Octavia, Commander of the Ninth Legion in the nape of the neck severing head from torso in one power stroke. The blood lust was coursing through Caratacus's veins and his victory roar had men from both sides cower in awe or fright. The victor now immediately struck down the man carrying the eagle before taking it and holding it aloft. His men soon restarted the fight their own desire for the battle amplified by such a crushing triumph, the opposite affected the few remaining Spaniards who foolishly threw away their weapons pleading for mercy.

The woodland was still burning feverishly, the orange rage now well up in the canopy with burning branches falling to earth sustaining the ground fire. It was into natures own furnace that the survivors were cast screaming for the clemency that would never come.

In the aftermath of the slaughter the three tribes shared the spoils equally. The silver coins carried by the troops and in the pay wagon was enough to make the attack worthwhile regardless of the impact it would have south of the wall. It was the ownership of the eagle that came under question by Alvor.

"The eagle stays with me!" was Caratacus's simple answer to Alvor.

"I will give you one hundred silver pieces for the trophy?" he persisted.

"The eagle stays with me. I took it in combat. It is mine. There is no more to be said!"

Alvor was not looking as if he was prepared to take no for an answer, even when Pononii agreed with the Brigante he still insisted that if he could not have it then it should be shared equally.

Caratacus suddenly became very assertive but in a deep low quiet voice. His tone laced with venom. "You would have been facing these invaders alone if it had not been for the Brigante bringing the three tribes together. You have followed our plan and won great riches and fame for yourself, your people will speak your name with pride. Take what you have got or we will fight for this prize and before I kill you I will cut off your balls and feed them to you. Your choice?"

Alvor managed to hold his stance and stare, toe to toe with Caratacus for a few seconds. "I should never have trusted you." He turned and led his tribe north.

Pononii looked at the disappearing Picts and shook his head. "That is why we have never formed an alliance with them before. They have no appreciation of what others have done. It is time we moved west Caratacus you have delivered a great victory that we shall all share in and I thank you for that. Beware of Alvor he will not forget!"

Just to the east of the Stainmore Pass was the fort of Lavatrae protecting two nearly deserted valleys that had the rivers Tees and Wear running along their base. This was the land that Caratacus called his home. The Brigante army had tracked south and used the same place to negotiate the wall that they had done moving north. The Roman engineers had utilised every natural feature that presented itself when they had constructed the wall. Instead of building a wall where there was a vertical cliff they incorporated it into the defences. Some of these appeared to the Romans as being impregnable and for that reason only "mile castles" were dotted along the wall. In bad weather the visibility could be so poor that these places gave easy access either side of the impressive barrier. To the determined it was no obstacle. The Brigante of the upper Pennines certainly were determined and would never be defeated by the Empire of Rome.

Gladiator.

A messenger arrived in the village looking for Caratacus. It had been a full month since the successful ambush that had wiped the Ninth Legion off the face of the earth. Caratatus had secured much wealth for the villages he led. His father had died from his injuries while he was away so it had been a bitter sweet homecoming for the victorious warrior. After he had shown off his prized gold eagle he went away telling Gluingel that he wanted to have time to think and mourn his father's death. The Druid had understood and had muttered something about not having anything else to teach his pupil as they parted. The old man watched him leave for the upper reaches of the valley of the Wear. Up on the water shed between the two dales and above the tree line it was a desolate place of moors and grit stone outcrops. He had spent so much time here as a boy and knew of the caves that he now used as his shelter. It was at the back of one of these he buried the eagle for safe keeping. It did not surprise Caratacus that the old Druid had left and his parting comment made sense when Aengir told him. He had arrived in mystery and he had left by the same manner. There had been no challenge to his rights to take over as chieftain and he had barely led his first sortie to raid the victus of Vinovia when the blue faced man arrived.

He brought with him important news of another strong build up of Roman forces at Vindolanda. It was strange that Caratacus's spies had not picked up on this but it was possible that units had gathered from across northern Britannia and individually these movements had not raised any suspicions. Alvor was suggesting that once again the Brigante rallied forth across the wall to join him and the Scoti in an amalgamated attack on the force when it mustered north as he was sure it would do. Typical of the arrogance of the man he was insisting that if the Brigante wanted a share of the spoils it would be, he, Alvor that would plan the lead the attack.

With such a successful ambush on the Hispana Legion it did not take much convincing for the other villages to send their warriors. Everybody wanted more Roman silver.

On their approach to their usual crossing point Caratacus sent out scouts to check that the mile castles were not unusually manned as his father had done when he had lead such crossings. They seemed to be in luck, the reports suggested that both appeared quieter than normal and that explained the lack of patrolling between the two. Although the rock face towered out of the ground with awe inspiring steepness, to those familiar with its cracks and ledges it was not more than a simple climb and they started their descent soon after checking out the area. Caratacus as always was one of the first down and the same process of scouting the area to ensure there was no welcoming reception took place.

As soon as he was down he felt uneasy and silently he gestured his disquiet to the others. They all fanned out and moved away from the base of the cliff having told the others to hold their position. There was something wrong and he could not put his finger on it. Everything looked as if it was normal but something had changed since their last crossing. What was it?

As normal, they had chosen darkness to make the climb so visibility was poor and just at the maximum range of his vision he could see a host of straggly bushes coming into sight. They were poor specimens that looked unfamiliar. He was watching the bush immediately to his front and it seemed to be growing out of a mound. It was out of place as was the mound which twitched slightly as he studied it.

He called to his men to fall back and those at the top of the cliff to prepare themselves for an ambush. It was as if every bush on the flat land in front of the cliff came to life. From being on there own and in silence blue painted men appeared but instead of being allies come to meet them they were menacingly, brandishing weapons.

Alvor called out from the gloom, "Caratacus my friend we had you worried did we not?"

"Damn you Alvor we could have killed some of your men surprising us like that!" he complained.

"That would have been unfortunate," called Alvor his voice having lost its jocularity. He continued. "Because if you had I would have had to have my new friend here, kill you." He had just come out of the dark shadows and beside him stood a Roman officer as several hundred troops appeared from round the sides of the cliff base. A wall of shield and Pilum creating a semi circle locking them against the rock face.

"Run! It's a trap, the little Pict bastard as betrayed us," called Caratacus to those above.

Marcus Valerius had shown restraint and a lack of wanting to wreck revenge on his enemy who had possibly been responsible for delivering such a body blow to the empire. He handed over a bag of silver to Alvor who smiled at the captured Brigante, turned and disappeared into the darkness along with his warriors. It dawned on Caratacus; Alvor would not want this officer to connect either of them with the Ninth's disappearance or he would certainly not have got his reward for his treachery he would have also been clapped in irons.

At least the main body of his army had escaped. It was only he and another twenty that were being marched to Vindolanda, chained by manacles round the neck and ankles.

You have done well Marcus Valerius. General Lucius Magnus was a happy man; he had been assured that the giant barbarian that stooped in the caged wagon before him was the leader of the Brigante rebels. There could be no mistaking Caratacus everything that had been said about the beast pointed to this being him, surely there were no more that size? This would earn him a fortune back at Vinovia when he sold them to the traders. Brigante warriors always fetched a premium, and the infamous chief would bring him twice what all the other would put together.

The general was taking no chances. The best part of a full Cohort accompanied the convoy that included the slave wagon. Cavalry front and back and near enough two hundred auxiliaries either side of the prisoners. Caratacus looked at the bowed head around him. Brelus, Ruadan, Caracalus and Venpasian, four of his most influential generals trapped with him in the same ambush, how naive to place all the tribe's leaders together and vulnerable. There would be no chance of rescue by an attacking force from their villages they had no one that would be able to take charge of the situation and command enough respect for the others to follow. They were on their own.

Sufficient Romanised Brigante's lived in the victus (a village that had built up around the garrison) of Vinovia to confirm beyond any doubt the Romans might have had that they did indeed hold the chieftain of the resisting barbarians that lived to their immediate north. With this confirmed and the information sent back to Lucius Magnus it gave the general the confidence to send his prize down to Eburacum where he was sure that the short life of a gladiator was the ideal career for the giant barbarian trouble maker and of course the most profitable for himself. He even sent word to the Roman capitol in the north exaggerating the fight that finally resulted in the capture of the most dangerous warrior in Britannia. This obviously had the general playing a large part in the fight where Caratacus took out twenty auxiliaries before the general took personal charge of matters over powering the beast-man with his own bodyguard. He generously mentioned a minor role for Marcus Valerius but kept quiet about using an ambush baited by the Picts.

The Ludus (gladiator school) of Eburacum was the most northern in the empire; as such it was limited in size but was immensely popular with the would-be Roman citizens and genuine ones alike. Its "Lanistae" who headed the "Familia Gladiatoria" was responsible for both training the legions as well as simultaneously entertaining the public. Polyneikes was an ex-gladiator who hailed from Thessalonica; he had won his freedom in the coliseum of Rome and was very proud of the fact. It was the first thing that he mentioned when he took a new intake of fighters. This was a man whose role gave him lawful power over life and death of every "familia member"; it also made him a social outcast on a similar footing with pimps and butchers. This did not bother Polyneikes, in fact in some way he revelled in the notoriety, just as he had done when he fought. It was the same across the empire, the Lanistae was despised by the normal civilian where as the gladiators themselves could become stars and adored by the crowds. The most honoured position was that that Lucius Magnus had become; the "Munerarius" or gladiator owner was associated with coming from a good family, high status and a man of independent means. It was everything Lucius craved, as he had come from a rather impoverished background. He was a proud citizen of Rome but had worked up through the ranks to a position that anybody who had known him as a young man would have doubted possible. Owning not one but five notorious barbarians he hoped would propel him further up the social ladder. That was why he had arrived in Eburacum, ostensibly on business of Rome but really wanting to keep a close eye on his potential route to fame and riches.

Great fanfare had preceded the arrival of the five Brigantes and Polyneikes had been in the training yard when the wagon had arrived. He glanced over as the men were prodded out by the guards who made sure they stayed at the full reach of their spears. The first four that dropped out and hobbled forward look like they would make reasonable gladiators if as the rumours he had heard suggested they were ferocious fighters. It was when the last man dropped onto the ground; even shackled he was surrounded by his own personal guard of three keeping their iron tipped Pilums aimed at his back. The three were clearly frighten of their charge as every time he moved they overreacted and expected him to turn on them. Polyneikes was not surprised by their nervousness, the man was huge, but his massively muscled body still suggested a level of athleticism in its symmetry. So the rumours were true, this must be the one they called Caratacus, rebel chieftain rebel slayer of twenty soldiers. He saw fame and fortune, but more importantly the prospect of taking this man all the way to Rome. Finally he might have his ticket out of this boil on the arse of the empire.

The first thing that Caratacus and his brothers faced was the *sacramentum* (a sacred oath) that would bind them to service of the Ludus. They were then given their stigma (tattoo), a branding that told of their owners. In the case of the gladiators in Ebruacum this was on the top of their right arm and appropriately enough, thought Caratacus, it was a golden eagle.

"What do you think Lanistae?" asked Lucius eager to hear the trainer's assessment of his new pupils.

"Well they look the part, but we will need to find out if they can fight and that means fighting in a way that is expected, not just barbarian warfare. But honourable combat. We will see tomorrow."

That night was the first night that Caratacus had spent out of chains since being taken captive. They were accommodated in cells, arranged in barrack formation around the central practice arena so at all times they saw their place of work. The five were crammed in together for that first night but looking around it was evident that there was some system to where you were billeted. They did not know it, but the potential that both Lucius and Polyneikes saw in them was the reason that they got the very good food as it was all part of the pair's investment.

The training was strict and precise, discipline harsh and sometimes lethal. Days confined in small dark cells were the prize for minor misdemeanours. The whip and even execution was for more gross misconduct. But death during training of any kind was not wanted by anyone that was to be reserved for the arena and the paying crowds.

From his cell Caratacus could see all that was going on in the training arena, just a small walkway and wall separated him from the sandy surface. High walls created the perimeter and he noted that people were walking around the top observing the proceedings below. By mid morning with the longer serving gladiators hard at it the guards escorted the new arrivals out. Caratacus stood facing a tall timber trunk with a cross member designed to mimic arms that had a net of one end and a timber sword on the other. Rope was bound several times round its waist so the men on either end could rotate it by pulling. It was perched on a round timber platform and the whole thing was buried securely into the ground. At his feet were several wooden replica weapons. One of the men who appeared to be assisting the Lanistae gave Caratacus a wooden sword.

"Let's see what you're made of, oh mighty one," came the sarcastic order as he threw him the weapon.

Caratacus was well aware of what was expected of him, he had watched from his cell for two hours. He had no intention of playing the games of these bastards as if he was a performing animal especially as it appeared that the people actually on the wall included women and children. He lifted the carved timber Gladius up in front of his chest and snapped it in half discarding the two parts with distain.

One guard and the assistant reacted to his insubordination. The guard approached his Pilum offered up too defensively to hide his unease at approaching too close to the colossus that seemed to grow even bigger as he neared. While the trainer pulled his whip out of the rear of his belt. He trailed the plaited leather tails out along the floor preparing the strike when Polyneikes stepped on it holding his hand up to stop the confrontation escalating.

"My friend I feel your rage that burns within. I felt it myself many years ago. But understand this; whatever you were in your former life that is over. Look around and see all this," he gave a long sweep of his arms encompassing the whole practice arena. "This is now your world, very soon you will be entering the arena for real and the only choice you have in the matter is whether you go in to fight or to be sacrificed. If you go in to fight you may survive to face more challenges and if you are really successful you may travel a little even to Rome maybe and if you are very lucky you, like me could win your freedom........."

Caratacus heard the man's voice become muffled and was replaced by that of the old Druids, "you will travel far and wide and be given the sternest tests before you will return to face the scourge of Britannia." It struck a chord with him.

He looked around at the Lanistae as if being reconciled to his fate and allowing him to think it had been his pep talk that had caused the change of heart. He nodded his head once in recognition.

Polyneikes was delighted not only had he got a giant warrior he had one that he could relate to. "Now my friend you may not have used one of these but see how it feels and take a few lunges at the target," he passed him a trident. The Lanistae was right he had never handled the three pointed spear before but as a boy growing up in his home village the first weapon they had used was a staff and he could not see that there would be many different moves.

He felt for the weapons balance point so he would be able to control it when in motion. It took him back, and some things you never forgot. Caratacus started a low growling as he sized up his target, the volume increased along with the weapon speed. Soon he was spinning the trident around in one hand them the next, after he had generated sufficient speed he fainted in one direction then the other, gathering it in to a two handed wide grip before stabbing forward into the would be throat of his target. It had been a mesmerising and a seamless attack which had brought the arena to a standstill, but the most impressive move was yet to come. Pulling back from the first attack Caratacus was still moving and with the deftness of foot that few in the arena could hope to match he danced round his target striking three further times before he was back at is starting point where he threw the trident like a javelin hitting the target in the chest with such force the triple prongs shattered. The entire move was lightning fast and the very essence of precision, it was capped off with a bear like roar that had the most primeval of under tones.

"It has been a long time since I used anything like that." He apologised to Polyneikes who was trying not to look too amazed. It had not been the twirling of the weapon or the thrusts although they were fearfully powerful and accurate. The big man's speed was phenomenal and he realise immediately that regardless of his weapons he should not be too heavily armoured or that would undoubtedly slow him down.

He went on to demonstrate his skills with the sword and then sword and shield. That brought an end to the target as it was flattened by the resulting charge where following a dazzling demonstration of heavy sword cuts alternating left then right he jabbed forward before smashing down the timber trunk with his shielded shoulder, ripping it out of its footings.

Caratacus was bathed in sweat and Polyneikes signalled for water to be brought. As he watched his newly acquired star pupil drink he asked. "So, you are a great warrior, what is your favoured weapon?"

"I always fought with the Gladius in my left and my war axe in my right," he replied.

"War axe! ermm...," he lingered on the final word allowing it to taper off thus showing he was thinking about it and it was causing him a problem.

Caratacus saw this seemed to concern the man so added, "what do you expect from a barbarian."

A smile cracked the concerned expression, "you have a point and that is exactly how we sell you. The giant barbarian chieftain, who put twenty legionaries to death single handed. We need you dark and unconventional. No chest plate to slow you down just arms shins and a black helmet. I will talk to Lucius Magnus we will not have any armour to fit you.

Since he had heard Gluingel talk to him Caratacus had a purpose. He had to win his freedom and get back to Britannia to prepare his people to face the scourge as the old man had called it. He knew deep down that his affinity with the gods of the earth; sky and forest, the protector of all beings, had singled him out for a reason and he had to fulfil his destiny. Whenever he had been searched he had remove the ring he had worn since Becuille had given him and kept it in his mouth, one time he had swallowed it when they insisted he opened his mouth. It had taken a few days but he had been aware when it had eventually reappeared. He spun it round on his finger as he thought of the beautiful daughter of Flidais.

Caratacus didn't like the heavily rehearsed choreography that most of the gladiators performed in the training arena, however he knew that by watching the others he would be able to read their moves if he came to face them for real. Even when he was not training himself he studied his potential foe. His commitment was now total; he could see how his current situation played into the old Druid's premonition. Each evening after they had been fed he would sit in a corner of his cell and muse about his past but more so his future and how he would make it back to his people.

A Dimacherus was a fighter who fought with two long knives or Gladius. Not that it interested him, but he was told that the name was derived from the Latin-language taking the Greek word διμάχαιρος meaning "bearing two knives". Caratacus was to be a slight variation to that theme. He, as discussed with Polyneikes would replace one of the Gladius for a war axe. Due to the degree of difficulty of wielding two swords the Dimacherus had to be a highly skilled experienced fighter, they were exalted as a class of gladiator, the ones most likely to be taken into the crowd's heart. Due to the addition of his war axe Caratacus was to fight some of the most heavily armed gladiator types including the, net and trident wielding Retiarius as well as the Mirmillo's, Samnite's and Thrace's who were similarly armed with sword and shield.

It was his armour that proved to be most problematic, due to his size it had to be altered. Usually the Ludus would have plenty of spare armour from men no longer needing it, but in Caratacus's case they had to make major alterations and combine two sets together to enable him to have the scale armour for his arms and leg protection for his shins. He was to wear scandals and these would have plates protecting him from blows across the top of his feet. His helmet was the style of a Spartan without any adornment so when he fought the Retiarius the flying net had nothing to catch on. This head protection had been split and a new section introduced to encompass his head and mass of dark hair. The cheek and nose protection allowed very little of his face to be visible just a glimpse of his ferocious eyes and the bottom of his beard.

He was allowed in the arena on his own on two occasions fully kitted out and armed with his true weapons. He moved round getting used to the new feel, but aware that someone in the cells looking on was the man he would be facing, he just did moves and air blows not attempting to engage the training dummy. At the end of both sessions he was made to place the axe and Gladius on the floor at one end of the arena before anybody entered. He had been covered by several archers all the time just in case he had any thoughts about escape.

His first two fights were almost an insult to a warrior of his stature. He was basically placed in the arena to execute two convicts. Both had been found guilty of raping women so he had no real problem with the task, in fact he would have happily done it without being forced. The first man had not even been able to defend against the power of the first diagonal sweep of the axe. He seemed rooted to the spot with fear and had been despatched in seconds. That was why he was given a second fight immediately afterwards, he had not even broken into sweat. This one was a different proposition as he was a soldier. Part of one of the auxiliary cohorts from somewhere in northern Britannia he knew how to fight and was only too aware that if he was to survive he had to defeat the giant that faced him across the dusty arena. He had been given a shield and a Pilum spear and Caratacus had to assume this was his choice and therefore was more than capable of using both. The noise began to grow in anticipation and penetrating his helmet he heard the crowd chanting his name. He had no idea why but he liked the adulation he was receiving and the sheer numbers of people who filled the amphitheatre made it all the more exciting.

The first thing he noticed about his opponent was that he had set himself in the centre of the floor taking the sort of stance you would expect if you were part of a defensive line accompanied by many like minded soldiers. He was flat footed with a wide stance his lead leg well forward behind the shield. It was a strong solid position and had been taken boldly enough. But what it did not do was enable him to be light on his feet and reposition if his adversary did anything other than a frontal assault. It was his left arm and leg that were pushed forward, his Pilum held tightly in his right and drawn back ready to strike. Caratacus could see his shoulders were tightly contracted and that his route would be a flanking attack to the left thus meaning his foe would have his shield in the way of his spear. The volume on the arena floor was growing louder as they neared. For such a big man Caratacus was keeping up on his toes speed and agility were every much as important as brute strength in this situation. He fainted right and then moved left. The disgraced soldier was drawn into the dummy and made an awkward lunge towards a body that was not there. His target had disappeared out of sight to his left. The soldier felt a hard wrap of the back of his helmet and the noise and pain of the blow had him continue the clumsy move he had initiated, tumbling to the floor.

He got to his feet, head spinning, breathing so heavy his chest was hurting as it rose and contracted with the effect of the exertion and adrenaline that flowed through his veins. He had blurred vision and the din from the crowd who he knew were calling for his blood made everything seem slightly unreal. If not frightened he was intimidated by the speed at which the warrior had moved he had to do something unexpected.

Caratacus was once again closing down on his prey, but not head on. He approached in a spiral pattern that kept the man shuffling and unsteady. He had reverted to his normal stance leading with his left so it was to this side Caratacus moved in. He was completely focused, the roar of the crowd blocked out of his mind he watched intently. Simultaneously he saw the shield just fractionally fall away to the left opening up the soldier's front. His right shoulder was just in the process of turning back winding up his muscles for launching the spear. With a brief acceleration into a forward roll the mighty Brigante warrior was too far round the shield for the throw to be successful and even as he was letting go of the weapon he knew he had lost his primary means of defence. Caratacus got back to his feet in one fluid movement and he glanced at the Pilum struck into the ground ten paces to his rear. He immediately moved back in the way he had come to prevent his target being able to reach the spent weapon. Now it was time for a frontal attack, driving the defender further away from any chance of him rearming himself. This was the time for speed but also the brute force and when it came it was decisive. He brought his axe up to bring the man's shield into play but never delivered the blow. Over extension of both arms locking forward expecting the hammer blow that never arrived, he never saw the half step back to the right that allowed the Gladius to rip into his neck slicing through his jugular, that had a fountain of rich red blood turn black as it hit the dusty floor. The shield had been dropped immediately with both hands clamped around the wound trying in vain to stem the catastrophic bleed.

Caratacus had been shown how to perform in victory as well as how he was to face an honourable death. The man under his foot was showing no fear just total courage but that was probably because he was either already dead or unconscious through the blood loss he was experiencing. He looked to the box in the audience where the governor watched on, to see what his instruction was to be. He was a convicted criminal it was only going to be one direction that everybody in the arena would turn their thumbs. With one mighty swing of his war axe the man's head was separated from his shoulders, the cheer that accompanied the head being lifted in celebration was immense and so was the buzz that went through the entire body of the big Brigante.

He had still not fought another Gladiator and that was to be his next big test. It was nearly a month until he took to the arena again. In the meantime he was given time for extra training this included fitness and strength. The later bringing the public flocking to watch the spectacle that was the "Brigante Barbarian" as the people had started calling him. He used a series of different sized timber trunks to push, pull and carry; maintaining his peak fitness was in everybody's interest. Lucius Magnus was beside himself with joy, all the Brigante prisoners had fought and won. He had sold Caracalus and Venpasian, to another owner. Brelus, Ruadan and of course Caratacus were not going anywhere without Lucius pulling the strings, Polyneikes would not be far behind after all

Lucius had limited knowledge of the gladiator business but both hoped these three were their passage to Rome.

Satonica was another disgraced soldier. Originally from a Cohort from Dalmatia, he had been reprimanded many times for his drunkard behaviour. Finally he had gone too far when in a fit of wine soaked rage he struck his commanding officer. He had been condemned to the arena with little hope of freedom. That did not mean he had given up, far from it he had already had four wins and stood a good chance of being moved to Deva Victrix (Chester) where one of the largest amphitheatres in Britannia was and frequently had significant gladiatorial games that made news back in Rome. To get noticed there was the first large step on the path to moving overseas where his name would not be so sullied and perhaps there he could win his freedom. He was only too aware that he had the small issue of defeating the giant and everybody's favourite barbarian, Caratacus, the Brigante Barbarian.

As was the custom the night before the games the men who were to compete were allowed out of their cells for a special meal and allowed to drink wine. Caratacus ate for two knowing he had the entire night to digest the food and by morning his body would be full of energy and he would be ready for the test ahead. Satonica reverted to type, but why not? He had drunk himself into near unconsciousness the other times and still won.

It was a hot sunny day, a rarity in Britannia. It would take its toll on both fighters if the battle went on. One man was suffering from dehydration before the contest started and the Retiarius regretted his over indulgence. Satonica nervously threw out his net repeatedly slowly hauling it back in as if he was showing it what he wanted it to do his heavy trident was carried in his left hand allowing his favoured arm to accurately direct the cast of the net. Caratacus had watched him out in the training arena. He had known all along that for him to win his freedom he would constantly have to fight the best and as Satonica had the best record it had figured he would face him before he was allowed to move to another arena.

The Retiarius had a well armoured trident arm and shins. His chest had a broad leather protecting strap which was part of the fastening of the arm protection. With a long reach with the net and trident the odds were evened up by him not having a helmet. He wore just a loincloth besides that. Caratacus had heard the singing and merriment the previous evening and the subtle scuffing of his sandals in the dust told him his opposition was not himself. The Brigante Barbarian boldly moved into the arena to great cheers and took his place with the sun at his back. This put Satonica facing into the sun ensuring his condition was exploited. He had watched the man from Dalmatia and had noticed that just before he prepared to cast his net that he would drop his triple pointed weapon opening up his shoulders to get better leverage it also left that side of the man vulnerable. That said Caratacus knew he had to fight what was in front of him and not have too many preconceptions of how the fight would unfold. As they started to move around facing each other, he remembered his training from back in the forest watching for signs of his opponent tensing and flexing anticipating when and where to attack would come, all the time keeping him facing the sun. Satonica tried to threaten with a couple of short casts quickly withdrawing the net and prodding defensively with the trident. Caratacus watched every move noting the drop of the weapon even on these half hearted casts. He counted with some intimidation of his own; the continual double rotations of the war axe were a blur and cut through the air with a "whoosh" while all the time the tip of his Gladius maintained its steady position ready to strike at a moment's notice. It took a few of these demonstration moves before Satonica tried for real; he was feeling the after effects of the night before and had to get the job done as he knew the longer it went on for the Brigante would have the greater condition. The cast came over from the right catching on Caratacus's arm protection. He in turn saw the dropped tips and smashed down with his axe with such force it broke the central point of the weapon but more decisively breaking Satonica's grip and knocking it out of his hand. He spun round against the cast so as to untangle himself and continued another half spin before coming back the other way and standing hard on the end of the net once again bring the axe to bear as close to the Dalmatians throwing hand. The power of the axe falling was far too great for Satonica to resist the energy which ripped the net away from his grasp and in blind panic he desperately turned to reach the broke trident. It was a move of sheer desperation having no other option and it had caused him to turn his back on his opponent. Satonica had seen the way the Brigante wielded the big axe and he always seemed to lead with that weapon so he turned the opposite way to attack the man on his sword side. Caratacus was well aware of never being predictable and when he saw the tension enter the back and shoulders of his adversary he knew which way the trident would be arcing. He was ready; he closed inside the length of the long weapon and dropped to his knee driving the Gladius forward burying it deep in the side of the gut. As the impact was made the tips of the remaining trident points hit the floor and Caratacus brought the axe over hitting the armoured arm. The scale armour had no protection against the sharpen axe blade from such a short range. The lower scale buckled allowing the blade to ride up into the overlap with the upper sliding between the two and snapping the leather binding before tearing into the flesh below. Satonica crashed to the floor bleeding profusely unable to hold his side wound as that was the arm that had been partially severed. He lay there motionless awaiting his fate. He had been a good champion and had made a reasonable fight of things the governor looked around the crowd and they seemed to be showing their appreciation of the defeated man. He was spared. It would have possibly been a more humane end if Caratacus had been allowed to despatch him swiftly in the arena as it took him a further three days to die.

Lucius and Polyneikes had known they had a special asset on their hand when they first clapped eyes on their star gladiator. They had not realised his speed and the exceptional way the man read a situation and reacted. Polyneikes had searched his considerable experience and memory for someone who might have shown such qualities. He couldn't, not even himself if he was being honest.

"I agree we need to take him to Victrix (the more widely used and shortened version for the name for Chester). But I will need to pay my contact over there to get him in and a high profile opponent," he warned Lucius that his idea was going to cost him money. "To make a big impact we need to get better, more striking armour. Something that shows off his unbelievable physique? It will also ensure word gets to Rome. That is not going to be cheap."

Lucius Magnus was not a wealthy man. His humble background had made him fight his way up the ranks and he had ploughed all his money into his families, Tuscany farm. He had little funds without selling off the family home and he was not about to do that. The man might lose his next contest!

Polyneikes could see the dilemma. "I have some funds put to one side and will use them for a tenth share in Caratacus. It will only get us to Victrix we will have to have a couple more wins before we look at the armour."

Lucius was in a predicament and had no other source of funding the bold strategy he had proposed. "A tenth it is, but you must come up with a tenth of the cost of his new armour?" he countered wanting to save a little face having found himself financially embarrassed by the situation.

"Deal, I will make sure he is given a larger cell and the best food, he can even have a woman or two in between fights I can source all that through the governors funding of the Ludus."

Caratacus was happy with his improving circumstances, meat, grain and good wine allowed him to work his body and hone his skills all the harder. He wasn't impressed by the women he was brought but then he was comparing them to a goddesses daughter. He was provided with more food then he needed so he managed to get some of the excess to Brelus and Ruadan so they could perform well and they too managed to win their contests.

Polyneikes was overjoyed by the news and could not wait to tell Lucius. "The Lanistae of Victrix had heard of the "Brigante Barbarian" and is proposing a two fight deal. The first would be an easy match up to build his reputation higher before he went head to head with their current champion in a multi fight extravaganza. His champion is Picti and there are a few of them so what he proposes is that we use our entire Brigante led by Caratacus against this Pict with his men. He assures me this will be all the talk of Rome and the winner will be sailing within the month!"

They entered the large Roman town of Deva Victrix to a large crowd who had been forewarned of their arrival. They clamoured to see the giant "Brigante Barbarian" shouting and cheering, treating them like celebrities. They were not chained nor were they in caged wagons they rode in a group but were clear that the armed guard that accompanied them would use their cross bows without hesitation if they tried anything. Polyneikes was ever the show man and before they had got to the out skirts he had stopped and had them put of their armour. By the crowd's reaction it appeared to have been a master stroke in publicity.

The training area was very much along the same design as that at Ebruacum albeit a little larger and knowing the long term plans Caratacus studied the training style of the Picts.

Training for the new arrivals was kept separate from the incumbent gladiators and this allowed Lucius to insist in charges to be levied to watch the Brigante train. It all helped to regain some of the money outlaid and following his warm-up contest the attraction was even more popular due to the manner and speed of the victory.

A recently arrived senator was in the city and he was a great follower of gladiatorial games, owning many of the top gladiators who fought at the great Coliseum itself. He was very interested in the new arrivals wanting to meet them in person.

Senator Brutus Aurelius had achieved great honour and fame in his younger days, leading part of the army that had suppressed and finally conquered one of the revolts in Gaul in the early years of the reign of Emperor Honorius. He came from one of the noble houses of Rome and was in Britannia on business when he had heard the stories of the Brigante Barbarian whilst watching the games in Victrix. It was his interest that had convinced Severous Synetos the Lanistae of Victrix to take Polyneikes's offer of bringing the "Brigante Barbarian" in to the city.

As the entourage had arrived Lucius Magnus had been surprised to get an invitation to dine with the senator in the Governors villa. It was exactly the circles Lucius longed to move in and he lapped up the opulence that surrounded him.

He was a little taken aback however when the senator made an offer for his prize attraction. It was an offer he could not refuse. In fact it was an offer he dare not refuse but at the last moment before the deal was sealed he came up with a master stroke that would see him set for life.

"Senator you will see what a great investment you have made at the games, but what if I told you I could let you have two more Brigante warriors? Think of the spectacle: five savage Brigante who resisted Rome fighting another group of Barbarians in the Coliseum."

"You have two more of these men?" he asked in amazement.

"Yes I caught them altogether but two have remained in Eburcum." It was a gamble. Lucius did not know where the two other Brigantes were or if they were still alive but if he was about to lose his star he wanted the biggest payoff he could. The deal was done and later that night when he met Polyneikes he explained the situation.

"Whatever it takes and regardless of the cost we need those two back as soon as we can."

Brutus Aurelius went to see his new stable of gladiators the day before Caratacus was to take on the warm up act. He was amazed at the sheer power the man possessed as he first watched him go through his training routine. He was heaving timber logs round that would take at least two maybe three normal gladiators to move and the combination of this and the speed with which he handled his weapons excited the senator.

The senator waited until after Caratacus had fought before seeing his new star.

The mighty "Brigante Barbarian" said Brutus Aurelius before recommencing with a more personal salutation, "Caratacus isn't it?"

"It is... err?"

"Brutus Aurelius, Senator Brutus Aurelius, you have just joined my gladiator stable and I have great plans for you and your four friends."

Caratacus had no idea what a senator was but could see from his clothes he obviously held a great deal of power. He hoped the man had not seen the surprise on his face at the mention of his four friends as he had not seen Caracalus and Venpasian since they had been separated weeks earlier in Eboracum.

You showed real promise out there today. He was a bit of a slow one but had reasonable skills and great strength but you managed to beat him in every section of the fight. Even when he resorted to that cheap trick with throwing the dirt at your face you had read it before he had even completed his dishonour. The governor was right to instruct you to put an end to his wretched life.

"He was just a man trying to stay alive, as I am."

"I don't think if the time comes you will stoop as low as he did?"

"My time will not come in the arena, I can promise you that."

If anybody but the giant that stood before him had made such a claim Brutus would have thought them foolish and misguided but there was an aura about this man that made him believe his words. "Do you still prefer to fight as a Dimacherus using that clumsy crude thing?" he pointed at the war axe that was leaning up against the wall in the area where all the weapons were kept.

"It is what I am used to and as I have said before, am I not the "Brigante Barbarian"? I would look foolish with one of them tooth picks in my hand."

The senator laughed, the beast actually had a sense of humour. He had taken a shine to this man already and just hoped the team fight would work out; he did not like his men being involved in such contests unless the stakes were in his favour. There were far too many loose weapons for his liking, a stray one could catch the best out if the fighters got too close to each other.

"You take care out there and watch your back in your next contest. Those Picts are devilish fighters."

"You have nothing to worry about senator. I have debt to collect on those little bastards and it will start in the arena and follow them all the way to the other side of the great wall."

The voice that Brutus Aurelius was listening to was calm and clear and was as if it was simply stating fact. This boded well for a profitable future on his considerable investment.

"On the day, I will take the leader. Brelus, watch that little bastard with the Thrace shield and curved sword you take him, see how he raises his sword to commit to that heavy chopping motion, see how at the same time he drops the shield. Be ready when his arm starts to move and a straight lunging jab will get him in the throat. Ruadan you take the Samnite watch him with that heavy Roman shield he always rams and tries to get in close to use the short Gladius, let him come on to you and deflect his charge, don't take it full on. If you push it right into his sword arm he won't be able to deliver a blow and you will be down his exposed flank." They were watching the Picts in full flow fighting against each other and against the dummies giving a good demonstration of their favoured moves. He studied his match up closely just to confirm his previous observations. He was a Murmillo and would be similarly armoured to Caratacus; the biggest difference was he would also have a Gladius and the standard Roman Scutum shield like Ruadan's opponent but his lighter armour made him much more manoeuvrable.

The worst thing about the day of the games was not the fight itself, but the waiting to take your turn in the arena, seeing the dead and wounded being brought back. Some could be so badly injured that just as Caratacus had witnessed it would have been better to put them out of their misery there and then. Some of them were screaming with the pain of their wounds but the Ludus surgeons still tried to sew them up or clap hot iron on them. The smell of burning flesh in such a confined space could be almost overpowering.

"Hey, Brigante half wit you are mine, I will take you in a heartbeat and have your throat in my hands and cut off your cock pushing it down your throat." It was the Pict who held the top billing in the Victrix arena.

"I'm pleased that you have chosen me. I wouldn't have it any other way. Did your mother favour pigs to men to hump her?"

He roared his anger at the remark and the fact that Caratacus had said it so dead pan, showing no emotion.

"I'll fucking kill you, you big bastard. Mark my words, I'm going to fucking kill you." He ranted as he was led down the passage towards the gates.

"Take a line on you men and turn them into the sun and remember what I told you about them. May Tuetates look over us this day my brother's," as he said it he used his thumb to rub against the ring that Becuille had given him. He felt the inscribed "TOT" on the outer face, representing the Druids tribal gods.

There was no more he could do for his men, at least until he disposed of the jumped up little wanker from north of the wall. The trumpet call started the contest and as soon as it sounded the Pict ran at top speed straight at Caratacus. It was not much of a serious attack he tried to ram the Scutum into him but it was easily avoided with half a side step. He noted in his peripheral vision that as they had planned the three simultaneous fights had spread out   so there was no fear of being caught by another fighter's weapon. The Pict ran twice more and only on the last attempt did he actually swing his Gladius missing Caratacus wildly to the left and short.

"Why don't you fight like a man you little prick or have you no balls at all?"

Caratacus's insult had its desired effect. It was again greeted by a scream of anger as he this time moved directly at his tormentor, shield up and heaving an in-swinging chop to Caratacus's head. Light on his feet and turning as the assault passed his left flank, Caratacus easily parried the blow but it had confirmed his observations of the training arena. There was another aimless charge that he let pass and finally the Pict started to tire so steadied his stance losing the lightness in his feet, they could now finally face of and fight for real. It was the Picts turn to feel the force of the mighty Brigante; he firstly prodded toward his opponents face with his Gladius while at the same time bringing over the axe with a thump, driving the man backwards into a stumble. He ended up on his backside and quickly recovered his prior bravado evaporating as he experienced for the first time the power behind the war axe. They took up their positions once again, face to face just a few paces apart. The Pict saw the great axe rise once again and steadied himself for the blow, bringing the scutum up to protect his head. This prevented him seeing what Caratacus did next; instead of delivering the expected hammer blow directly down on to the awaiting shield he twisted his shoulder to allow the axe to fall backwards and delivered an undercut that brought its blade underneath the bottom of his protection. The Pict was tensed waiting for the force in one direction, when it came from the completely opposite direction he had on strength to prevent it. The axe's shaft drove the Scutum up and over the hapless Murmillo's head while the axe blade continues upwards smashing into the loincloth burying itself deep into the groin. The severing of the Femoral Artery is a death sentence, the recipient having less than a few minutes before they bleed out. The Pict wasn't given that. With his defence shattered and his sword arm coming down to try to hold his torn manhood he had lost his weapon. The movement to try to hold himself together brought his face forward and it met Caratacus's Gladius as the tip ripped into the heavy helmet visor. This pushed his head back with such violence that his neck snapped his body hammering into the ground. The fight was over. Caratacus looked for his companions and all had their opponents in trouble. Within a few seconds the three Brigantes were looking up at the Governor to see what the outcome was to be. It was death on all counts.

Polyneikes had been busy in the days following the meeting between Lucius and the senator. Good luck favoured the general as the man who had bought Caracalus and Venpasian had move south to Camulodunum (Colchester) and it was there that the deal was made to buy back the pair of warriors at no little profit for the man who had only owned them for a few weeks.

Brelus had taken a heavy blow to his shoulder and Ruadan one to his side, both awaited the iron to burn the wounds closed. They sat head bowed in the area where the surgeons had the brazier blazing away, irons deep in the yellow hot glow.

"You two never could fight. Hey, Caratacus could you not look after them?"

The voice was familiar, as all three men looked toward the doorway, even the thought of the pain that was coming their way melted in the joy of seeing the return of their two friends. Suddenly the conversation that Caratacus had previously with his new master made sense.

That night was one that they were allowed to celebrate paid for by an appreciative Brutus Aurelius. Even the two new arrivals, although they had not fought were allowed to join the party. It all took place within the confines of the cell block, the central communal room that led to the rear of the cells allowed all the days victors to salute each other's success, supplied with copious amounts of wine, food and some of the better class whores from the brothel next to the arena. Caratacus had drunk too much; he seemingly could never eat too much. But he did manage to take a dark skinned woman back to his cell. In the morning he vaguely remembered she was called Midbia or something like that. He had stripped her naked and laid her on his bunk before removing his tunica and loincloth, returning to his prize his hardness sparked by seeing Becuille had taken her place through his wine fuelled haze. It was hard to see how she had taken Midbia's place as she was far more rounded and dark skinned than the petit, pale skinned daughter of Flidais, but in his head it was the beauty for the forest he was burying himself deep inside. She even reacted in the same way that Becuille had the final time they had been together when he had eventually been on top, hooking her heels round his lower back and pulling him close with her arms round his neck. But he had to try and hide his disappointment when in the morning it was Midbia who left his cell, her nights work complete.

Caracalus and Venpasian were made to pay for their unearned celebration, the following morning they were out in the exercise yard being put through their paces, being assessed by the Lanistae of Victrix, Severous Synetos who had been instructed by the senator to see how good they were and if they would be a good inclusion to his stable. All five of the Brigante new the importance of the session and the outcome of the mock fight with their wooden weapons they faced at the end.

Senator Brutus Aurelius was planning his return to Rome. He had a busy year ahead of him. His son would be coming of age and had to serve the empire by taking a small private force with him to join General Flavius Stilicho back here in Britannia but first he had the hold a commemorative games event in the Coliseum. It would be an enormously expensive affair but it was the tenth anniversary of the death of his father, like him a great general of Rome and just as all the other noble houses it was something that needed to be rejoiced, money would be no object. It was the reason he had bought the Brigante warriors and why he now lavished them with the best armour he could have made. They were to play a central role in the culmination of the three days of the games. In the meantime he would have them travel the provinces building their reputation until they came to face their greatest challenge in the greatest arena in the world.

Five sets of armour were made specifically for the victorious Brigante Barbarians. Both Caracalus and Venpasian had successfully come through an encounter in the arena proving their worth to the senator. So it was, that they had some of the best craftsmen in Victrix measure the men and produce the appropriate armour for each other's style of fighting. The protection oozed quality and was finished off with hardening in oil which gave the metal a black mat finish. Only Caratacus had a difference; the edges of every individual plate was polished brass and gleamed like gold. Their weapons were treated to the same ornate finishing with handles finished with black, tipped with highly polished amber coloured stones. Each helmet matched the rest of their battle uniform and had the unelaborated style of the Spartan. It was all designed to give the barbarian effect, hard, unpretentious and deadly.

Their journey started by travelling down the impressively engineered Roman road of Watling Street. They stopped off in Loninium (London), which had become the provincial capital of Britannia following the sacking of Camulodunum during the Iceni rebellion by the she-warrior, Boudica in the early days of the occupation.

The place was immense and Caratacus had never seen so much humanity squeezed into such a small area. A dark cloud hung over the entire city as the smog from thousands of fires burnt, their smoke adding to the stench. They were accommodated in the fort that was just at the end of the road while the Senator stayed in the Governors Palace. With selective choice each of the five were put through their paces with a contest in the amphitheatre that was just adjacent to the garrison. It was another step up in size and it appeared by the reaction of the crowd that the five warrior's notoriety had preceded them.

They eventually boarded a ship at a wharf on the river that someone told them was called the Tamesis (Thames) and it was from there that their first ever voyage departed. They left a damp and miserable Londinium heading into the grey sea before seeing another coast in the distance, after many days hugging that coastline on their left until the weather started to pick up and their bodies started to warm for the first time since they had embarked. They had landed at several ports during their journey and had been allowed on shore to stretch out their sea legs that seemed to be unable to do as they were being told. It was strange but for the first time since their capture they had no guards or chains.

"Where are we, where would we run to and who lives over those next hills are they friend or foe?" Caratacus understood why that they were now given so much freedom and explained his reasoning when the lads had been discussing their rapidly changing situation.

The sun was shining and the sky was blue. Apparently it was always like that in the countryside to the south of Rome. Italia was the name of the Peninsula and the entire territory was the property of Rome. Along with the mainland it claimed the islands of Corsica, Sardinia, Sicily and Malta. But the names of the Brigante gladiators would not get Roman tongues wagging enough by entering contests on the islands so it was Regio III, Lucania et Brutii that formed the toe of the boot of the peninsula where they landed. Reggio Calabria was a coastal city, separated from the island of Sicily by a narrow strip of water called the Strait of Messina. It was here that the ship finally docked and the five gladiators first stepped on to real Roman soil.

There was a small amphitheatre in the port city and the scene of all the gladiatorial events. Brutus Aurelius met his personal Lanistae who had arrived from Rome to take charge of several shipments of gladiators that were being shipped in for the senator's games. It was a busy time in the city and the small cell blocks around the arena were full so the five got to stay in a disused barrack room within the garrison. Lanistae Titus Cyprian stayed just outside the garrison as a guest in the commander's villa while the senator headed back to Rome. Each day Titus had them taken on a run into the nearby countryside before returning for combat training. He had heard a lot about the "Brigante Barbarians" and was pleased it was not just exaggerated boosts from his master, the old man had actually brought some real talent home this time especially the giant who was built like Mars the god of war but he would dare not say such a thing in this age of Christian faith. Titus was always angry when he had such thoughts, why he should be fearful of worshipping the old gods he didn't understand he was sure the empire had weakened since Christianity had raised its ugly head the one god merchants were even attacking the games, the very heart of the empire. It wasn't any wonder that barbarian hordes across the empire were rising up in revolt. He snapped out of his inner rant.

"Hey you big man, let's see you in action. Are you as good in a fight as you look?" Titus picked up a wooden trident and a net and faced off with Caratacus. He repeatedly rammed the forked points in a jabbing motion towards the opposing torso. He wanted to see the man's reaction and to observe how he dealt with a lazy weapon that wasn't being withdrawn quickly enough. The first three prods were just parried and it was obvious by the intense concentration his opponent was measuring him up. On the forth jab the big man slotted his short gladius between two of the prongs and twisted it ripping it free of his grasp. As fast as a lightning bolt from Jupiter himself the Brigante moved down that free flank in a forward roll bring his wooden axe to rest against his knee.

"Bravo, bravo my big friend they call you Caratacus do they not?"

"Sir," Caratacus had learnt to show humility to all Romans, it made for an easier life and as Polyneikes had told him he would need the beggars on his side if he was ever to win his freedom, so he bowed his head as he replied.

"How often have you worn that fancy armour that our master bought you?"

Caratacus liked the way this man tried to make out he was one of them and serving the same master. He was not setting himself up as superior and seemed to be a man that could be trusted. "Just the once sir, when we fought in Londinium."

"Ah, Londinium they say it is a city where a good man could prosper?" without warning he attacked Caratacus by trying to cast his net over his head. Caratacus had not taken his eyes of the Lanistae and had seen him drop his near shoulder and tense his far arm ready for the cast. He bent at the hips dropping his head at the same time as he took two steps back to his original position, his axe drawn back ready to strike. Titus Cyprian had been bettered twice in a matter of seconds. This man was quite exceptional. He got the feeling he had fame standing at his side.

"Excellent Caratacus, you are correct never to drop your guard. Go and put your armour on we need you working in what you will fight in, getting used to the weight and its restrictions." He watched the muscled back flex and relax as the giant slowly but very smoothly with great grace moved out of the arena. Yes with luck this man would bring him fame and fortune; after the people of Rome see this beast perform they would all want to know his trainer.

For a full month they trained in the same city. "We are making sure you men from the colder parts of the empire get used to the climate before we give you your first outing and that will be next week here in this arena against gladiators from one of the senators greatest rivals. We obviously need you to win, but we also require you to humiliate them, beat then quickly and with ease so you need to be in peak condition."

The day before the games in Reggio Calabria another consignment of gladiators arrived for the Aurelius stable and to everybody's fascination there were two gladitix (female gladiators) amongst the group. They too had a training session in the arena and seemed to be able to handle themselves.

The Lanistae explained to Caratacus who he had taken a liking to as he saw the prospect of his fame on those great shoulders, that the women would fight each other but without any despatching at the end. They were light entertainment something to whet the appetite before the main show. As far as he knew there would be no real competition for the women until they reached Rome and that would be months away.

The crowds had been watching the Aurelius Ludus train for weeks, enthralled by the power and raw animal barbarism that these men possessed. When the opposing gladiators arrived in the city just a few days before the contest they were strangers, interlopers who had come to challenge the might of the gladiators that they had come to call their own.

On the day of the games it was very clear who the public were backing. Caratacus entered the arena to a massive cheer, the applause needing to be ushered down so the contest could start. He was facing a stocky man but rather short and therefore saw his opportunity for the swift attack using his superior reach. The man took the style of a Thrace so carried the heavy circular defensive shield and a curved sword so commonly used in the Thracian part of the empire. Without any niceties Caratacus rained a torrent of crashing axe blows that splintered the shield leaving just the leather strap handles hanging uselessly on his arms. In desperation the Thrace tried to parry the next blow with his sword, leaving his right side open for Caratacus to plunge his Gladius into his gut. It was all over in a blink of the eye. The crowd roared their approval amazed at the raw power of their hero who stood, foot on the chest of the defeated man waiting for the decision to be made. He had not put up a very good show and there was little sympathy for him. The thumb was turned downwards.

Whether that knocked the wind out of the rest of the opposition gladiators no one could tell, but none managed to put up a very stern test for the Brigante fighters. Two of the new men were beaten one being granted "missio" (allowed to live) as he had put up a valiant battle, coming away with a leg wound that was repairable.

From Reggio Calabria they went to Cosenza, from there to Salerno and then on to the city of Neapolis (Naples), dominated by volcano Vesuvius that lit up the night's sky with a display of red magna iridescence. Its enormous power had been on show as they passed through the town of Pompeii, a once thriving and sophisticated city. Pompeii had been buried under huge mountains of ash and pumice after a catastrophic eruption many years earlier. It had only just starting to be resettled and regain some of its former glory.

The city of Neapolis was where Caratacus was to face his stiffest challenge to date. Although they were not aware of the fact the Aurelius Ludus was not one of the major players in the Roman gladiatorial world. That prestigious honour was constantly shifting between the emperor and the most prominent senator of the age. The emperor would not be sending his own Ludus to compete in anybody else's games he would never risk being up staged. When he held his events it was between his gladiators no other Ludus was invited, this did mean that he had to foot the entire bill. But there were advantages of being the emperor.

Augustus Cicero was the most powerful man in the senate. He was also one of the wealthiest, his riches rumoured to be greater than the emperor himself. It made for a very fractious political situation but that was nothing new. He was a man who held on to the old ways and had never taken to Christianity although he did not publically condemn it, needing the many believers of the new faith for the support he required to challenge the Theodosia dynasty that the emperor belonged to. On the other hand Brutus Aurelius had thrown his lot in with Flavius Honorius Augustus who was the current emperor of the western empire, his brother Arcadius was emperor in the east. Their father, the last sole ruler of the empire, Theodosius I, had not only split the empire between his sons he had ruled over a period of great unrest, campaigning against the Goths and other barbarians who had invaded the empire. Unfortunately for him he had failed to kill their leaders, or drive them out of the empire, the result being that they had established a homeland in Illyricum, south of the Danube, within the empire's borders. It was seen as a sign of the empire weakening. As a result he had to fight two destructive civil wars, in which he defeated the usurpers Magnus Maximus and Eugenius at great cost, which further undermined the power of the empire. For his enemies the final straw had been the acceptance of Orthodox Nicene Christianity becoming the official state religion of Rome as well as banning all the pagan rituals that he knew were still part of everyday army life. He had even tried to bring an end to the games his people loved so much. His son Honorius had seen that as an error and in an attempt to regain some of the lost popularity he had openly embraced them even funding huge events and having his own Ludus. This hint at a return to the old ways, the days of the empires greatness was why he had held on to a lot of support including that of Brutus Aurelius. It brought the two senators head to head many times and Augustus Cicero would never pass up a chance to get one over on his senate rival even in the arena.

On the day of the Neapolis games rumours flooded the city of the heightening tensions in Rome and of civil unrest stoked by a split in the senate. Talk of groups of violent thugs running riot attacking supporters of the other side seemed to fill the air. The guards down in the cells that fed the main arena seemed more interested in this news than doing their jobs. Caratacus had been drawn to face a Syrian Secutore and followed the display of the gladitix. Even during the somehow erotic scene of the two women fighting there was unrest in the crowd. Billed as two mythical "Amazonian" warriors the scene of two scantily clad, dark skinned fighters usually had the crowds enthralled but not today, certain sections were actually booing them hurling objects on to the arena surface screaming abuse at the women condemning them as Aurelius whores, chanting the name Augustus Cicero over and over again. But most of the Cicero supporters disquiet was for Cassius Aurelius the senator's son and one of the privileged guests.

Caratacus entered the arena to a mixed reception, his supporters cheering hard to ensure a good welcome for the famed "Brigante Barbarian". His opponent was a little known man who had just arrived in the city, in fact that was the same for all the men who were fighting for the Cicero Ludus. Following on from his challenge would be the contest on horseback where Equites would do battle. They entered from a different gate but could be seen waiting in the wings.

The Syrian Secutor moved and danced around without making much of an effort to attack just the occasional faint forward them quickly dodging back out of reach. Caratacus kept moving forwards following the man's retreat but stopping occasionally to get up on his toes trying to remain light on his feet. He could not put his finger on what troubled him but something did. His opponent was expending a lot of energy keeping out of his way something that he surely knew he would not be allowed to continue. Every gladiator knew if they failed or refused to fight they would be executed by either their opponent or the archers around the top of the arena walls. So when he would eventually stop to fight he would have already exhausted himself. Something was wrong.

The Syrian had moved back towards the Equites gate and Caratacus could see the mounted men in the tunnel over the Syrian's shoulder. With them being the next contest on they would need to be ready but he would not have expected them to be mounted and armed when both horse warriors were in the same tunnel. His peripheral vision picked up some of the crowd getting uglier in their behaviour and small scuffles had broken out. It was time to put an end to this.

He shot forward and struck the round shield with three fast and heavy blows while at the same time jabbing his Gladius. The two pronged attack had the tired man stumble backwards, but he had already backed himself up against the side of the gate and without being totally conscious of his exact position in relation to the arena wall he crashed his head which pushed the rear protective brim of his helmet forward and down cracking the bridge of his nose. It was the break in his opponent's concentration that Caratacus had been trying to create and he now took full advantage of it. The weight of axe blows had the man on the floor in seconds and Caratacus stamped on his sword arm as it moved to get into a position to strike. The Syrian gave a kick trying to knock him off the stance that held the sword flat to the ground. The kick only annoyed the Brigante who used his other foot to stamp on the exposed loincloth driving all the breath out of the now condemned man. Finally the shield could take no more punishment and split in two exposing the helpless man. He looked round for the judgement of the clearly nervous governor who had Cassius sat at his side. A mob was making its way to the privileged enclosure just as the gate went up releasing the two horse men, who were carrying a Pilum each, a Gladius in their belt and a heavy round shield. They charged into the arena and headed directly for the pair of dignitaries in the enclosure. As the second one passed Caratacus he tried to stab the Brigante fighter with his Pilum jabbing it towards his side but a swift sideways move resulted in nothing more than Caratacus taking matters into his own hands the plunging his Gladius into the Syrian's throat to finish the contest. As the sword thrust execution was completed he turned all in the same movement and hurled the axe ten paces into the back of the retreating rear Equite. The first rider had arrived in front of the magistrate or editors box, cried out the name Cicero and threw his Pilum missing both targets wildly wide striking a member of the crowd adding to the chaos.

An Equite would enter the arena on horseback, starting their contest with lance or spear but would usually finish dismounted with sword and shield. Caratacus had retrieved his axe and was screaming to the guards on the other gate to let his men out so they could protect Cassius and the governor. Being totally overwhelmed by the situation and not having any orders that considered this eventuality they gave in to the loudest voice. That was Caratacus's.

The treacherous Equite had turned to see his fellow conspirator dead just as Caratacus was pulling the war axe out of his back. He started his charge expecting to see the barbarian run for his life. He obviously knew very little about the man he faced. Instead of running away he charged at the horse. The gap between the two shortened at a pace, just before the collision Caratacus threw himself at the horse's front hooves creating a natural instinct for the beast to jump. It had not been expected by the rider who was unseated and crashed to the floor, his helmet bouncing off his head. Dazed the rider stumbled to his feet and looked up in the direction he had come from. A dark vertical line started to appear in front of him; it was rapidly growing larger and just below it was a much thinker solid upright shaft. The barbarian war axe was the last thing that the would-be assassin saw on earth. Caratacus had quickly got to his feet and followed the horse until he reached the floored rider, as the man was getting up he started to look up just as Caratacus was unleashing the death blow via his axe. The weapon was embedded so deep that the eyes of the dead man had been separated by the blade, causing them to burst from his head as the extreme internal pressure of the force exerted got to the point that the sockets could no longer hold them.

The other four Brigante warriors had arrived at his side. "With need to help the young Aurelius," he called as he led them towards the enclosure that was now being overrun. The attackers were now far too close to the pair for the few remaining archers to take safe shots.

"Cassius Aurelius! Jump down here. We will protect you," he called trying to make his voice heard above the pandemonium that was going on above them. The two bodyguards died valiantly doing their duty, trying to protect the governor but it was just the two dignitaries that dropped to the arena floor, being immediately surrounded by the five gladiators who held their shield high to prevent the torrent of projectiles hitting anybody in the group. As a unit they moved back, weapons out shields up but the mob dropped down and continued their frenzied attempt to get at their original targets.

Finally the attackers were exposed so the archers who had not been attacked could fire at will. The gladiator bodyguard took its toll on many and when what seemed like an age a unit of infantry soldiers came into the arena the mob was despatched without mercy.

The young man was trying not to show he had been shaken by the assault. The governor was a different matter he was ashen and dropped to his knees gasping for air. With the immediate danger over they moved away to give the man some fresh air and Cassius comforted him pleased to be able to do something constructive.

That evening it appeared that the whole city was in lock down the entire garrison was out on the streets ensuring that nobody could continue the murderous acts of the afternoon. The governor, Cassius and the Brigante bodyguard took refuge in the garrison commander's villa. Here they waited until a cohort of Cassius's men arrived to take responsibility for his safety.

With a heavy military presence the Aurelius Ludus accompanied by Cassius marched to Rome. The Ludus Magnus was the training school for the very best gladiators in the empire and the five were given their own cells. That evening with guards on every door the senator visited and thanked the five personally for saving his son. He had arranged a feast for them and entertainment from the local brothel. But first he needed to talk to Caratacus.

"I have heard the accounts of your actions from my son. I appreciate the others played a great part in his survival but he is in no doubt that without you taking charge of the situation things could have turned out far worse." He stopped and placed his hand on the huge shoulder that was nearly above his head. "This is going to seem a strange plan I have for you Caratacus but hear me out..." he waited to see Caratacus head acknowledge he was being requested not ordered before he continued. "The games that take place in two months time are in celebration of the memory of my father and I need my very best gladiators to pay justice to his memory, but those who come out victorious will be given their freedom to serve with my son as his personal bodyguard and he is bound for Britannia with General Flavius Stilicho. After three years service you will be given your complete freedom, in the meantime you will have the full pay of a serving centurion with the others on regular soldiers pay."

Britannia, freedom two words that rung so sweetly they sounded like the gods had sung them. He tried to hold his composure but failed, his broad smile breaking through his tight lips. "Thank you, senator. I pledge I will protect the young man with my life and so will all my men. You have the word of Caratacus, Chieftain of the Pennine Brigante.

"Until the games you will have the freedom you deserve as top gladiators but please train hard and well I would dearly like all of you to win your freedom at the munus (memorial) games."

The conversation was relayed to the others and it made that evening celebration all the sweeter, but all agreed that it would be the last time they would take a drink until their freedom had been secured.

The gladitix and a few others joined in on the celebration. But even as the first of the drink had started to flow Caratacus was thinking about the road to Britannia and Amergin Gluingel's prophecy. He did not feel like drinking. He was inwardly pleased but also now nearing the finish line he did not want to become complacent. The laughter coming from the others cheered him but he would keep a clear head. Only when he had drawn his first Centurion pay would he take his next drink.

"Why so glum Caratacus?" It was the Thracian, Arbella, one of the gladitix. She was the beauty of the two and had a body as well proportioned as it was muscled. He had talked to her a few times but although he had seen her physique it had been more of professional interest as she trained in the different Ludus arenas they had lived in. Tonight she looked different; no headgear just long straight jet black locks that reached the base of her back. Her light armour and chain mail skirt and small top replaced by fine fur garments that still showed off her womanly assets.

"You should be happy with the news of your impending freedom not sat here quiet on your own," without asking she sat alongside him offering him a cup of wine.

I am happy and I intend to taste my freedom so I have no use for any wine until I can say I am free once again. They spent the next hour telling each other of the homeland and how they came to be in the Ludus Magnus. Caratacus stretched his shoulder he had been having a certain discomfort since the events in Neapolis when the horse had actually kicked him trying to avoid his flying body.

"Are you still in pain from that shoulder?"

"Yes it seems to stiffen up when it is idle, it will pass in time."

Here, let me help, it needs gentle stretching so that the muscle can release its tension." With that she had stood behind him and had started to knead her fingers into his shoulder and rotating his arm gently pushing it until he winced and then expertly sank her fingers once again exactly where the pain had been. After a little time she stopped, much to Caratacus's disappointment, however she was repositioning to work from the front. With him sitting she had spread her legs so she straddled his and this placed her ample bust almost in his face. It felt good and her soothing work was helping him in one area but causing some growing tension in another. He looked up at her face, she was looking beyond him at the back wall but must have sensed his attention so looked down at him and smiled as she saw how close his face was to her. Her smile said it all, she knew what she was doing and he did not have a problem with that. He placed his free hand on her hip and started to massage his giant hand across her smooth dark skin. She responded by slowly gyrating to his hand movements.

"I think we should go back to your cell." It was a statement not a question she whispered in his ear. He took the offered hand and followed her.

In the cell where they could get as much privacy a gladiator ever did get, she turned to face him. She was tall for a woman but still considerably shorter than the man she was looking at with a passionate hunger. He was wearing a short course woven toga tied around his waist by a thin rope which accentuated his massive shoulders. She longed for this man, it was not very often that she was ever in the presence of anybody who made her feel small and vulnerable like a little girl but this man of Britannia did just that. She sat back on his bunk and used the rope round his waist to pull him towards her. As he arrived beside his bed following her none too subtle encouragement she let one end of the rope drop. As she continued to pull it unfastened and fell away. She smiled at the bulge that was so pronounced in the front of the toga and with one hand gripping one of his buttocks she reached inside the stretched garment to ease the strain in his loin. For all she was a fighter she had soft hands as far as Caratacus was concerned. He stood, his eyes were shut tight, his head bent backwards towards the ceiling as Arbella worked his hardness cupping him gently and caressing him. She stopped her magical work and stood, taking the bottom of his toga and pulling it up towards his head. He finished off removing the garment as she returned to her previous delicious intimate attention. Again she made the move turning him round then pushing him back on to his bunk, now she towered above his semi prone inclined body his manhood paying tribute to her skilled work. The soft fur, cropped top was held together on one shoulder by a rough metal clasp which fell away on releasing. The top had been under pressure by the magnificent contents resulting in it falling forward where Caratacus caught it. It was still warm from her beauty which added to the eroticism of the moment. She stood there knowing just how good she looked, daring the man in front of her to resist her charms. For the first time Caratacus made the next move. Moving forward out of his inclined pose he reached to the short fur skirt and traced his fingers round the waist band finding the bone pin that held the overlap together. She was so different to Becuille in every way other than the effect she was having on him. Her skin was a dark rich bronzed colour and unlike his tan it was all over, even in her most intimate places. The gorgeous colour was constant with the exception of the two dark buds that tipped her full rounded breasts that he was now feeling under both of his rough hands. He leaned forward and kissed her ripped muscular stomach dropping one of his hands to begin exploring her most inner sanctum that had her moving in a slow rocking motion following his lead. Arbella's breath was becoming faster and more erratic as she lifted one leg on to the bunk giving greater access to his ever increasing hand speed. She dropped forward placing both her arms round the back of his head pressing her chest into his face as she started to convulse crying with pleasure. His hand was wet with her passion and as she collapsed on to the bed she took his hand in her mouth greedily tasting her own love juices. He pulled her down the bed until she was laid flat where he entered her. Their love making was intense; each move was firm and powerful as they started their synchronised sexual adoration, growing faster and more frenetic as their excitement culminated in an explosion that would have impressed Vesuvius the fire mountain herself.

In the early hours of the morning, Arbella returned to her own cell as the guards had left the victorious and heroic saviours of their maters son free reign on the back on the senator's orders.

Caratacus had his head full of conflicting emotions. He longed for Arbella to return to him but knew her safety was now a concern to him and that deflected his focus on winning his next contest and ultimately his freedom. And if he did win his freedom he wanted her to be free with him. Things had just got complicated.

The emperor was in a rage when he heard what had happened in Neapolis. He was not one to let such a slight on one of his biggest supporter go without a swift riposte. But when it did it was far more violent than anybody had expected especially Augustus Cicero.

When you have just announced your violent intentions towards a powerful enemy a wise man would not continue to follow his regular routines. That is unless your arrogance blinds you to your own mortality.

It was the standards of the time that the noblemen of Rome would regularly use the services provided by some of the more colourful bathhouses in the city. It consisted of having the very close attention of a selected slave or slaves depending on your purse.

Just as he had done every "dies Mercurii" (Wednesday), Senator Augustus Cicero had spent the latter part of the afternoon and early evening in the company of his favoured girls. It was dark when he left the bathhouse brothel that was situated in one of the seedier parts of the city. His bodyguard had been waiting for him since he had entered the establishment hours earlier and were thoroughly bored and miserable. They guided their master down the same back streets as always so he would re-enter the acceptable side of the city far from where he had been conducting his business. There were no witnesses to the attackers who appeared out of the shadows of a semi demolished home. But they must have vastly outnumbered the bodyguard to overpower them so quickly. In the morning there was reports of a large group of men found floating in the River Tiberis (Tiber). That in itself was not too surprising, unfortunately in a city of the size Rome it was a regular occurrence. What was unusual was they seemed to have a uniform that suggested they all belonged to a private army. The other news of that morning rocked the city. Senator Augustus Cicero had been found murdered, his body floating in the baths of a brothel with his manhood cut off and pushed down his throat.

With one fateful swipe Honorius had dispensed with his main enemy in the senate. The other senators who had backed the anti-emperor movement fell silent and did not bother to attend the next few sittings effectively accepting defeat. At the same time the fortunes of his supporters soared, especially the man who had been so badly wronged in the arena at Neapolis. It was Senator Brutus Aurelius who took the mantle of the most senior senator in the senate.

The senator's "mundus" for his father was honoured by Emperor Honorius himself. Arbella performed her ritual fight that as usual did not end in either contestant's death. Where normally there would be no bloodshed there was a twist. Many of the lesser conspirators of the Cicero plot had been rounded up and were to be executed in the Coliseum. Both gladitix had to do their duty and remove the heads of one man apiece. It was the same for the other fighters the victorious man would be given the honour of despatching the "Noxii" (enemy of the state). This bloodletting gave a more conciliatory mood to the crowd when it came to the decision for ant defeated gladiator and with what had been the Cicero Lundus having been shared out between the emperors supporters nobody really wanted to lose men. That was with the exception of Caratacus.

The emperor had heard so much about his deeds in the arena he wanted to see the Brigante Barbarian fight. It was the Cicero champion that was selected as his opponent. It would be a true battle of the giants as this Nubian was almost the same size as Caratacus.

Caratacus has been given two light workouts in the first two days of the games. Each day he had faced one of the conspirators, unlike the others they had been armed but it really had been nothing more than a practice session and the would-be battle was over after a rain of axe blows had driven the condemned to the ground and his death followed with the head removed with a single sweep of his war axe.

The entire three day event was built for the final day to culminate in this great showdown. The arrangements had been changed to appease the emperor. Brutus having decided to have the Brigante gladiators as his son's bodyguard did not want Caratacus to be risked especially when there were plenty of killings going on in the arena. But it did not pay to displease your emperor even if you were part of his inner sanctum.

As the pair walked out of the gloomy tunnel into the glare of the daylight the contrast hurt their eyes, burning into their retinas leaving yellow spots imprinted on their brain, for a few seconds they could not see at all, just hear the unbelievable din of over fifty thousand people. His eyes had started to become accustomed to the new light and he noticed his opponent was looking round awe struck. Caratacus realise it had been a shroud move to have him fight both the previous days, gaining experience of the surrounding without having to face such a serious threat. His Nubian friend across from him did seem to be on edge.

"We who are about to die salute you," they called out in unison with their weapons across their chests in tribute. The emperor waved his hand giving the pair permission to take their places. The Nubian carried the two swords of the Dimacherous so both men were armed and armoured similarly, Caratacus new that with two Gladius the man opposite him was going to be quick. When the trumpet blast sang out to start the contest Caratacus quickly moved round to get the sun on his back and therefore in the other mans eyes. If he had trouble seeing he would be slower and that should even up the contest. The Nubian moved in and out making exploratory jabs and was rewarded with parries. Caratacus went on similar attacks and his ended in the same way. Both attacked at the same time and ended up shoulder charging each other and although he was surprised by the man's strength it was Caratacus who won that little encounter and the Nubian failed to stand up to the collision needing to take a few steps backwards to regain his balance. Every time they came into close quarters Caratacus had the upper hand of sheer brute strength and he used this to regain the advantage of the sun because it was evident his opponent had realised the disadvantage he was at. Time and again one would attack only for the other to counter and the battle of the giants had been going on for nearly an hour. Such huge men were showing their grit maintaining the work rate. Hardly surprising, as to drop it could mean death. It was incentive enough for them to keep going at full pace. Gladiatorial contests were occasionally considered a fighting draw when both had fought bravely to a standstill, but it wasn't what Caratacus wanted he had never failed to win a contest and had no intention of accepting such a result. The Nubian made another attack and his right was parried so he followed up with the left. Just as before this was knocked away with Caratacus's axe.

What was that? A slight flat ring from the Gladius as it was struck by the thick broad axe head. As the man stepped back Caratacus attacked with more vigour than he had for many minutes. It pushed his adversary back and when he brought up his Gladius that rang with the flat note attempting to parry the axe, Caratacus turned the axe head to strike a direct blow on the sword blade.

Ping! Just as he had suspected the metal of the blade had been showing signs of stress and the blade had shattered close to the hilt rendering the weapon as good as useless.

A great cheer rang out as the crowd saw a possible end to the stalemate. So did Caratacus who was not going to relent from the attack that had given him an edge. He brought his axe down once again only for it to be blocked by the last remaining sword in the Nubians hand. His gladius was free and his foe had no blocker until the wily fighter turned and backed towards Caratacus so he was inside his sword arm and no blow could be delivered.

The crowd was screaming wildly and drove the men into one last great effort. The Nubian tried to duck down and use Caratacus's momentum against him trying to up end the Brigante. Caratacus saw the dark muscular skin flex and tense and seeing this he anticipated his intentions before he had even started the move. The sword that had not had chance to strike the winning blow on the previous attack got a reprieve, still too far forward to use to slice or stab it could be turned into a hammer by using the hilt in his hand.

Oohh! It was as if even over the crowds din the crack to the back of the Nubians helmeted head rang out and gained their attention. A deep dent was left in the rear section as his face was planted into the dusty ground. Before he had time to react Caratacus's gladius point was resting on his back while he knew the axe would be held up high, waiting. Still face down the beaten man raised his hand in submission. The contest was over; all that was left was for the emperor who as expected was the acting editor to give his decision. Life or death?

Even an emperor in these circumstances would be foolish to ignore the will of the people and why would he? He had just witnessed one of the best contests he had ever seen. It was missio, the Nubian was spared and the crowd once again went wild with joy. Caratacus dropped his weapons and offered his hand to the defeated man. The vanquished took the gesture as it was meant, two gladiators respecting each other after a hard fought contest.

It was the end of the games. All that was left was for the Emperor accompanied by his family and Brutus Aurelius to present the laurel crown and purse to Caratacus with all the other victors of the day getting a reward. Finally Honorius raised his hand and gave a speech that ended in Caratacus receiving the highest reward that any gladiator could, the *Rudi* (wooden sparring sword) which offered Caratacus the opportunity to stop being a gladiator. It was the final part of an exceptional games and one that sent the people of Rome home happy and that pleased the emperor.

Brutus and his son Cassius were both relieved. Caratacus had not only survived, he had further enhanced his reputation. It couldn't have worked out any better, for during the sharing of the spoils of the Cicero Lundus Brutus had won the Nubian that Caratacus had just fought. He had resigned himself to losing at least one of his gladiators but as it was he had not and Cassius had been quick to ask his father if the Nubian could join his already awesome bodyguard.

"Will you share wine with me?" asked Caratacus of the Nubian. The games had finished hours ago and it was time for the post games celebration. It was just for the Aurelius Ludus and it was back at the barracks where Cassius's small army was based. As they had filed into the empty barrack room it had just started to seem real. The entire band of "Brigante Barbarians" had survived the gladiatorial trials and would soon be heading back to their homeland. They had had their ankle irons removed by the smith and it felt good. Wine and food was plentiful, supplied by a grateful sponsor and not soon after they had started their banquet the women from the nearby brothel had arrived.

"What is your name friend?" he continued offering the jug of wine to the rather deflated looking Nubian warrior.

"Axios," he replied holding up the rough earthenware goblet.

Well Axios you gave me the hardest fight of my life this afternoon, we both survived and are free of the games for good. I know you are likely to feel unhappy about losing but you courage is without question, the emperor himself acknowledged as much and from now on we fight on the same side. Caratacus pushed his goblet towards Axios offing the little speech as a toast. Axios smiled weakly and raised his goblet responding to the attempt at cheering him up.

"It is not that Caratacus. I was beaten by the better man today and that man it quite rightly the toast of Rome. You and your brothers have every reason to celebrate you are heading home. Me, I am heading even further away from mine. In Britannia I will be on the other side of the empire to my family."

Caratacus suddenly felt bad about how he had presumed that his good news would be everybody else's good news. It also hit him that Arbella would not be feeling as good about events as he. Sure she would be happy he had triumphed but it did mean if she was to remain with the ludus he would be leaving her behind and they had become very close since their first passionate encounter.

It was father and son, Brutus and Cassius who brought the female company with them when they came to welcome the new recruits to Cassius's Cohort. Both were clearly inebriated but not that far gone for Caratacus to pass up the opportunity to immediately ask if he could use all his prize money to buy Arbella's freedom. The pair looked very serious when each turned to face one another. Brutus finally turned back to Caratacus.

"You will give me all your prize money for her freedom?" he repeated as if trying to make sense of a stupid request.

"I will master."

"Stop right there! I am not your master; you won your freedom from the ludus today. I am Senator Brutus Aurelius so you address me as Senator as do the citizens of Rome, is that understood?" He was looking back at Cassius and Caratacus wasn't sure if he didn't see a little wink towards his son. "I will let my son agree how you should address him when you have time together, but I am sure as Centurion of his personal bodyguard he will expect a little less formal salutations between the pair of you." Cassius's head was slowly nodding. "It seems to be my lucky day today Cassius," he started to address his son. "Not only is the emperor very happy with the outcome of recent events and the games, but my two star men both survived and just when I was about to give Arbella to Caratacus as a tribute for his services to me he gives me his winnings for her. The pair burst out laughing; amused at the clumsy way Caratacus had tried to win his loves freedom.

It was Cassius's turn to have fun at his expense, "Caratacus, it has not exactly been a well kept secret about you and Arbella. It never could be in the ludus, but watching her make every move of your fight from behind the gates confirmed it. I asked father to grant you her freedom if you survived the arena yesterday and he agreed. All you had to do was win." He smiled as he saw Caratacus's joy. She is outside in a court yard and the blacksmith is standing by. She has no idea what is happening, I think it might be good for you to break the new to her?"

Arbella was flanked by a guard who left as Caratacus approached.

"Oh, Caratacus. I died a hundred times during that fight," she threw her arms round his neck and they embraced. Kissing passionately he picked her up off her feet and moved across to the smithy shop. He saw the same perplexed expression on her face as he had worn when he had been teased earlier.

"Put your foot up on the anvil. It is time to remove this damn thing," he arranged the heavy ankle shackle for the smith. "Besides no woman of a chieftain of Brigantia is going to Britannia with the markings of a slave."

A soldier of Rome.

It had taken longer than expected to return to the shores of his native country. But just as the Druid Amergin Gluingel had foreseen here he was. They had sailed from Rome and had first landed in Dubris (Dover) before sailing up the east coast in a large convoy to Eboracum. They had stayed in the port city for a few days waiting for the convoy to build to a size that would give security against Pictish attack before heading north. Hearing this news Caratacus thought of the little bastard who had betrayed him to the Romans so long ago. It was nearing the time he had promised himself as they had been trapped on the wrong side of the wall. It was time for pay back.

They could tell something was wrong as they moved up the River Ouse from the mouth of the Humber Estuary. Three telltale signs of vertical columns of dark grey smoke contrasted against the silver sky. Each plume was too large and dense to be the work of rather over enthusiastic inhabitants.

The victus of Eboracum had taken the worst of the Pictish raid. The painted faces of the dead warriors were testament to the strength of the forts defences, even with the majority of the garrison missing. To vent their frustration at not being able to breach the sturdy walls the raiders had turned their attention to making the locals pay the price.

The attack had been launched from the dense fog that habitually hung over the surface of the Ouse, it allowed the flotilla of small vessels to arrive unseen and by the time they left there was little need for stealth. As was common place on raids such as these anything of worth had been taken. That included men, women and children of tradable age who would fetch a good price as slaves. Too old or young had been slaughtered; it was a simple case of economics, the Picts would have considered the attack a good haul. They had obviously had greater ambitions if their own dead were anything to go by. Their intelligence had been accurate and ever watchful as the assault had come just five days after most of the garrison had marched north up Dere Street to help against the growing unrest and attacks on the wall around Vindolanda. It was of little surprise to Caratacus who remembered his days as a rebel leader; he always had men watching the Romans movements.

The fleet docked and to the great relief of both the civilian and military population the newly named Cohort of Brigantia started to disembark. It wasn't that the entire, near five hundred men were Brigante, just the lead Century had that distinction. With Senior Centurion Caratacus heading the eighty strong group, they had been acquired by Brutus Aurelius for his son's bodyguard. The rest of the cohort were made up of various mixed groups of barbarians from across the empire but all knew Caratacus by his hard earned reputation and his iron discipline and training regime. It was all five of the original Brigante gladiator's that saw to it that the training followed the gladiator's strict codes and dedication. Even on the voyage over they had never missed a single opportunity to drill the fledgling fighting unit into the formidable war machine it had become in the few months since the end of the games back in Rome.

There might have been initial resentment on hearing that the senior Centurion role in the cohort had gone to a man who had just joined the military. Some of the other's had got years of experience serving Rome behind them. But it did not take long when they met the awesome gladiator for this to fade and their acceptance gained. Even as barbarian soldiers of the empire they were all kept updated with the gladiatorial news and all five of the "Brigante Barbarians" had been grabbing the headlines for the last year. So it had very quickly become something of an honour to be serving alongside these proven celebrity warriors.

Cassius Aurelius had only just set foot on Britannic soil and found himself in charge of the garrison of the provincial capital. With the capture or slaughter of all the principle families of the city he even had to oversee the reconstruction of the victus. General Flavius Stilicho had been forced to take the greater part of his force north and not wait for re-enforcements to arrive from General Flavius Claudius Constantinus legions in Deva as they had been coming under attack from the marauding Scotti from across the western sea. It was obvious to Caratacus when he was listening to the situation report from Sarus the Goth, the garrison commander, who was one of Stilicho's most trusted lieutenants that their main foe were the Picts. He even had to ask about any ongoing trouble from any local Brigante rebels. Sarus had made it clear that according to his information the Northern Brigante tribes were having just as much trouble from the Picts as they were and this kept those particular rebels very quite. In a way it pleased Caratacus that he would not be going up against his own but it also suggested his people were suffering. However it was with pride that he thought of his people still free and had not been totally suppressed by the Roman war machine, joining the rest of the Isurium Brigante in their acceptance of Rome's rule. This gave him an idea.

"I am sure we could swell our numbers by at least a few hundred if not an entire cohort of my people," offered Caratacus when he got the opportunity to talk to Cassuis.

The young commander was torn between the obvious advantage of an increase in numbers and having to trust his number one soldier to return following any reunion with his people. He tried to put himself in Caratacus's position; Finding himself back in the bosom of his own people and then returning to serve Rome? He like his father held the mighty warrior in the highest esteem but doubts filled his head when he weighed up the situation. It wasn't as though he didn't trust him, it was more to do with Cassius not being able to place himself in that situation and consider that his word of honour would hold him to his pledge if the roles were reversed.

Caratacus could read the young man like to tracks on a forest trail. He quickly dispelled any doubts, "I could have disappeared the first day we landed back in the land of my birth. I could do it every time I lead a patrol out. Within a short distance from here I could find the Brigante watchers and return with them into the northern valleys, but that would not only be betraying an oath I made to your father, I would also be turning my back on my closest of friends as well as Arbella. It would also mean letting you down when you most need me, something that I simply would not do."

Cassius was embarrassed, his lack of trust must have been so obvious, and the logical reasoning of Caratacus with his heartfelt support convinced him. "I apologise if I seem to be a little mistrusting I have a lot more on my plate than I expected I would when we left Rome."

"You have nothing to apologise for, I will visit the Brigante watchers up on the northern moors." He was sure that even with their lack of recent activity they would still be keeping an eye on the invaders from Rome just as they had done in his time. "I will be back in a couple of days with a report for you. I only need Ruadan to accompany me. If necessary he can take my word back to my people."

The pair set off at dawn. All their uniform and armour carried on a pack horse. They would look just like any other trader plying their wears along Dere Street, but also able to regain their true identity for their return. The Roman roads made for very easy travel, but it did also make it very easy to keep track of any traffic coming and going. For this reason it was necessary for the pair of would be merchants to ride north until they were out of sight before they doubled back to where they expected to find some of the old warrior comrades.

They had tied their horses and armed themselves as fellow Brigante fighters for the last few hundred paces of their approach. The distant hidden equine mutterings brought them to five tethered mounts. It was the first sign that all was not as they expected. He as chieftain would never have used five mounted men for this task in his own land, that size party would be used in other territory where you might need the larger number. When they got to the unaccompanied horses their suspicions were confirmed, Roman mounts with blue painted symbols on the neck and hindquarters that matched the blue face painting of Pictish warriors.

Caratacus and Ruadan dropped back deeper into the undergrowth to consider their next move when simultaneously they felt a blade at their throats and a hand across their mouths.

"There can only be one fucker that size!" was the strange greeting whispered into Caratacus's ear.

The last time Severus had seen his tribal leader he had been looking down from the top of the rocky outcrop on the great wall watching despairingly as a treacherous ambush had been sprung. The last words he had heard from Caratacus was for him to retreat and save the rest of the men from capture.

Caratacus smiled as he recognised the voice of the man who was laid on his back. "You always were a sneaky little bleeder and I hope that is you scabbard sticking in my arse and that you are not overly excited to see me!" He turned to see the familiar face grinning back at him.

Severus and Arvirelinus who everyone called Arvi for short now embraced the pair of men who apparently had returned from the dead.

"I think it is time to deal with our friends," Caratacus pointed with his thumb in the direction of the Picts. "Later, I will be interested to know why they have our old observation point and we have to lurk in the shadows?"

Only one of the Picts was looking outwards of their camp and his attention was to the south in the direction of the garrison, not north back to the wilderness of the high moors. Two others slumbered lazily while the final pair busied themselves preparing a couple of leggy hares that they had snared. Severus and Arvi would have helped in the attack if they had been given the opportunity, but instead with a click of his finger and thumb their chieftain signalled to the pair to take the sleeping duo prisoners. He and Ruadan moved across the small clearing stabbing their gladius into the backs of both cooks. Caratacus had no sooner driven the blade between the man's shoulders as he transferred his Pilum to his right hand and sent the javelin flying, taking the turning guard in the chest. The sudden disturbance brought the remaining two out of their slumber with a snap. As their consciousness returned they were both knocked senseless by the hilts of the two short swords without ever seeing their assailants.

That night under the stars overlooking the garrison the four reunited friends ate well on roast hare washed down with the best wine Eboracum could supply. The two newcomers listened in amazement to the tale of their well travelled friends adventures. As only Ruadan could, he told such a saga that even Caratacus was spellbound, not just in the way he told the tale but in realisation of it actually being a true. He had never really stopped and thought about it before. Typical of Ruadan he did not spare Caratacus's blushes, he was not about to leave out the detailed recollections of Caratacus's passionate relationship with Arbella the "Amazonian Gladitix" going into great detail of their less than discreet pairing. This obviously brought much delight and merriment to the three especially as they saw it made their chieftain uncomfortable.

After the amusement came the shock as they discovered their new roles within the Roman Army. As if to reinforce the message they even brought their armour and uniforms out of the packs. It was evident by their expressions that both Severus and Arvi did not know what to make of this part of the saga.

"So just why do the Romans tell me that the Northern Brigante no longer poses a threat to them and that their only real concern is the Picts? They seem to think that we have a common foe in the blue faced bastards," asked Caratacus wanting to move away from the story telling and to the point he had sort a meeting in the first place.

It was Arvi who answered in an almost ashamed tone but in a way that appeared to give him some relief as if he had not been able to speak his mind for a long time and this was the opportunity for him to purge himself of his frustrations. "We have not had a real leader since you were captured, not a single man who could unite the tribes of the valleys. All we do is talk and bicker like women. When the Picts attack a village nobody comes to help or to support so we are being picked off as individually we have not the numbers to defend ourselves. All we do is keep a watch on them so we can avoid their attacks. It has been a long time since any of us have killed one of these little shits," he jerked his thumb over towards the two bound prisoners.

Severus's nodding confirmed his friends lament; he added nothing as Arvi had covered the worst of it.

The following morning two soldiers of Rome, two Brigante warriors, three dead Picts and two prisoners entered the garrison gates. Every soldier within sight came to a standstill to witness the new Senior Centurion make his statement of intent; the great name he had acquired in the arena was going to be maintained in the ranks, if not bettered.

"Now that is a rapid result," beamed Cassius. "Four prisoners and three dead." He had come out of the commander's office on hearing the commotion that had greeted their arrival.

"Err, just two prisoners, these two are here as my guests, that is unless we no longer want the Brigante to join us sir?" Caratacus was quick to come to his friend's defence whilst at the same time ensuring all those listening heard that the pair were friends. He continued, "This is Severus and Arvirelinus they were two of my best warriors and both honourable men and are perfect to arrange for the other leaders to attend a meeting providing we make them welcome and show them they have nothing to fear."

"Yes of course forgive me, my misunderstanding Caratacus," Cassius corrected himself. The way he accepted he had made a mistake endeared the young man to Caratacus; many a man would have let pride stand in the way of overcoming such an error.

Turning to the two strangers he smiled and reached his hand out in salutation, "can you express my pleasure in meeting them? What about these two then?" he pointed at the two men whose coloured faces were even bluer from the substantial bruising. "They seem to have had an accident, what happened," Cassius chuckled at his own joke not really wanting an answer. But he did take a long hard look at his first living Pict warrior.

"Oh, that blue mess is what they all paint their faces with; the other mess was Severus and Arvi's work. They really dislike Picts!"

A great shout came from behind them from the other side of the training yard, "by the tits of the Goddess Brigantia, where did you dig those two lazy bastards up from?" It was Brelus, Severus's brother and he was followed by the others. With the exception of Caratacus the reunited group disappear to catch up and drink to each other's health.

"What do you suggest we do with our prisoners Caratacus," asked Cassius knowing the big man would more than likely have a plan for them.

"If you don't mind I would like to take them out into the forest. One I will kill and the other I will bring back and having seen his friend fate he will be a lot more prepared to answer our questions."

Once again Caratacus could see the doubt in Cassius's facial expression so added, "You are welcome to join us but it may offend your one god when I use an old ritual to scare the shit out of the weaker of the two."

"No, I think I will leave it to you," was all he said.

All seven of the Brigante friends from the northern valleys set off the following day. Right across Britannia you never travelled very far before you came to a vast forest, so they did not have far to find a suitable location. Just to the west of the garrison the forest in question ran as a solid block to the mountain range that some called the "Backbone of Britannia". They followed a smaller river that cut off from the Ouse and traced its route back until they came to a place that Caratacus was happy with. The minute they entered the small clearing along the bank he had immediately known it was the place.

The waterside glade was next to a gentle slope leading down

to the river's edge rather than the steep, sometimes near sheer banks previous. It had an uncanny likeness to the area where he had experienced his first ritual. It even had a sharp change in water levels crossing some slabs of rock that over the years had formed a tumbling cascade. It wasn't exactly the impressive waterfall that he, Becuille and the old druid had as a backdrop but its presence gave even more significance to the site.

His war axe was firstly used to fell a nearby tree and chop wood for the fire. It was again used to strip off the braches to bare the trunk which was placed in a hole at the water's edge. Just away from the water on the first dry ground a fire was lit. When night came Caratacus watched the skies for a sign. It did not come; the celestial lights flickered their iridescent best but all above remained stationary. As morning started to dawn Caratacus was drawn by some gut feeling to look across the river.

Just as he did someone quietly said, "who is that, over on the other bank?"

"Don't know," came a reply, "but it appears to be a young woman, I can hardly see through the fog."

"Is that a child by her side?" asked another.

"Stay there!" commanded Caratacus as he stood and moved to the water that lapped up the gentle slope. There on the other side of the river shrouded by the light grey swirl of mist was the daughter of Flidias, Goddess of the Forest. Becuille appeared to be beckoning him to her and he was not about to disappoint her as he started to wade into the frigid waters. It was deep and he soon was up above his waist. He could now clearly see a small child holding her hand, instinctively he knew it was her child, the child they had conceived during their passionate encounters back in that mysterious and enchanted forest. She was beaming her radiant smile across the water, it warmed him even though he was in such a cold current, the young child seemed excited by her mother's words and gave a small wave of acknowledgement. The water was even deeper so he kicked forward into a swim and in doing so he momentarily lost sight of the pair on the far bank. When his head resurfaced and his sight returned the bank ahead was empty, no sign or tracks of mother and child existed when he scoured the heavily vegetated bank. The only thing left where they stood was a small goblet with a familiar earthy smelling elixir in it. His return crossing was slow and his disappointment beyond words, the river temperature seemed to have dropped several degrees matching his demeanour. But he did manage to keep the goblet free from contamination and out of the brown mud coloured water that carried him back to his friend who had watched spell bound by the unfolding events.

He rejoined the others who confirmed they had also seen the two figures on the far bank and that they had just melted into the drifting fog that at that moment had thickened before completely dispersing revealing the couple's mysterious vanishing. What Caratacus had not seen, because of his temporary submergence was Gluingel place the goblet for him to retrieve.

Arriving back at the small smouldering fire the two prisoners were both jabbering wrecks and Ruadan pointed to the appearance of a strange headdress wreath of Ivy and Mistletoe that had been placed on top of the nearest man's head. Both now knew that what lay in store for them did not bode well for either having a long term future.

The following night three stars feel from the sky. One had a bluish aura to it, the other flamed orange while the last was a blood red. If Caratacus had not been certain about his path he was now, every sign he could have hope for had been clearly evident, the victim chosen.

After the heavy work of chopping through timber it had taken a lot of painstaking attention during the day to bring the edge of the war axe back to the kind of sharpness that was needed. It would be precision and not blunt trauma required for its next task. The slow constant rubbing of stone on steel had been torture to the prisoners not just the sound but the sight of their executioner preparing had lasted hours.

The Pictish warrior who had been mysteriously singled out by the placement of the headdress was fastened to the tree stump. A strange calm had come over him from his earlier panic. This contrasted to his comrade's complete ongoing breakdown which had resulted in him fouling himself as he had voided his guts from both ends, chattering incomprehensive gibberish like a simpleton. He of course expected that he would be next to receive whatever treatment his braver fellow warrior now faced.

With the first stroke Caratacus started to re-enact the ancient chant he had heard just once before, years ago. It was word perfect. It sounded like his voice but he was making no conscious attempt to move his lips or remember the words, they just presented themselves in his head for delivery by his mouth.

"I live with the moon," he raised his arms knowing that he was following the exact same movements the old druid had made.

"I live with the stars," as soon as his words had left his mouth a shower of the embers from the fire danced up into the nights sky.

"I cherish the earth as she cherishes me," his arms swept down, gesturing to the ground.

"I am the trees, I am the waterfall, I am the air that you breathe."

The slice opened up the prisoner from one side of the abdomen to the other; his guts were hanging down towards the floor. Caratacus looked at the gruesome sight studying the pale pink intestine, before ripping out the liver and taking a bite out of it and handing it to his friends. They, shocked by what they were witnessing as this was not part of their tribal traditions it was only something that the druid had practiced in secrecy, hesitated at first. Ruadan had heard all the rumours of the druids work and had seen the transformation in the young Caratacus who had disappeared with Gluingel to return just weeks later the giant he was now. There was no hesitation for him and it was then the next Brigante warrior's turn.

"I am the wolf, I am the bear, I am the eagle," he reached up into the chest cavity tearing the still steadily beating heart offering it to the sky. The fire crackled once again glowing orange into the blackness. Once again he took the first bite, before offering it to the others.

The Pict head was swaying from side to side as the embers were placed in the empty cavity.

"I am your servant, the appointed one and have returned to defeat the coming tides." With that Caratacus pushed the trunk over into the river.

"Accept this sacrifice, killed threefold as the ancient would have it. Blade, fire and water. Give me the blessing of mother earth."

With the ritual over the headdress was retrieved and placed on the second Picts head. Warrior or not he was now prepared to answer any question he was faced with.

"Well it makes sense and typical of the sly little bastard." Caratacus was commenting to Cassius having told him what they had gleaned from the now very talkative man from beyond the wall.

"Yes, unsurprisingly they have no intention of being drawn

into open combat. Whatever he is, he does not appear to be a fool. They just maintain a hit and run war, attacking where we are most vulnerable before disappearing back into the forests," agreed Cassius. "I will send a rider north to inform General Stilicho that Segedunum (Wallsend) is next but not until he and his men are seen returning south."

"We can set up a trap to catch them," offered Caratacus.

It had been a month since Severus and Arvi had returned north. Cassuis with the main section of the Brigante Cohort remained garrisoned at Eboracum while Caratacus with his eighty strong unit of true Brigante took Dere Street up to the meeting that he hoped would be well attended by the elders of the tribal villages of the northern valleys. It was to be close but not too close to Vinovia so as to allow his guests some security. As they crossed the bridge at the fort of Morbium (Piercebridge) they turned off Dere Street to the west. Overlooking the surrounding area on a hill top they awaited their invited friends to arrive.

He had chosen the site wisely. It was in the territory where his people hailed from and gave a good vantage point, so any movement in any direction would be easily seen. The village elders, for that was all they were without one man having been accepted as their leader in his absence, would feel safe.

Severus and Arvi arrived alone. It didn't look promising. "They agree to meet with you, but the bunch of women who now lead the different faction's fear it could be a trap so are insisting we take you to another place of their choosing."

"They do not take the word of their rightful chieftain, the man they swore an oath to and as not been succeeded by any other?" snarled Caratacus his anger, momentarily plain to see. It was something he very rarely let happen and soon cooled down, but the snub would not go by without somebody feeling the wrath of their chieftain.

It was a short journey to the alternative meeting place, a shockingly poor selection. The clearing in the small wooded area was in the bottom of one of the many side valleys off the principle one that carried the River Wear down towards Vinovia. It would have taken a hundred men to stand guard with any assurance of success but there were but a hand full and they were positioned on the periphery of the wood not the tops of the valley sides where they could give early notice.

"Which dim headed arsehole chose this as a secure site for a meeting?" Caratacus demanded as he dismounted, leaving all those present that he was not at all pleased or impressed. The fact that he had left most of his force back at the original site made it evident that he did not intend spending much time there.

There was near to one hundred men present and most seemed to be smiling with delight to see him and hear his uncompromising style as his first address rang out. He had rode into their midst with his helmet off so he could be recognised more easily but also so he could pick up on the mood of the majority of the crowd, it all seemed fairly positive. That was all but for a small group in the middle, a group of stern, anxious looking older men that appeared to have a small bodyguard around them who made space so the elders could move forward to greet their returning leader. The bodyguard took up their given position directly behind their charges, their hands resting on the hilts of their swords and shields at the ready in a rather menacing manner as if they expected trouble. It was another poor way to express their happiness in seeing the chieftain return.

Zebrus was probably the most accomplished warrior amongst the elder's protection and as such stood as their hand. It was a position that would cost him. Caratacus knew him well and made straight for him ignoring his father the man who had stepped forward to act as spokesperson.

"Zebrus is that the way you welcome your chieftain on his return?" The threat in Caratacus's voice was such that it left no one in doubt what was to come if Zebrus didn't show fealty immediately. "You like all here swore an oath of allegiance to me on the death of Conorus, my father. Yet here you stand hovering behind these old women," he gestured to the line of elders almost spitting his displeasure as he snarled. His aggressive reaction had the man drop his hand off his hilt and lower his shield to his side. It was not how he expected his former leader to have approached when he wanted the tribes to unite with the Romans.

Caratacus had them on the back foot, literally. He pushed past two of the elders to get closer to Zebrus. He nearly knocked the pair off their feet but he didn't, that was reserved for the bodyguard who took the full force of his anger square in the face. He went down like a felled tree as did the man next to him for no other reason than Caratacus felt like it.

"I am Caratacus your chieftain," he bellowed. "I am the champion of Rome, winner of my own freedom and now Senior Centurion of the Brigante Cohort, son of Conorus, chosen by Amergin Gluingel the Druid, bestowed with the will of the goddess of the forest and Brigantia herself. If any man amongst you dispute this now is the time to step forward and stake your claim!"

All was quite but for the groaning of the two men who had just started to regain their sensed after being floored.

"Then we return to my original meeting place where we can defend ourselves from all comers instead of sitting here in the ambush pit that could only have been chosen by fools," he turned and looked directly at the elders. He was sure he heard a ripple of suppressed laughter pass through the crowd. It just took a cry of support from Severus and Arvi to have the whole band cheering and calling the name of the leader.

"Caratacus!" a voice called out nearly swamped by the rest of the din.

Caratacus, Caratacus!" it was a young man's voice and the owner pushed to the front of the jostling crowd who was now trying to mob him. It was the son of Aengir, his father's second wife. Although he wasn't, he had always called him his half brother, it was Vesutius. The small boy had become a young man during Caratacus's exile.

There were more reunions when they arrived back at Sharnbury Top their original site. It was after this that Caratacus started his story. He let Ruadan tell the colourful sections but when it came to stressing exactly what the Roman Empire consisted of and what resources it had to call upon he stepped in. They spoke of the vast armies that were spread over the whole of the known world that could be brought to Britannia if required, the wonders of the magnificent cities of Naples and Rome as well as those they had heard talked about but the most chilling was their technologies of waging wars such as their mobile war machines like the huge crossbow called the Ballista and the heavy catapult that could hurl huge stones hundreds of yards that shattered fifty men at a time and the much more manoeuvrable Trabucchi that could fire smaller projectiles many times quicker than the heavy catapult.

"At the moment they fight us and take the lead and silver from our lands and you have proven since I have been gone that you are powerless to stop them. Now it appears you are unable to defend yourselves against the Picts," he emphasised his dismay at this, before continuing. "If we have an alliance with the Romans then we can destroy our real enemy, the one that will annihilate all of us if they get the chance. If we join Rome we will be freer than we are now and with trade routes across the world. When the painted faces are wiped off the map we can then decide our future beyond there. If we like what we see then we can remain as part of Rome, if not we rise up and have a fight with just one enemy."

He looked at the faces that surrounded him and he was sure he had them but he made his final play. "I will not have you pledge your allegiance to Rome as I and these men have done," he waved his hands across the men of the Brigante Cohort. "No we will have to follow our oaths until it as expired, but you only need to renew you oath to me and follow me into battle. Rome will have no claim on you."

Questions were asked and answered well into the night. There were still a few dissenters but on the whole the overwhelming feeling was to follow their well travelled and experienced comrades with Caratacus at their head and by doing so would bring an end to the Pictish attacks into their land.

Messages were sent back and forth and very shortly Cassius was proclaiming that his legion had increased its strength by an entire cohort of Brigante warriors. General Stilicho arrived in Vinovia a few weeks later to witness this additional force for himself. He watched them train and go through the regular drills. He had no doubt about their potential ferocity in battle, but what did impress him was the iron discipline that the ex-gladiator officers had distilled into the rebel barbarian force.

"I watched you fight in arena at Deva early in your career before you won Rome's heart. I listened with interest as your fame and notoriety grew, there cannot be a more famous centurion in the empire," the general complimented as they finally met. "You might remember this officer?"

Out of the shadows stepped Marcus Valerius. The pair had not met since Senator Aurelius had persuaded the officer to sell Caratacus to him along with the other Brigante Gladiators.

"Caratacus it is truly a pleasure to see you again. The fact it is as a comrade in arms makes it all the more special. I salute your success. He brought his right arm across his chest in the traditional Roman military gesture then offered his hand.

"So I hear from young Cassius Aurelius that you conducted some sort of ritual on a blue-face and it enabled you to gain vital information?" Stilicho worded his question in a way clearly designed to put Caratacus at ease but even so he was careful how he answered.

"I conducted a forceful interrogation in front of the other Pict so he knew the consequences of withholding information. Sir!"

"Caratacus, relax. You may not know it but you are amongst like minded friends. Friends who realise that this religion of "Christ, the one God" is the path that the Politian's in Rome have turned to, but the soldiers who have to deal with all the empires shit, see it weaken us to a point where we are under attack from all sides. In the lives of real soldiers Mithraism is our following. The old Gods of natures elements and of war, warriors across the world might know them by different names but they are all the same to a man who is about to go into battle. Your beliefs are your concern my friend, but remember when Rome asks Christianity is the only faith," he slapped the big man who towered before him on his shoulder. "Now what is it you are proposing?"

"I like it. Marcus Valerius will accompany you but I will make a big show of marching back down south to Eboracum. I will send word to Segedunum to expect an attack but not to make signs that they are on alert."

On the same day as Stilicho and his troops moved south a caravan arrived in the opposite direction. Caratacus was overjoyed that Arbella had ventured north to join him.

Having been separated for many weeks he was only too pleased that she was as eager for him as he was for her and an evening of unrivalled lustful sex followed. She had always had the most perfect rounded large breasts but that night they seemed all the fuller and he was drawn to them more than ever. She really was the perfect specimen of the opposite sex, her skin of dark perfection, her muscles ripped and taunt as when she was in the arena, her stomach rippled with tense power as he pumped back and forth having drawn himself up on his arms to look at the glorious sight beneath him. Her grip on his back tightened signalling the growing urgency in her loins, attempting to pull him deeper within trying to extract every possible fraction of penetration, crying for more, demanding more. It was only afterwards as both rested, exhausted in each other's arms recovering from their exertions that she shared her news. She had come bearing joyous tidings, she was with child. She had purposely not told him until after their reunion for as she explained; she knew her man would immediately start to treat her like a delicate little flower when what she wanted from him was a good fuck! How like Arbella he thought, still a warrior at heart. His love and the bearer of his child.

"Caratacus I want to come with you and fight the blue faced bastards," Vesutius pleaded his case to be allowed to go with the main force as it prepared to move out to Segedunum.

"Vesutius I need you to lead the bodyguard protecting Arbella. She is with child and I need my family to protect my family. You are the man I am relying on." What he really meant was he did not want the young lad in danger. He knew if it came down to a real fight it would be Arbella that would be protecting the lad. It was only a small lie and was a means to an end.

With the pride of his young half brother placated Caratacus and the cohort of Brigantia moved off two days after Stilicho. They moved west initially before dropping south and doubling back to their objective; the eastern extremity of Hadrian's Wall, trying to fool any observers that they were sure would be watching.

Using a local warrior as guide and under the cover of darkness they moved into a covert base where they could remain unseen but still have a clear view of the fort and the river estuary. The tree covered rolling hills was a perfect setting to wait for the expected water borne attack.

The Picts hailed from lands far to the north of the wall and many miles separated them on these forages from where they would call home and felt a degree of safety. Coming the distance they did on their plundering was a risky strategy by land compared to the seaborne alternative. It was why Caratacus was happy with the vantage point. He overlooked both target and watery access point.

The first thing that Caratacus noted was the sluggishness of the small fleets approach. Even with a full set of oars propelling them they struggled to make headway as both tide and wind was against them.

Even at distance it could be seen the warriors from the north were far from ready to give battle. Men were stretching and shaking off aching muscles as they pulled their fleet on the mudflats. These craft had far too little room to allow slaves to man the oars that was the job of the warriors as well as doing the fighting.

The garrison runner was sent back to allow them to prepare for the impending attack. The Picts had left a small force behind to guard the fleet, protecting their escape route while the main force of no more than two hundred set off immediately. It was the relatively small size of the force that surprised Caratacus, according to the witnesses there had been near twice that when they had attacked Eboracum. But even the chance of ridding the world of two hundred Picts was not to be passed up. The enemy moved off using the river bank as protection against being seen. They had no idea that it was a pointless exercise as every move they made was being closely monitored as they were sucked into the awaiting trap.

When the main Pict force was out of sight Caratacus led a similar sized group down to the embankment and used the same route to move on the anchorage. The morning's low sun was in the guard's eyes, it allowed them to be almost on top of the defenders as at first they thought it was their own group returning. Another smaller group led by Ruadan had entered the sea and had waded neck deep to the rear of the beached vessels. Their positioning was not observed as all the Pict guards had gathered to look at their prematurely returning comrades appearing out of the dazzlingly low golden glow of the rising sun and light mist that was slowly being burnt off by the steadily increasing heat of the morning. When their calls were not answered they started to become agitated and anxious and when the approaching force broke into a charge accompanied by the unmistakable verbal challenges of Brigante battle cries they hastily gathered close and formed a shield wall.

The fight would have been an uneven contest based on numbers alone. But with the wall of shields and speared directed at the charge they were left totally exposed at their rear. That was exactly where Ruadan and his men appeared from using the partially beached craft to hide their approach until they were only a few paces away. A call from the furthest boat that had not been grounded gave the defenders a split second to react, but it was all too late. The resulting disintegrating wall was swamped by the frontal attack as the trapped men turned and realised all too late they were too closely packed to face the rear with the spears in their hands. Some managed to lift them vertical and they were the few that managed to maintain their best defensive weapon. Others twisted and rammed the shafts into the neighbour and simply dropped the spear and fumbled for the swords. Many even dropped their shields while others tried to cut a dash for the far vessel that had always been their means of escape if attacked. It was a lost cause from the outset. Most of these few trying to get to their escape vessel were cut down by Ruadan and his men before they had moved a few paces and as the splintered wall moved to attack the smaller group of enemy from the sea they were hit by a tidal wave from the main assault.

Caught between the hammer and the anvil they were mercilessly pummelled. Their leader bravely cried his defiance, brandishing his weapon over his head wanting to take the fight to his assailants but such was the chaos in being caught front and back he didn't even get the opportunity to deliver his threatened blows as each man was struck down from the metal points of a hundred Pilum. The dead fell where they stood and covered no more than an area of a few paces square but three men deep.

Caratacus had headed straight for the man making the greatest noise. His speed reduced the distance rapidly, the sight of the twisted screaming blue painted faces causing the burning hatred in his Brigante heart to glow white hot with the rage of battle fever. Encouraged by the sight of their leader in full assault it generated even greater speed from the rest of the attackers as they neared the broken defences. Just as they had been drilled hundreds of times they dropped their upright Pilums into a horizontal, lance like position and plunged them with all their force, deep and hard into the bare-chested foe. The Pictish leader was driven backwards by the power of the spear point that impaled him in his gut. He had taken several backward steps before he and Caratacus were close enough to use their swords. The weapon of the man from north of the wall was still held aloft when his dying grip released the handle. Both of his hands then grasped the wooden shaft of the Pilum that was the source of the searing sharp pain that had punched deep into his stomach. It was as if by cradling the offending object it would lessen the trauma to his soft flesh. This allowed Caratacus to bring down a sweeping side cut of his own sword onto the side of the condemned man's head. The crack of the sturdy metal blade smashing the brittle bony skull just above the ear announced the end of the assault.

With the exception of a couple of men each warrior had been despatched in a similar manner with only two lightly wounded attackers. One of the men who had made for the sanctuary of the floating ship had managed to avoid the fate of his fellow fighters. He was running down the mud flats of the estuary his direction taking him deeper into the softer terrain and his progress growing ever slower. Two men followed both carrying Pilums and chasing the Pict down like wolves on the heel of a deer. The first spear was thrown javelin like at the slowing target, it fell just short of the broad back that had been its intended target but found the soft fleshy section of his rear thigh. His end was watched by Caratacus who was in the process of calling for the man to be spared so he could be questioned. It was to no avail. Blood lust had overcome the pair and before their leader's words registered they had hacked the fallen man where he lay, face down semi submerged in the rivers silty, mud.

Caratacus was spinning back to the main scene of the fight, his back having been turned to the floating escape vessel when Brelus hurled his Pilum up at the bow of the ship which towered above them. He saw the man who had given the warning of rear attack to the shield wall holding a war axe readying himself to launch it at Caratacus's back. Slowly, ever so slowly the pent up tension in the tall figure softened, his up stretched arms bent and fell down dropping the axe safely into the breaking waves. The body that sported Brelus's Pilum in his side followed with a crash as the dead man fell into the cold grey sea from a height.

Before setting off to Segedunum they drew the escape vessel further up on to the shore so nobody would be able to re-launch any of them in a hurry. These would be a welcome bonus to the spoils of war. But they had no wish to preserve them for any escapees to use the head back north after the trap was sprung.

They had little time to waste as the main enemy force would not be far from their objective.

Arriving at the fort it appeared the Picts were mainly focussed on taking the fort. At least at that point they had left the few civilians of the victus who had not taken refuge behind the great stone walls alone and many of these ran straight towards the pursuing Cohort of Brigantia amazed at the arrival of their saviours apparently from nowhere.

The first the Picts knew of the unfolding threat was when a giant Roman centurion smashed into their leader's bodyguard. While still in full charge, Caratacus had hurled his Pilum, it found its target with a thud. The full metal tip was buried in between the unfortunate recipient's shoulder blades knocking him to his knees, the dead body falling slowly on to his face which brought the shaft of the spear equally as slowly to the vertical position. It was sufficient to alarm the others in the guard detachment but as they turned to face the impending assault Caratacus had already swept his Gladius with a forehand slice across the neck of one man before maintaining his momentum to deliver a backhand from the left to another. Simultaneously the metal boss of his shield was driven into the face of a third. Across the whole of the southern flank of the garrison Brigante fought Pict all the time the later was getting unwelcome attention from the battlements above.

With his initial impetus stemmed by the sheer number of bodyguards around their leader Caratacus could see his target draw his blade and raise his shield. It was disappointing, it was not the face he had hoped to see, but he was one of Alvor's kinsmen that Caratacus recognised from their brief alliance so long ago. The melee of bodies were too closely packed to even give him room to use his short stabbing sword so he heaved forwards with his shield to create the space he needed. The limited room only allowed him to drive a couple backwards so he could smash the nearest face with a head butt. He felt and heard the crunch of his metal helmet colliding with the nasal cartilage causing it to disintegrate in a shower of blood and snot. The man dropped like a stone, finally allowing the extra space he needed. Two short sharp stabbing jabs into the bare midriffs of unidentified assailants was followed by a parry and a block from his shield as the full force of an axe blow deflected striking his main objective a glancing blow to the back. Caratacus hammered the hilt of his weapon down onto the rear of the axe man's head as he had followed through far too far following his attempted delivery. A heavy stomp of a hob nailed boot ensured he would not get up. The space had materialised as the bodyguard was being decimated on all sides, Caratacus lowered his shield to make sure his opponent saw who was facing him across the field of battle. He was pleased at the reaction on the Pictish leaders face; it was one of complete recognition. It wasn't the revenge he wanted but for now it would have to do. He sheathed his Gladius and drew his very "unroman" war axe that had been his signature weapon as a free Brigante warrior and one the man would have known was Caratacus's most devastating killing tool. Once again he could read on his oppositions face that he knew what was coming. If his size did not, then this weapon set

Caratacus aside from any other centurion across the empire. As he moved forward he lunged with his left hand smashing his shield into his oppositions, his size and strength forcing him back, driving on to his heels. The axe rose into the air, its long shaft above the mighty arm set it higher than anything still standing on the battleground. The parry that met the brutal heavy blow was just in time but propelled the defensive action into a retreating fight as there was no chance of standing up to the onslaught. The Pict knew that such a heavy weapon should have been slow to manoeuvre in close combat but not in the hands of such a powerful and agile adversary. Each of his parries were slightly later as Caratacus continued to send a torrent of quick blows, just using his wrist to keep a continuous rotating spinning attack, probing for the first signs of exhaustion in his foe. It was appearing; desperation had entered the now clumsy footwork and his sword and shield were being constantly driven apart. Both knew the next parry was going to be too late and Caratacus had read his oppositions body movements along with the tensioning across his chest and shoulders. He was about to put all his strength into his shield and this took the danger of the sword away as he turned sideways dropping his sword shoulder back and well behind his badly damaged timber defence. With the threat of the sword removed Caratacus dropped his shield and now re-drew his Gladius and waited for the over commitment that the Picts desperate situation would bring about. To bring his sword back into play he needed to get back on the front foot and with the giant having discarded his shield it was his one and only hope. He pushed with all his might, both his hand behind the shield hoping it was enough to turn the tables on the worryingly familiar centurion he faced. It was the tired over commitment that Caratacus had been encouraging by dropping his shield. With the enemies arms fully extended and his feet having not kept up with the pressed reach, a huge gap had appeared behind the Picts shield. Caratacus had a long reach and it was doubled by the shaft of his war axe, as he jabbed his Gladius forward with his left the blue painted face and body turned slightly to face it square on. It left even more space for the subsequent looping chop to get round the corner of the protection, driving the axe blade deep into his shoulder. After several minutes of one on one combat the end came quickly and it was as if every other man on the field of battle had one eye on what their leaders were doing. The traumatic damage had almost severed the arm from the torso and left him totally incapacitated with the agony he was experiencing.

"Kill me you Brigante bastard!" he still had enough fight left in him to snarl his defiance to the victor.

Caratacus kicked away the shield he was still gamely but limply trying to hold on to and this caused the man to stumble backwards, falling on to his back. The Brigante was quick to step forwards and stamped on the useless arm that still gripped his sword forcing it to relinquish its hold. It was then flicked out of reach by the tip of Caratacus's Gladius. Two swift, short jabs torn holes into each thigh, causing muffled cries of pain. Caratacus backed off slightly, looking around aware of the fact that many were watching the outcome.

The rest of the Picts were hopelessly outnumbered and without their leader when the gates opened to allow the whole of the garrison loose it was finished in a matter of minutes. Losing their leader had taken the fight out of them and men threw down their weapons wholesale like a wave sweeping across a beach, finally reaching all parts, smoothing out its chaotic tumbling struggle into a peaceful scene of victor and vanquished.

It was the sight of this victory and the relative ease in which it had been achieved that had Caratacus worried. The attack on

Eboracum had a reported five hundred attackers and this had a few more than half that. Where were the others? He immediately set guards and put the garrison back on full alert. But he was sure he had not missed any signs of another force.

It was after his ritual despatch of the Pictish leader who right to the bitter end, even with his entrails handing out showed his bravery and hatred for his enemy. Each prisoner had been made to watch and was then led away one by one assuming they were to face a similar end. It didn't take long for Caratacus to learn of the whereabouts of Alvor and the rest of his band of Pictish warriors. That information made his blood turn cold in his veins as he realised his mistake.

The Picts had never as far as anybody had been aware split their forces and carried out synchronised raids. They had always found strength in numbers being so far away from their homeland. This was of little comfort to Caratacus who had just learnt that the main Pict force had sailed past the mouth of the Tyne estuary and had sailed up the Wear which would bring them close to their target, Vinovia. He had left his pregnant wife and half brother exactly where the enemy was intending to strike thinking it would be a place of safety.

The scene of destruction was total. To leave the garrison even more vulnerable a large patrol had left on a routine trip north to Vindolanda just before the attack. That had been the first group to be massacred before the savagery of the blue faced warriors had descended on Vinovia. Caratacus half heartedly tried to convince himself that Arbella and young Vesutius might have been taken prisoner and that a quick sortie north might win back their freedom. But in his heart he knew that the pair would have fought to the death rather than being taken into slavery. She was the Amazonian Gladitix and he the son of a Brigante chieftain they would never surrender. He found them side by side where they battled and fell; the blood soaked ground around them suggested they had made the bastards pay dearly before succumbing to the insurmountable odds that had been stacked against them. It was little comfort for the man who for all his power and strength, regardless of being touched by the gods had failed to protect the ones closest to him. As survivors came out of hiding they confirmed that the Pictish leader had been Alvor. He had announced it in his victory celebrations as he slaughtered those who were worthless as slaves.

The inconsolable senior centurion returned to Eboracum. His sadness at failing to protect his own kin was only outweighed by his further energised motivation to reap the bloodiest of revenges upon the person he knew had committed such an act. He would make a pact with friend or foe to bring Alvor and his blue faced bastards to heel where he swore they would face the slowest of slow deaths.

"You were not to know that these heathens would be planning their first ever two pronged attack. Until you had the information from that prisoner nobody in all of Britannia would have suspected it." Both General Flavius Stilicho and Marcus Aurelius were trying to comfort Caratacus. Somehow his size and power seemed to make his sorrow seem all the greater his might shoulders hunched and his head was bowed.

Neither men would mention it but the victory at Segedunum was the only news that would get back to Rome. The loss at Vinovia would be understated to such an extent that it would appear to be no more than a slight inconvenience with just a few locals and some auxiliaries being lost in a battle where the attackers took just as many losses. To build further on the positive result Caratacus, the famous gladiator now centurion would be allowed to take centre stage as one of the main belligerents in the fight. It was great publicity. Even without knowing it Caratacus the one time champion of the arena was now a hero of Rome. It all helped boost the rather lacklustre performance of Stilicho's legions in Britannia.

He might have been one of the best fighting generals of Rome and had spent years away fighting very successfully on behalf of his Emperor but he knew how the politics of Rome worked. Whichever and whoever's news got back to the heart of the empire first, providing there was a thread of truth in it, it would be that version of events that the people believed.

Stilicho was the highest ranking man in Britannia; he was Magister Militum, all the more impressive considering he was half barbarian himself having Vandal blood flowing through his veins. He had worked and sometimes fought his way up through the ranks finally marrying a niece of the Emperor Theodosius. He had even been given a brief period of being regent while the young Honorius came of age. The list of his military triumphs was impressive, barbarian and Roman armies alike had been vanquished by his superior tactics and that meant he had enemies as well as friends back in Rome. He did not intend for any ammunition to fall into the hands of those who might have vengeful intentions within the senate.

The generals early military victories had been on behalf of Theodosius I, who at the time ruled the eastern empire out of Constantinople, but with Stilicho's military guile Theodosius had won several battles against his opposite number in the west, unifying the empire back into a single entity. The now emperor of the entire empire had recognised Stilicho as a major asset, the strong arm of his reign even using him as an envoy for important peace talks. Following this success he had proved his political savvy which added to his military record made him a man wanted as the closest of allies so the emperor had strengthened their bonds by arranging his marriage to the lovely Serena. With the couple having a son and two daughters he was an accepted member of Roman society, no mean feat for a half barbarian who found himself a major player in Rome's Military and political merry-go-round. After the old emperor's death the empire was once again split between his two sons, Arcadius in the east sat on the throne in Constantinople while Honorius reigned in Rome. Both young men seemed out of their depths when it came to the task of ruling and although Stilicho claimed he had been given the same powers to assist and advise Arcadius as there was no doubt he had in respect of Honorius it was his rival, Rufinus that filled that role in east. He had many powerful friends but also just as powerful enemies and it was a difficult challenge to win the man's trust and respect. Cassius's father was one of Stilicho's greatest supporters and through that friendship Cassius found his favour. The history between Cassius Aurelius and Caratacus, along with his own hard earned reputation promoted the Brigante Warrior into the limelight of Stilicho's most trusted inner sanctum. Following the victory at Segedunum his trust was clearly demonstrated with him being promoted to head of the general's bodyguard along with the rest of the Brigante Cohort.

It had been several months since the action at the wall. "You are not going to like our orders Caratacus," was the statement that greeted him when he reported to the commander's villa as ordered. Stilicho let Caratacus read the document for himself so he knew that they came directly from the imperial throne in Rome, the broken seal still clearly visible.

Time had eased the pain of his loss. The deep sadness in his heart had eased from that raw burning to a festering open wound that gnawed bluntly in his soul. The Picts had been very quite since that fateful day, after all they had lost a huge number across the two battles, and it would take some time to rebuild back to their former strength.

"Pulling out all together sir? But that will leave all Britannia open to the little bastards up there," he swung his arm animatedly in a northern direction. "If all the forces Rome have here leave they will have so few trained fighting men left there will be wholesale slaughter right across the land!" His concern was obvious and not unexpected to Stilicho who raised his hand to silence his friend.

"I know you are right. But we are soldiers of Rome sworn by oath to do the bidding of our emperor." He again raised his hand to prevent Caratacus butting in before he had heard him out. "Let me finish Caratacus. That is my official position. We have as little as six months before the last of the legions will be withdrawn. Britannia will then be up for grabs by whoever is the stronger. As you know there are the Picts to the north but they are far outnumbered by the Saxons, Jutes and Angles that have been raiding the southern shores since before you arrived. Of these barbarians I would say the Saxons and Angles are the strongest and are closely related that they regularly combine to fight their common enemy. If that was to happen they could drive out the others and even if our armies remained they would probably be too powerful for us without major re-enforcements. The empire is under siege from all sides and when we move back across the water the Jutes and Visigoths who are attacking Gaul will be our main focus. A wise ruler would let the protagonists fight and then when all were weakened threaten the strongest while offering an alliance from a position of strength.

Caratacus was now listening with intense interest. Where was the general going with this and could that be what the old druid, Amergin Gluingel had been predicting in his visions?

Stilicho smiled as he saw how the mighty warrior had realised there was more to the conversation that just passing on an imperial order. "I suggest you travel north and spend a little time preparing your forces to defend themselves and in the meantime I will see to it that our armourers work flat out to supply the base at Vinovia with enough weapons to last your forces at least long enough for a year's worth of fighting." He paused and took a deep breath knowing the next part of the conversation would not be as warmly received.

"My advice would be to let the Saxons and Angles take the fight to the Picts and for the Brigante to stay in the shadows at least until you can get back to lead them." He stopped at that point until he saw the recognition on Caratacus's face.

"But I need to stay here with my people; you can't expect me to desert them at such a time?"

"Yes I can, if you stay here your people will be emboldened to take the battle to all their enemies and you will be defeated, even with the great Caratacus at their head. Besides you are still sworn by oath to serve Rome for nearly another year and I need you behind me in the battles we have to face. If I let you go and defy the imperial wishes I will be seen as being weak and unable to command my own men and the wolves will be at my door in no time. When the time comes you and your men will be honourably released from their pledges. When that comes I will ensure all the Brigante Cohort is given the very best arms, horses and provisions to see you back to your lands, you have my word on that."

It made sense even though it was frustrating. He was surprised how much the word, honourably meant to him. While continuing to fight for the good man who stood before him had a surprising draw. His people needed him, but at that moment in time, if they followed the plan it was not quite as much as Flavius Stilicho did.

Caratcus nodded his head appreciating his general's wise and generous words, "How soon can I leave?"

"How soon can you be ready?" was the reply.

Just as the men readied themselves to head north back to

Vinovia, Ruadan looked up and whispered to Caratacus that the general was approaching. He turned to see Stilicho was leading his favourite white Persian stallion.

"Caratacus, Vulcan here would like to see the north one last time, I would ask you to allow him that, so long as you promise to bring him back fit and healthy?" It was a great honour and a very generous gift although it had been suggested it was no more than a loan. Caratacus was not fooled by the generosity it was another promise he was making, solidifying further his promise to return when the time came.

The seven mounted Brigante soldiers of Rome set off along Dere Street heading north within two hours of getting word from their proud leader who rode the most distinctive horse in all Britannia. While they rode leaving the sprawling vicus and fort of Eboracum behind, he explained the situation. Ruadan, Brelus, Venpasian, Caracalus, Severus and Arvi listened, stunned by the recent turn of events, but allowed their leader to finish. All had the same initial reaction that Caratacus had shown but started to see the logic in the long term plan as well as agreeing that the honourable thing to do was to see out their pledge providing their people could be persuaded to go along with the plan of laying low. They first moved to the provincial capital of the kingdom of Brigantia. Isurium Brigantium (Alborough) was the seat of the puppet ruler of the Brigante. He was a weak man who was so immersed in the ways of Rome it was hard to see any sign of his lineage. Epaticatus was a direct descendant of Venutius, but it seemed that every successor since the warrior king had lost more and more of his heritage. He was so stricken with fear of losing the protection of Rome that with a little intimidating from Caratacus along with his promise to return to lead his army he agreed to the plan that Flavius Stilicho had suggested. He got permission to raise an army of the entire tribe and have then assemble in the upper hidden reaches of the valley of the Wear. The seven riders split carrying word from Epaticatus to all the regions of the kingdom, their task was to bring the fighting men of the tribe together to be armed and trained.

Within two weeks hundreds of men of all ages had arrived at the given rendezvous. They had answered the call as it was delivered by Caratacus and made it clear that if it had come from Epaticatus they would have ignored it. Yes they would fight for their people but only behind a true warrior.

As the training proceeded the fortresses along the wall were taken over by the Brigante allowing the Roman Auxiliaries to move back to the given assembly points under Stilicho's command to the south. These takeovers were completed under the cover of darkness so as not to give any chance of Pict or Saxon spies realising what was happening. Segedunum was to be the last fortress relieved. It had been gradually weakened in strength with each patrol that left not returning but heading south. It had obviously been seen by the Picts as with only a few weeks remaining before the legions were to head back across the sea a rider arrived from Stilicho:

"Segedunum attacked by a Pict war party. Praetorian Governor and his daughter who had been visiting taken prisoner when entourage had been leaving fortress. Reports from Votadini spy says the war party are holding the captives and some of their bodyguard just beyond the wall on the coast. They have sent word that they are willing to trade. I require you to attempt a rescue."

It was all that the general's message said; by the time the rescue mission was ready the garrisons at Vindolanda and Segedunum had been taken over by Caratacus's men. For the first time in centuries, there were no Romans north of Eboracum.

Caratacus knew he could not use a large force to march on the Pictish stronghold that the Votadini spy that was to accompany them had identified. If they did then the Picts would just use their raiding ships to sail further north towards the safety of their homeland. The military cross over from Rome to Brigante had gone smoothly but Caratacus knew at some point an entire withdrawal would be needed. If they were to stay in the shadows of the battles to come he did not want to antagonise their enemies by letting them see it was in fact native forces facing them so the men he chose for the rescue were all from the Brigante Cohort, genuine soldiers of the empire. The group would also be small, moving fast and stealthily hopefully remaining unobserved.

Severus and Arvi were left in charge of the continuing training while Caratacus and the other four planned their assault. They knew that even if they were successful, by the time they got back to Eboracum they would be just in time to join the evacuation of Britannia as they would be leaving with the rest of the legions. The two men left behind had not sworn the oath and represented the two most trustworthy men Caratacus had, they knew the plan and would take advantage of the confusion of the rescue to withdraw all the forces back into the valleys where they could defend themselves awaiting the return of Caratacus.

Pledges of undying brotherhood and kinship were exchanged as the five riders along with their Votadini guide called Ingarm moved west to cross the wall over the now empty battlements of the greatest Roman defensive build in the empire. They chose the high mountains, down the back bone of the land. It was one of the most desolate areas in all of Britannia, inhospitable and least travelled. It was also the easiest route to journey if you wanted to remain unobserved before moving back to the east coast and approaching the Pict camp from the opposite direction that any attack would be expected to come from.

Stilicho's message had been delivered just one day after the Pict envoy had arrived carrying the ransom demand. The message promised that the general would stall but could not promise more than a week or two so they had very little time to waste. But the requirement for speed had to be tempered with the need to move without being seen, this was the reason they moved along the mountainous spine for two days before crossing over into the hills of the Votadini lands using the treacherous exposed terrain. Even Vulcan's brilliant white coat was draped in a heavy blanket with his legs covered in charcoal to hide him from view.

Ingram hated the Picts just as much as the Brigante did. They had constantly raided the Votadini lands until it was impoverished and it became worthless especially when compared to the riches of the Roman Empire that lay just beyond the wall. It had taken four days for their guide to bring the group into position. They were looking down from the sweeping hillside on to the enemy camp, which sat along the side of the sandy cove of the cold, grey, eastern sea.

Over the next few days they watched the daily coming and going of the camp identifying the temporary lean too which served as the prison. It appeared that the vanquished bodyguard had been disposed of as there only appeared to be three figures tied up to the frame of the makeshift jail. Raiding parties kept leaving venturing south on the hunt for easy plunder and soon the force left behind was relatively small.

That evening with most of his men and ships out on raiding missions trying to find provisions, Alvor took one last turn around the perimeter of his camp. Down on the beach the moorings of his remaining ships seemed to be fine, their anchors driven into the sand. Caratacus was close enough to drive his Pilum into his gut as they hid neck deep in the sea to the rear of the bobbing craft. Most of the Pict warriors were onboard enabling a quick getaway in case of coming under attack, but by the light-hearted banter it appeared they did not expect any trouble. From the centre of the camp roared a large fire which illuminated the Pictish leader, these fires were reciprocated by brassieres burning onboard the upper deck of each ship giving a little warmth against the brisk offshore breeze. There was too much light to make their play at that moment without risking being seen so they all had to wait in the frigid sea until the banter had been replaced by none too melodious snoring and the fires had died down a Caratacus confirmed his plan by hand gestures.

More snores had joined the raucous choir and the lone guard onboard each ship allowed the fires to burn back not wanting to use up all the fuel before day break. With the exception of Caratacus each of the men picked a ship and climbed up the steering oar that protruded out of the stern of the vessel. Having got to the top they moved across to whichever side of the ship gave the greatest protection from being seen. One prominent timber stood out down the entire outer length and on this rested the oars with their holes directly above. The two features allowed, firstly for each man to move down the outer length of the craft and secondly to get close enough to the onboard fires to push their Pilum through the oar holes and push over the glowing hot brassieres. One by one with a crash, orange glowing embers spilt across the decks. The sails being stowed down the centre of the ship was the first thing to ignite and within seconds a raging inferno was tearing through each of the ships as spare sails, ropes and eventually the actual timbers conspired to condemn the vessels. With most on board soundly sleeping the reaction of each crew was delayed and took far too long to give any hope of saving any of the targeted ships. Fanned by the north easterly winds all but the end two were engulfed by the growing conflagration.

Four of the six craft that lay anchored to the shore were ablaze as the shouts and screams of burning men woke Alvor and the few men on shore from their slumber. With four consecutive ships lighting the night he looked in horror at the wall of flames that was about to reduce his small fleet by two thirds. He could not understand how the fire the thought had started on one had spread so quickly to the others, but his main focus was to save the two remaining vessels and worry about what had started it later.

"You men, they can save themselves," he was calling to his warriors who had been in camp with him and had gone to help the men who were jumping into the water on fire. "Help save the two ships that are not burning, quick with me let's get the anchor ropes and move them up the breach." He clearly had no interest in his men, just the ships.

Just two men stood guard over the prisoners. Caratacus had left the water and got behind his target before the pyrotechnics had started. Both seemed fascinated by the giant floating torch display that was so bright against the darkened backdrop they needed to shield their eyes. Even this far away they could feel the radiant heat and while it warmed them they knew it was doing serious damage to many of the kin. With a left-handed plunge the Gladius severed the lower spine of the first man incapacitating his every action a brief moment before he was dead. As he fell the Pilum flew, gleaming orange in the reflective flames the iron tipped point was never going to miss its target at such a short range and with the power that Caratacus packed it was always going to be fatal, but just the ensure the death sentence the mighty war axe was drawn and with three side steps the huge brutal blade took an undercutting path tearing into the man's groin ripping up into his gut. With three more slightly precise cuts the bindings of the prisoners had been severed. Retrieving his weapons Caratacus led the Praetorian Governor, his daughter and a servant away into the distant dense bushes where they were met by the others who had finally got out of the numbingly cold sea.

The next part of the plan was for Caratacus to re-enter the camp on horseback and free the few horses that were corralled nearby. Once again the chopping of the war axe did the trick. The horses already skittish from the flaming commotion did not have to be coaxed, the beasts fled as their opportunity of freedom was given. They thundered along the beach into the darkness keen to leave the burning chaos behind. What was not part of the plan, but just an afterthought when he tried to justify the risk to himself later was Caratacus seeing the chance to take his vengeance on Alvor as well as saving the prisoners.

He charged forward towards the growing group of survivors who shocked and suffering a range of burns and the effects of smoke had turned when hearing the sand muffled stampede behind them. Alvor was wide open and even on a fast moving horse in the surrounding confusion Caratacus would have been certain of hitting his target. What he didn't expect was a quick moving warrior diving into his direct charge causing Vulcan to veer off to the left and unbalancing his rider to such an extent that he barely managed to hang on to the reins and Pilum. Using only his impressive core strength he managed to blindly lung forward catching Alvor's brother in the gut snapping off the iron tip that was left embedded in its victim. Regaining his balance quickly was not enough to give him time to strike a second time the Pictish leader was safe. Caratacus was fuming with frustration but he did manage to work a little of his irritation out on one man who was staggering around the beach still stunned from his fire engulfing experience. His skull was crushed with the broken Pilum shaft being smashed across the top of his head as Vulcan flew his master to join the others.

"I am coming for you, you blue painted piece of pig shit!" he boomed as he vanished into the darkness.

They rescuers and rescued met up at a point further down the long sweeping beach of the cove. One of the spooked horses had been captured and the servant was calming the nag trying to steady it for the young lady to mount when an arrow implanted itself in his back with a thwack! Without a moment's hesitation and with his daughter still bending over her servant seeing if her faithful man was dead Felix Cato, Praetorian Governor of Eboracum had brushed her to one side and mounted the free horse and started to flee into the darkness leaving everybody aghast at his blatant lack of concern for his daughter and the total panic he was showing.

The Picts had surprises the Brigante rescuers by the speed in which they had pulled themselves together and covered the long stretch of sandy ground. It was now that Caratacus's impulsive action started to tease him as to whether or not his attack had been purely driven by his overriding desire for revenge. It was evident in his own mind that if he had not given such an early warning they would have been long gone by now with the Picts still fighting the fires. Had he jeopardised the whole party just for his selfishness lust to kill one man?

All this passed through his head as the cowardly governor galloped down towards the opposite end of the beach where Ingarm had warned them that it was hemmed in by tall rocky cliffs offering no escape route.

"I see you Caratacus, bitch of the Romans, I swear the next time we meet I will kill you!" it was the voice of Alvor that called through the lightening gloom of early morning.

Caratacus hauled the girl up behind him and spurred Vulcan on leaving the corpse of the servant behind following the others who had moved off up the track that lead to the higher ground that overlooked the cove.

It was a long steep haul and without horses they knew that when they got to the top they were safe from further pursuit. The dawn was fast defeating the darkness as a new day beckoned the silver grey gave them enough light to see back down below where a lone horseman was trapped by at least fifty warriors. They closed swiftly and menacingly grabbing horse and rider pulling both to the ground. The coward that was Felix Cato was separated from the struggling, flailing horse which once again ran free up the beach while a hail of blows from sword, axe and every conceivable weapon rained down ending further possibility of rescue. Vengeance had overtaken the Picts greed for ransom, payback for lost ships and killed brothers. As the group parted there was barely a sign of a body, it being almost battered under the soft surface, just an area of blackened sand told the tale.

The young woman showed astonishingly little emotion, she was either a very cold individual or her disappointment in her father's earlier behaviour had created such a surprising lack of reaction, nobody knew her well enough to make that judgement. She just looked away when they had turned to see how she had taken watching her father being butchered.

Without knowing how long it would take the horses to be recaptured but with the knowledge that their foes were excellent trackers they had no time to waste. Having watched the events down on the beach they had revealed their position on the high ground being almost silhouetted against the rising sun. They moved off following the lofty terrain until it started to drop into a small valley that housed a small river which emptied back into the sea a mile or so to the east. They entered the water course and followed it up stream several miles travelling at ninety degrees to the direction they had last been seen travelling. It would be two days of riding before they reached the wall as they dare not take the obvious shortest course so they would head inland before turning south. The wall no longer promised the safety it would have just a few days earlier and they did not want to lead the Picts to Vinovia and the Brigante. They would have to pick up Dere Street further south only considering they were safe when back inside the fortress of Eboracum.

As they rode Caratacus could feel Aemilia Cato's thighs pressing against him. Her arms were wrapped around his waist tightly and although he was now wearing his armour he could swear that he could feel her breasts pressing into his back. His imagination was working as hard as his self discipline was, unfortunately they seemed to be antagonising each other. What wasn't his imagination were her hands with their interlocking grip slowly dropping down off his waist until they rested on his inner thigh and the jostling of the horse's movements caused them to tease him into a state where his indiscipline had become all too evident. Through his peripheral vision he could just make out her head turned sideways and resting on his armoured shoulder, her eye shut. Never in the hours they rode did her grip slacken, she remained intimately tight to him until it was time to rest the horses.

They had little provisions left but between the five warriors they managed to find a little for Aemilia to share. Ruadan was stationed on the high ground acting as their watch out as the horses lazily helped themselves to the lush grass and water in the stream close by. The Praetorian Governor's daughter told of her ordeal of being attacked as they had left Segedunum and how those men that had survived the attack had been separated and put on a boat that headed north. She was only mildly upset for their loss and that of her servant but never mentioned her father and nobody pressed her on the matter.

"Where are you going?" asked Caratacus as she got up, "don't wander to far, we have no idea how far behind the first of their tracker will be."

"I wish to wash in the stream as I am sure I am quite a sight."

Caratacus had removed the blanket off Vulcan to keep him cool so offered it for her to dry herself on. "It is only a horse blanket but you are welcome to it if you want?"

"Thank you. So you must be the mighty Caratacus the Brigante Barbarian who won his freedom in the coliseum and is now the senior centurion and favourite of General Stilicho?"

Caratacus suddenly realised that he had not introduced himself or his men. His lack of Roman education and social skills on display he apologised and pointed each man out in turn.

She told them her name and asked them to address her using her first name as having saved her she considered them her close confidantes.

"If there is the possibility of the enemy arriving would you accompany me down to the river and watch over me while I bathe?" she asked Caratacus. Her innocence was so exaggerated it was almost amusing to all the others, but it was further embarrassment for Caratacus.

"Could you raise the blanket up so you screen me from your men? I wish to remove my rather dirty clothes and wash them as well as myself."

When they finally got back underway she was wearing a much cleaner but very damp toga praetexta and her hair was hanging long and loose rather than the bound fillet it had been. The horse blanket had once again been used, a hole cut in the centre of it to create a over shale type of garment to keep

Aemilia warm as the wind whistled by the fast moving horse. As if this was not enough she positioned herself as before, drawn tightly to Caratacus but this time she kept her hands warm, pressed between his legs and the saddle. He knew he was being teased but could not help his reaction which was very much the same as before.

Ideally they did not want to move too far west before travelling south so picked on one of the mile castles just east of Vindolanda. Wanting to check that the passage was safe they took refuge in a dense part of the forest they had been negotiating and Caratacus and Brelus moved forward on foot. It was clear but they waited until dark before they made the crossing so as to reduce the possibility of being seen. The delay cost them, as just before they set off they saw movement at the small fortress. Forced further westward they continued for a little way before they made camp for the night. It was to be a cold one and there would be no chance to light a fire.

The horse that had been separated from Felix Cato was being ridden by the best tracker the Picts had in their army. They had caught the beast surprisingly quickly considering how spooked it had been. It meant that he was no more than an hour behind his target. Having lost their tracks at the river he had known to travel slowly up the water course looking for the overturned rocks, broken vegetation or even the more obvious hoof prints that would spell out where his prey had departed the water. Every now and again he made sure he left tell tale markers to enable his comrades to follow without delay. Having heard the stories of the mileposts of the great wall being emptied over the previous months he suspected his quarry would head for the populated fort at Vindolanda, but he had been warned by his leader not to take anything for granted when following the man who led the raiding party.

Caratacus was never more at home in his surroundings as

when he was in the forest. It was as if the trees talked to him, he was at one with them and them with him. He knew someone was following them. It was to be expected but he knew this man was close and having no difficulty in seeing through any of their attempts to hide their route. He also knew in his gut that the tracker was a stranger in these parts and not as at home as he in the dense cover of the Caledonian Forest. A sixth sense told him he travelled alone and he knew he needed to be dealt with before he brought the entire war party down upon them.

Darkness had descended and in such impenetrable greenery the light could make a man easily disorientated. It was becoming near impossible to see tracks even for a skilled man. Caratacus dismounted on a nearby fallen log that lay by the side of the winding animal track they had been following. Ruadan had taken Vulcan's reins while the others began making camp adjacent to the trial.

As he dismounted Aemilia looked concerned realising that something was amiss. "I will be gone just a little while, you should try to rest as best you can," he whispered trying to reassure her. She instinctively grabbed his hand which he gently shook free as he turned. As Ruadan led Vulcan forwards her face was etched with worry showing just how petrified she was. She continued looking back towards him, watching him applying mud on his face from the underside of the downed tree trunk and slip back into the gloom of the arboreal night.

"He is going back down the trail," explained Ruadan in a hushed voice, "he is aware that someone is following us and needs to put an end to it."

Caratacus felt he was not alone as he moved off deeper into the tree line. He knew Becuille was watching over him and guiding his path. His sensors were heightened to a point that he could see and hear the smallest of disturbances in the darkness. He looked up and saw the usually silent owl in a tree stretching its wings and a squirrel scampering across the floor. He was moving back parallel to the trail they had been on, sure footed without as much as a twig snapping underfoot. He stopped dead in his tracks sniffing the air. A horse some fifty paces ahead, it was tethered as it was not making the expected regular strides but instead was scuffing the ground waiting to be fed. Yes there it was the smell of cut dry grass being spread out. His target had set up camp for the night and was feeding his mount. The animal knew of his presence but made on sound that might give any warning, it too was at ease knowing this stranger was part of the natural environment of the forest and bore no threat to it so continued eating its meagre ration of hay.

His approached slowed even more as he moved off, the tracker was wise not to have a fire lit as it would have left him vulnerable to anybody in the area that would have smelt the wood smoke trapped beneath the canopy. What the young Pict had not reckoned with was an enemy so at home in those surrounding that he could pass almost ghost like maintaining the night's natural equilibrium. Whether that was the old druid's training and spells or the powers of the goddess of the forest the Pict had his fitful slumber rudely interrupted by a kick in the ribs which expelled all the air from his lungs before he even opened his eyes. As he forced them to open gasping to replenish his empty chest he saw the butt of a Gladius hilt loom out of the darkness growing ever larger in his vision, just before darkness flooded his brain accompanied by a crunch of his collapsing nose.

He was brought back to consciousness by water running down his face. He was tied to a tree next to a fire. They were not in the same place he had set up his camp as they were next to a small stream which he could hear running nearby. A huge giant of a man stood before him and he was chanting some strange incantation that sent his blood ice cold. As this feeling of a deep chill passed he suddenly felt peculiarly light headed as his midriff became weightless and a burning pain erupted in his gut. He felt as if he was spinning uncontrollably but just as the world was about to leave him he was plunged face down in cold water. He would never know but he had just suffered the triple death of blade, fire and water. The hapless tracker had paid the ultimate price to the goddess of the forest.

Caratacus was back in the camp before his men knew anybody was approaching. Aemilia was rooted to the spot where Ruadan had lowered her from Vulcan nearly two hours earlier. Her fear had not dissipated it had completely disabled her ability to move until she saw Caratacus return. She grabbed him once again as a small girl would look for comfort from her father. Caratacus checked his horse had been cared for then set out his bed roll on a pile of leaves.

The pair lay together, she holding on to him tightly as he looked up through a break in the tree tops. A star shot across the black sky, its silver, streaking movement so striking set against the other motionless celestial bodies. He was totally absorbed by the sight until a voice whispered in his ears. "We have a beautiful son Caratacus, you saw him the last time we met." It was Becuille; she had been with him during his attack on the tracker. It was her lying beside him. "Our son will come to join you when the time is right and carry on the fight for the people of the earth. But he needs a sister, one that will continue my line after my time and become the next Goddess of the Forest. There was a little tremble in her voice as they embraced and their passion ignited around them. She arched her back and opened her legs inviting his exploring fingers to enter her while his tongue played, brushing across her hard nipples. "I am the only one who can bare your children, that was our pact; any women conceiving from your seed will die along with that child. Beware." She whispered the frightening, almost silent warning in his ear as he rhythmically moved inside her, while she used her hands on his back and heels round his legs to pull him deeper, extracting every last seed after what seemed like hours of joyous love making as night became day and back to night again. Her skin so soft and pale and her nakedness so tempting he could not resist. He wasn't sure but he imagined he had seen two dawns before he fell into a contented exhausted asleep.

When he did awake the camp was just stirring and beside him laid Aemilia. Sound asleep, her clothing having been discarded but now pulled across her to guard against the chill of the night. He could see her rounded olive skin was every bit as blemish free as Becuille's pale slender body but so completely different he could not see how he could have been fooled into believing she had visited him.

"By it didn't take you long to get between her legs," Brelus giggled quietly looking at his leader as he approached.

"Not a word of this to anyone Brelus," he warned.

"I don't think there's anything for me to keep quiet, with the amount of noise she was making. Just as well you despatched the Pict tracker last night or he would have come into camp to have a look at what you were up to!" he was still giggling as the others joined them and gladly, added to their leader's discomfort.

Alvor and his men were several hours behind their tracker and travelling much slower. It wasn't a problem the young man was good and he was leaving clear signs to direct them to their prize. The revenge that would be metered out on the man who had killed his brother would be slow and painful.

It was a warm morning and they were in probably the

densest part of the forest. So thick was the vegetation that it was impossible to see just a few paces off the track that they followed. Alvor's horse caught its hoof on a low lying ivy vine that seemed to have been strung taught across the narrow trail. As the horse dipped its head in the stumble Alvor's quick reaction brought his head and shoulders back in counterbalance. It meant that when the butchered body of his tracker crashed out of the trees it struck him directly in the face. He would not have wanted to react the way he did but the sudden appearance of the partially disembowelled carcass dropping on his lap, suspended by his feet by Mistletoe vines along with the plague of bloated shiny blue bodied flies disturbed in their lazy early morning feast was too much for anybody to remain calm. As the buzzing cloud managed to get airborne from their banquet they swarmed and covered him. The smell of both burnt and raw flesh made him turn away and wretch as part of the remaining intestine had deposited itself on him. It was the first time in his life that the Pictish leader had experienced real fear. He had heard many stories about Caratacus and his allegiance with the super natural beliefs of the ancient druids and their Gods. Everybody knew that the druid tribe had been one of the native bands the Romans feared the most of any in all of Britannia. Even when they had bettered them in combat it was said that these demons just melted back into the forests which was said to be their fortress. Was this what he faced in Caratacus? Not only a mighty warrior but a demon bless by some ancient deity? He could not help but think that this was the man he had betrayed and vowed to kill. He was unsettled by the prospect and every one of his warriors saw it etched in his strangely deflated body.

The murmuring of disquiet around him snapped him back from his internal lament of doubt, but it was too late his men had witnessed his qualms. He called them to cut the lad down, although he did not relish the prospect he urged himself forward in pursuit of a prey he wasn't sure he really wanted to face.

Without knowing it the Picts had managed to get one of their raiding parties in front of Caratacus's group. The Pictish warriors had just discovered that the garrison of Vindolanda was deserted and they were on the rampage destroying all that they could not carry. This included all the nearby mile castles. If Caratacus was tracked moving further west it would encourage Alvor's band closer to Vinovia and the valleys where his people resided but he gambled that the draw of ran sacking the Roman strongholds would be too great, keeping their enemy too busy to look south of the wall. To be safe he moved the rescuers west whilst still in the cover of the forest. Cilurnun was a substantial fort just a couple of hour's ride to the west of Vindolanda and by good fortune it was not suffering the same fate as its neighbour. Ruadan went forward to check and was quick to wave then through when he established that the scene was safe. They were now in Brigante territory heading south as fast as their horses would carry them. Ingram their guide north of the wall was happy to stay with the group as he explained there was little left for him on his own land. With the horse gathered from the tracker everyone in the party now had a horse so progress was good.

They were not going to get to their destination for another two days so that night they took to the safety of the hills so as not to expose their presence on Dere Street until they were much closer and likely to run into Roman patrols. That night they made camp in the high moors.

Not only had Aemilia been given the dead trackers horse she now had his warm bed roll and furs. However it did not mean that she wanted to be alone during the coming night.

"I am going to freeze if I sleep on my own," she whispered

kneeling over Caratacus having appeared silently by his side. Without waiting for an invitation that he did not want to seem to be too eager to give she laid out her bed beside him pulling herself in close so as to benefit from the body heat of her liberator.

"I have not had a chance to really thank you for saving me from those heathens, last night we said very little but it was delicious," she said her mouth almost pressed against his ear. "Now where shall I start?" Her hand that was wrapped around him once again pulling her close moved purposely between his legs and started to gently massage him into erectness. It didn't take long.

The following day and night followed a similar routine to the day before the bleak deserted moors were safe to travel but made for slow progress. They managed to catch a couple of hares by snaring the burrows they located close to their chosen campsite. Now feeling safe they risked lighting a fire so feasted on roast hare roots and berries before retiring, Aemilia and Caratacus making the most of their last evening in each other's bed, her appetite for his animal magnetism seemingly knowing no bounds and he happy to oblige. By the time they entered Eboracum they clearly did not care who saw that they were an item.

"Congratulations Caratacus my friend you have out done yourself this time," was the welcome from his general.

"I'm not sure about that, we failed to bring back the Praetorian Governor back alive," he questioned.

"Ah! Once again you show your lack of knowledge for the Roman greed for stories that fire their imagination. How many Picts did you kill? How many ships did you destroy and all this can be confirmed by the beautiful daughter of the governor who the Brigante Barbarian, champion of the arena, darling of the people saved and won her heart." He pronounced the achievement like he was introducing a play. "Rome will love this and you, even more!" Caratacus knew that although the general was using the word "you" he really meant "him".

It was with a heavy heart that within the week they sailed down the Ouse into the Humber, out into the sea and headed south. He had spent each night in Aemilia's arms, stopping in the governor's villa in surroundings he had never experienced before but Aemilia told him of the inheritance that she stood to gain providing she arrived back in Rome quick enough to stop the rest of her more distant family stealing it.

The fleet landed on the shores of Gaul where the army disembarked. But for the general and his bodyguard it was on to deliver Aemilia and to get word of the problems that had befallen the empire that had required the evacuation of Britannia.

Citizen of Rome.

General Flavius Stilicho was not surprised by the muted homecoming he received. Gone was the hero's welcome he had experienced when returning after defeating his Roman foe bringing the two halves of the empire under Theodosius's rule or the victories he had presided over when taking on the Visigoths, rescuing the young Emperor Honorius. Things in Britannia had not gone as he had hoped even with the imaginative reports he had sent back to Rome. What he was surprised by was how highly Caratacus seemed to be viewed by both the citizens and senators alike. He was quite the celebrity and with his new found relationship with a daughter of one of the provincial governors he had been elevated up the social standings without really threatening the politicians. At least for now he could do no wrong.

Aemilia was also very pleased by his popularity. Although her father had been a Praetorian Governor his death would mean she would need to find someone who could help maintain her status. Without knowing it, Caratacus had another crucial role to play in her future. She was the only remaining direct family member of Felix Cato and therefore should have been the unquestionable inheritor of is money and estates in Rome and Tuscany. But his affair with a low born woman following Aemilia's mother's death meant there was one person who might stand in her way.

Davina Claudius ran a successful local lupanar (brothel) and following the loss of his wife Felix Cato had started using the establishment. In Roman society both women and men of the highest social standing engaged prostitutes of either gender without incurring moral disapproval. It was big business and as "Lena or Madame" she was not lacking in wealth. What she did crave for was respect and a step up in social standing for her and her family. That was why she had given her daughter the task of satisfying Felix's needs. The older man had been besotted by such an energetic girl and very quickly would not have the services of any other but his Fabia. It was to Fabia he had a son, half brother to Aemilia and just five years her junior. The young man was working as part of the security at the lupanar where there was often trouble with drunkard clients and competition who wished to get one over on them. Decimus was a nasty piece of work and had to be considering his business, he and a few of his associates had a reputation that nobody wanted to mess with and the few times he had over stepped the mark and got in trouble with the authorities his father had pulled strings to arrange for any charges to be dropped. Davina's plan seemed to have fallen flat when Felix had been posted to Britannia but the news of his death brought other possibilities.

As soon as news of the Praetorian Governors' death had reached Davina's ears she had started petitioning for her grandson's recognition as a rightful heir even before Aemilia had set foot back in Rome.

"It has been so long since I have been in Rome I got lost today," Aemilia's story started. "I lost my bearing and ended up walking through an unsavoury area when I was set upon by some thugs who tried to get me inside a Lupanar to work for them." What had really happened was she had visited the brothel to try to head of Davina's plans by threatening her with calling in favours with the authority's to close the establishment down. She had even used Caratacus's name in her threat but with Davina having lost touch with the political goings on in Rome she was not too sure who he was and had called to her grandson to introduce himself to his half sister while throwing her out. Inside such an establishment in such a seedy area of the city she had been man handled during her ordeal and Decimus had taken the opportunity to get very familiar with his estranged family member. Aemilia had seen a plan immediately that would end Decimus's claim to her fortune. She had used her personal slave girl to grip her hard around the tops of her inner thighs so that she left her finger marks. It hadn't taken much force for the lovely Nubian slave to bruise her. She had seduced the girl not long after buying her and thus started regular, sexual encounters. On this occasion the girl was ordered to be a wild animal while with her. It was ironic that she had used that phrase as it was that animal like characteristic that she had grown tired of in Caratacus and had already started to look elsewhere for her pleasure. But that would not be until she had used him to rid herself of her father's bastard son.

Caratacus was totally unaware of Aemilia's love for him having waned she seemed just as eager to please him as she ever had been. She was so keen to please him that she had even started to get the dark skinned slave girl involved doubling his pleasure. So when he was told of her terrible experience there was only going to be one outcome.

Caratacus had been watching the front door of the lupanar for a few nights and was well aware of the number of friends that Decimus had working at his side. But when the door shut for the night he always walked home via the rear alley and one by one his friend left him until he was alone for the last few minutes. It was during this short period when Decimus was to see a giant shadow appear at his side and take his life with one enormous smash of a heavy club which crushed his skull. His lifeless body was dragged to the River Tiber and unceremoniously dumped, weighted down with some old heavy chain, leaving behind just a bloody pool where he had met Caratacus for the one and only time in his short life.

Aemilia didn't even flicker when he told her that the man had paid the price for his treatment of his beloved but was more than happy to agree to be his alibi if he needed it. He didn't. For all Rome was the most civilised city in the world it was full of rogues and villains and death awaited round every corner if you entered the wrong area. Decimus was just one of the hundreds of people who ended up in the Tiber every year and with the exception of his immediate family would not be missed by anyone.

Following the inheritance settlement Aemilia had no further use for Caratacus. Her excitement for his body and powerful love making had died so she was continually making excuses not to sleep with him. She even encouraged him to find a slave of his own or to visit a lupanar and enjoy some different excitement. He naively still seemed to think she wanted to ensure he got maximum pleasure from their life together. So when after weeks of hinting, when he had still not managed to get the message she moved out to her estate in Tuscany explaining that with the summer having arrived she had to oversee the harvest. He travelled with her to ensure she was safe but had to return as the emperor had finally got round to dealing with the growing crisis in Gaul and had granted Stilicho his audience.

"That ungrateful, little upstart!" The general was obviously furious and was waving his arms animatedly pointing in the direction of what he imagined was the emperor's palace. "He seems to think that because another one of his generals as rebelled and announced himself emperor of the west it is my fault as I serve with him in Britannia." He was pacing back and forth and extremely agitated. Caratacus had never seen him in such a rage and what he had been told at that moment made little sense. Stilicho must have sensed the unease and calmed a little.

"Sorry Caratacus you have walked right into my venting off and probably have little or no idea why I am in such a fury?"

He smiled at his general who had brought his temper under control in a flash and followed the gesture to sit down. A slave poured Caratacus some wine and topped up Flavius Stilicho's goblet.

"Not long after all the legions left your homeland and landed in Gaul readying themselves to face several different rebelling barbarian tribes, Flavious Claudius Constantinus pronounced himself Emperor of the Western Empire in an attempt to usurp Honorius from his throne. He has taken most of our forces, only one legion as stayed loyal. Apparently his betrayal is my fault according to that little wet pup that I have kept on the throne since his father died. We need to travel back to Gaul with all haste and stamp out this treachery before it gains momentum. Prepare the bodyguard for travel Caratacus. I will be coming shortly afterwards I need to contact an old adversary and an even older friend so try to arrange a meeting. It will be an interesting meeting, I have defeated Aleric of the Visigoths twice since we were comrades. You will like the man and he you, so you will accompany me when it is arranged."

Arriving back in Gaul and expecting to meet up with the mighty army he had left, Caratacus realised just how many men had taken Constantine's side. Marcus Valerius was first to meet him and he was taken to the tent of one of Stilicho's most trusted subordinates, he had meet the man called Sarus the Goth who a few times previous.

"How many men do you bring with you Caratacus?" was his opening welcome.

"I have the bodyguard and the rest of the Brigante Cohort

plus some auxiliary units of cavalry and Persian archers that the general could muster at short notice. No more than five hundred men unfortunately."

"Damn, I was hoping for more. But that will have to do; we need to move quickly if we are to cut their vanguard off before the main army arrives to back them up." He turned to Marcus Valerius. "I need you to return on that ship back to Rome and convince General Stilicho to bring an army up through the Alps.

Marcus Valerius saluted his superior with the customary forearm across his chest and left.

"So Caratacus this is our situation;" he went on to explain that due to an attack by the Jutes the main body of Constantine's army had been delayed and the vanguard was now isolated. He intended to strike and take out the smaller unit before they got to the mountain border on the northern territories of Italy where they would find good ground to defend.

"Sir, do we have any locals who are friendly to our forces?"

"Caratacus. I am like Flavius and yourself, a barbarian fighting for Rome. When we are together we are brothers and call each other by our given name, so a little less of the sir my friend. Yes we have but only a few hundred old men, women and children, what is on your mind?"

"Well, I would expect that the enemy is watching us, so if we can dress up the locals to look like the force is still in camp and then use the ships that Marcus is taking back to Rome to take us a little further up the coast we can get in front of them and catch them off guard?"

Sarus nodded his head and a slight smile across his face. "Stilicho said you were a good thinker as well as a mighty warrior. It appears he was not mistaken.

The entire fighting force was packed into the holds of the

ships under the cover of darkness. All spare Rome clothing was given to the locals as well as all the tents being left behind for them to live in. The following morning as would be expected the fleet set off on the morning tides but instead of sailing direct to Rome it landed Sarus's force just a few miles southeast where they immediately struck inland.

A captured deserter had told of two generals of Constantine leading the vanguard. Sarus knew them both. Iustinianus and Nebiogastes were two of his most senior officers; both held the rank of *magistri militum* in Constantine's army of Gaul. The later was best known to Sarus and he had a plan for him if he could separate him from the staunch Constantine supporter, Iustinianus.

The two rebel officers were in no hurry. They were not even concerned about being separated by such a distance from the main force. Their watch outs had only the day before said that Sarus was still in camp and the word from Rome was that Stilicho had remained there when barely more than a cohort had sailed to meet up with his pitiful army in Gaul. Within the next day or so they would be in the foot hills of the Alps where they intended to wait for the entire army to regroup.

Sarus and his force had arrived in the foothills a full day in advance of the rebels expected arrival. The road that led several miles into the pass had been built and maintained by Roman troops for the last three hundred years and was the only route a Roman army would consider using.

"It makes them very predictable," was the only comment Caratacus made when he heard Sarus's plan.

The solid Roman road took the high sided valley between two low mountains before reaching its terminus on the plateau of an alpine meadow. It was there that it turned back to its original dirt track for the rest of the crossing of the massive range of the Southern Alps.

With Sarus's own bodyguard knowing the area they acted as the small forces vanguard, so he chose to use Caratacus and his Brigante by his side. He pointed out the high meadow in the distance.

"That is where they will most likely camp and wait for the rest of the army to join them." He smiled to himself remembering Caratacus's comment about being predictable, adding. "Yet again easily predictable as you have said."

"Any large force will have to look to the easiest route so they do not get strung out and lose contact across their army. But when they are moving between those two hills that's what is going to happen."

"And that is exactly why we will wait for them there."

Caratacus was looking around at the numerous woods they were passing and new that deep inside there would be large amounts of dead foliage and other combustible vegetation. It reminded him of the attack he had led on the doomed legion in the Caledonian forest. He also noted that the sides of the mountain pass were littered with bushes and scrubland which would hide any preparation they might want for an ambush. He discussed his idea with Sarus without actually mentioning the annihilation of the Romans.

"I intended using the pass for the ambush, so if you can arrange the flank attacks I will sort out the cavalry charge from above and the blocking infantry behind. If you can make enough of an impact we can have this battle won with minimal loses."

Caratacus and his men moved off to examine the sloping ground and found a section on either side that was perfect for his plan. He set the Persian archer on gathering flammable materials and vines with which the huge bundles could be bound into balls, while his men cut tree trunks from the blind side of the woods and carried them onto a rocky platform which the road passed directly below.

Sarus had sent scouts back to locate the approaching army and when they reported back he came to check on the progress of the ambush.

"Are your men ready Caratacus? They are no more than two hours away."

"Just finishing off. All we have to do is clean our tracks up so their scouts don't suspect anything."

The vanguard was nowhere near the number of an entire legion. With the formation they march in, it suggested five or six cohorts with cavalry at its head, and a large baggage train bringing up the rear.

From the lack of interest shown by the scouts it was obvious that they did not expect to find anything of concern. The small army was approaching the end of the day and the entire force seemed tired and looking forward to reaching the high meadow where they could set up their camp and rest. Heads were bowed and feet dragged, shields and Pilum were dragging along the hard surface of the road. It made a man weary just watching the sorry sight making their sluggish progress.

As the mounted scouts crested the top of the road and moved onto the plateaux they disappeared from their leaders view. Caratacus was not to know it but it was Iustinianus at the front and Nebiogastes was in the centre of the column. The riders never got the opportunity to dismount and were set upon by a small party of infantry that waited behind a few large boulders at the entrance to the meadow. While one drove his spear in the rider another took the horse's reins to prevent them bolting and warning the men below.

Iustinianus was just as exhausted as his men. They had been taking their time but it had still been a long journey, in hot dusty conditions and as the road had been gradually climbing for the last two hours he was ready for a rest. Looking ahead he saw one of his scouts come back into view and waved from the head of the road with the sun at his back signalling all was well in the alpine meadow. He heard the murmuring of the troops behind, it was the first noise they had made in hours, anticipating the rest in a cool meadow fanned by the gentle mountain breeze. He had camped here before and it was a good place to spend a couple of days waiting for the main army to catch up. It appeared his men agreed.

The scouts signal was designed to encourage their continued progress, but it was also to let the ambushers know that the real scouts had been dealt with and all was going to plan. The front of the column was reaching the steepest point of their climb where the flanks took an equally sheer gradient. Just as the column started to bunch up as the rear now moved faster than the front a few pillars of grey smoke started to waft, languidly skywards. It was Nebiogastes in the centre of the column who had been dealing with a discipline issue who called forwards. The chain of calls eventually drawing Iustinianus's attention to it, it snapped him out of his daydream. He realised it was the sign of an ambush and he cursed his exhausted stupidity for not paying more attention, of course it was the perfect place for an enemy to spring a surprise.

It was all too late; their tired response would be too little. Bushes above them started to burst into flames and cascaded down the hillside, scattering the cavalry horses, which bucked and panicked throwing their riders as they tried to escape the flaming balls that bounced down upon them. Caratacus had positioned the frontal assault to be just ahead of the cavalry so it drove the terrified horses back down the road clattering into the infantry who were only just reacting to the mayhem ahead. To the rear tree trunks crashed of the top of the cliff top pounding the men below and cutting off the baggage train from the rest of the column. At the same time the sky darkened with two swarms of Persian arrows flying inbound from each flank, before the shield wall was constructed by the startled infantry. The balls of flame had come to rest against their targets burning and obscuring, the smoke having darkened as the fuel had taken hold. The few remaining mounted men suddenly quadrupled in numbers but the newcomers were riding with the momentum of fresh horses charging downhill. The defenceless riders who had survived the ordeal of the flames were quickly despatched on the business end of a tide of lances that swept through their ranks, continuing on until it smashed into the stationary infantry beyond.

The initial onslaught was so devastating to have put the result out of doubt, with no cavalry and half their infantry dead or wounded the remainder gathered round their only remaining leader. Iustinianus lay on the ground with his gut ripped open by a glancing blow of a lance that had pierced his armour just under his armpit tearing into his lung. He could still see the smoke swirling round in the sky as his vision was fixed upwards and a bloody pool flooded his moulded rear back plate. The smoke slowly got thicker and thicker until he was lost in the forever darkness of death.

With Nebiogastes being further down the column and having been the first to react had been allowed more time to arrange some sort of response. He had luckily been spared the fate of many of the men around him who had fallen victim to the hail of arrows propelled by the powerful Persian composite bows. His horse had not been so lucky, it had taken two arrow strikes, one in the neck and the other into its fleshy muscled rump and had collapsed flailing pathetically trying to gain its feet while the life blood drained out of it. He called his men to fall back and they took shelter behind the fallen tree trunks that had caused such devastation to their comrades. Less than two hundred men survived and many of those carried wounds from the swift assault they had experienced. They would have tried to continue their retreat down the pass but they had soon realised that the baggage train had been stopped lower down by more enemy infantry.

"Nebiogastes! It is I, Sarus you are hopelessly outnumbered and surrounded with your main force many days away. I offer your men the opportunity to reconsider their allegiance to Constantine. Come and discuss terms." Sarus had moved forward in full view of the demoralised men. His mount was pawing its hoof into the ground emphasising its eagerness to continue the fight.

Caratacus dismounted with Sarus and the pair walked down to meet the defeated leader halfway between their positions. Both lieutenants kept a few paces to the rear as the two leaders moved forward and took each other's arm in the salute of old soldiers. With lightning speed Sarus drew a short dagger and drove it up under the bottom of the man's armoured breast plate and took one step back. Instantly Caratacus was at Sarus's side his war axe drawn looking the opposite second in command in the eye.

"He was the only traitor, you and the rest of the men were purely following orders, if you are prepared to take those orders from me you will all be saved." It was a statement not a question and the officer knew he had little choice so nodded his head in submission.

It was Stilicho's army under the command of Sarus that camped on the high alpine meadow, but it was not for long. A rider came into camp bearing news of the approaching army of Constantine under the general ship of Generals Edobichus and Gerontius. The numbers described suggested it was the entire army of Gaul and that did not bode well if they stood their ground. With Stilicho expected to be moving towards the other side of the Alps it was not a hard decision.

The Bacaudae were Roman bandits and rebels, frequently men who had deserted or had escaped military punishment for some misdemeanour or other. The group that operated in the area that accommodated the alpine pass was more than happy to lead the small force to the safety of the Italian side and to their appointment with Stilicho in return for the baggage train that had been won during their earlier battle. It was a small fee to pay to ensure they took the quickest and most direct route across the treacherous path even during the summer.

With a successful rendezvous with the army that Stilicho had managed to convince Honorius to let him take to secure the northern border the pas was sealed and although scouts appeared the pursuing army seemed to have lost its appetite for a battle with a full strength opponent under the masterful leadership of General Flavius Stilicho.

"Unfortunately we will need to stay here for some time until we know that Constantine's army has left the other side of the alps and no longer threaten Italy," explained Stilicho when he was once again reunited with his bodyguard. "But while we are based here we can make use of the time by going to see Aleric of the Visigoths, the man I told you about when we were in Rome, for all I am part barbarian the Visigoths see me a true Roman you on the other hand will hopefully bring some much needed trust to the discussion." He stalled for a little while then continued, "Marcus Aurelius as something he wishing to discuss with you but before he does let me remind you that we have work here and I need you by my side when I ride to see Aleric!"

"What on earth did his general; mean by that?" he wondered But just as he was finishing the thought, as if he had been listening Marcus entered the tent and beckoned Caratacus to follow him.

With the exception of Alvor, Caratacus could not think of anybody else who had ever betrayed him. It made what Marcus Aurelius told him all the more unbelievable, but deep down he knew it was the truth: Aemilia had been seen around Rome at many society events and private parties in the arms of several consorts including a young officer from the emperor's personal guard. Not content with that she had taken over the Lupanar that had formerly belonged to her half brothers grandmother Davina. Rumour had it that the young officer had ensured that both mother and grandmother had succumbed to the same fate as the young man had at the hands of Caratacus. It finally clicked in Caratacus's head that he had been used to secure her inheritance and the attempts to ensure his pleasure were in fact nothing more that her trying to rid herself of him. He felt a fool, a naive fool, who had been blinded by the excesses of the great city of Rome and could not see what must have been clear to all around. The fact that he was more ashamed of his own stupidity than her cheating put it in perspective. He had had his fun with her and her slave girl, whether Aemilia had been doing it with ulterior motives didn't change the fact he had enjoyed it.

Marcus Aurelius watched the big Brigante's facial expression, dreading the thought of trying to stop him riding down to Rome and crushing the bitches head between his bare hands. His surprise and relief was to say the least overwhelming when he heard his reaction.

"It was fun while it lasted, we have work to do up here and when it is over I will see to it she gets her just rewards," Caratacus shrugged his shoulder and walked back towards his general's tent. He was using every sinew of self control to hide his wish to deliver his sentence immediately, but he now knew what Stilicho had meant when he had left the tent.

It was just Stilicho, Caratacus and the other original Brigante Gladiators who rode north to a meeting that an envoy sent by Stilicho from Rome had managed to arrange.

Aleric's career as a warrior had started without promise as a soldier under the then Gothic king Gainas. Wanting to make a name for himself he joined the Roman army and did just that. Aleric became known as a ferocious fighter and great leader, returning to his people where he led a mixed band of Goths and other allied tribes. He had assisted Theodosius to reunite the divided empire and it was during this time he had struck a friendship with Stilicho. But as the battles came thick and fast it was his force that was always being used by the emperor as the shock troops or diversions that would feel the enemies' wrath while the legions of Rome struck the death blow and took the spoils. They had split in acrimonious circumstances and since then Stilicho had defeated the Goths twice but had failed to weaken them. Once again they threatened to invade but Stilicho wanted to rekindle the alliance and that was why they sat as honoured guests in Aleric's camp being entertained, fed and watered.

From the first meeting Aleric seemed to have an affinity with the Brigante warriors and when he heard that they had all won their freedom in the arena it seemed to impress him all the more. It was of course exactly what Stilicho had wanted and he heaped compliments on Caratacus and told Aleric of his feats in battle and the arena, most of which were greatly exaggerated and the general certainly could not verify many of them personally.

"You know Caratacus I could do with a good man like you; your men would be a most welcome addition to my army as well." Caratacus had been taking a piss in the bushes when Aleric had joined him and the two talked in the private of the bushes that acted as the latrines.

"I am sworn to serve Rome until the end of the year, Stilicho says he will release me from service then to allow be to go back to my homeland and lead my people against the Picts and Saxons," he explained his situation not wanting to spoil the promise of the alliance that Stilicho was trying to furnish.

He needn't have worried; as usual it simply came down to money. Stilicho had agreed to pay a disputed payment that was outstanding from their early battles together with the promise made the two men were allied once again.

By the time they had returned to northern Italy all the scouts were reporting that Constantine had moved south into Hispania removing any immediate threat. More worrying was the summons for Stilicho to return to Rome to appear before the senate and the emperor himself to answer for his agreement with Aleric, the death of Rufinus year's earlier as well as explaining his woeful leadership in Britannia and against the usurper Constantine who he had failed to bring to heel.

"It is my death sentence," he said calmly to Caratacus as he was signing a series of documents.

He could hardly believe what his general was telling him and was amazed just how cool he was about it.

"I would have you come with me and take my wife and children to safety as your last task in your service of Rome," he pushed over the signed release documents that annulled their service to the empire. I fear my eldest son will already be in custody as he is in the service of the emperor, but if at all possible I would like you to try to free him also?" It was a request not an order but one Caratacus had no problem in agreeing to.

The proud general said farewell to his men, some who he had served with for years. Men he had led from one victory to another. Men who had, like Flavius Stilicho, placed

Theodosius and eventually Honorius on the throne. They openly wept for their leader as the bodyguard conducted their final mission for their general.

The small party moved down into Tuscany and to Stilicho's country estate where he was relieved to find his wife and two daughters, the news of his son Eucherius was not so good. He had been taken into custody until Stilicho had presented himself to the senate. Once again the general's calmness was almost unnerving.

"You mission stops here my friends," he announced to them all. I am afraid that my son is already lost. He will never be allowed to go free as he would pose a threat to the men who are about to condemn me. We are both dead men and I will not have good men die on my behalf. As your release states you have paid your debt to Rome you are free of any oath you have taken. It has been a pleasure serving with you." With that he went to each man and gave them the soldiers salute. When he finally came to Caratacus he finished the salute by embracing him as a father would a son.

"I have personal business in Rome and will accompany you general."

"I know you have but you cannot enter wearing the uniform of a soldier of Rome or you will be arrested along with me."

The next day they headed for the great city leaving behind a grieving wife and daughter who were about to lose a father, husband, son and brother.

Outside the city walls they parted, his loyal band were more than happy to enter side by side with the man they still saw as their general but Flavius would have none of it. He did not want to jeopardise their freedom that had been so hard won. They followed at a distance until he reached the forum that created the outer square adjacent to the Senate.

The last time the Brigante warriors saw him he was climbing

the steps up to the Senate, head held high, proud and defiant.

Just as with so many of the political witch hunts that forever plagued Rome, Flavius Stilicho had been found guilty in his absence. His enemies had found the ear of the emperor and poisoned his opinion while his friends, fearful of their own survival had melted into the background. He found the Senate a friendless place but was not surprised. He did not plead for pity or leniency for himself, just his son who had little to do with any of the allegations. It fell on deaf ears. The great general of Rome the man who had been the driving force behind the Theodosius rise to power and the defender of the young Honorius was executed and his son followed soon afterwards.

While they passed through Tuscany Caratacus had visited what he had considered was his estate to see if Aemilia was still there. As he expected, as soon as he had left she had returned to Rome and had stayed there ever since. As soon as they had parted from Stilicho the band had headed for the Lupanar that Caratacus knew so well. They had been richly rewarded by their general who knowing his fate was sealed had removed most of the wealth from the army he had left in the north. Most of the wealth had gone to his wife but he had been generous towards his bodyguard who had more money than they knew what to do with. The Lupanar was as good as any place to start spending it.

Unsurprisingly Aemilia was not there in person. The woman who managed the brothel on her behalf was as pleasant as you would expect when new clients entered her establishment. She enquired about their tastes and had a young girl take them to the changing rooms where they prepared to bathe. A bevy of beauties had paraded along the side of the large bath. Women of different colours and shapes represented all the corners of the empire, taken as slaves and bought by the Lupanar to serve the pleasures of the good citizens of Rome.

One dark skinned Nubian girl caught Caratacus's eye. Her shining skin contrasted with the pure white of the short flimsy toga that hardly hid her assets. She was far more reticent in coming forward than the others who seemed to boldly flaunt their wares. After the parade he asked the Lena about her and it was explained that she was from a Nubian background but her father had fought for the empire with great valour and had won the right to become a citizen of Rome, following his death during a battle in Gaul both mother and daughter had been destitute. While the honoured soldier was still alive they were treated with a little respect and she had been able to find work, unfortunately once he was dead they were mere foreigners and given no reputable work. The mother being older was not up to the level of beauty required to work in a high class establishment such as the one they were in so had to find work out of a local tavern. She was telling the story as if making her sales pitch to explain why his pick would cost so much and her final gambit was that she was also the favourite of the proprietor and this instantly had Caratacus on the hook.

Business was business when all said and done. Even the chosen one of the proprietor, Aemilia Cato the well known socialite was up for sale when she was not busy pleasuring her owner. So when Caratacus supplied the require funds and the Madame saw the size of his purse she did not hesitate. The best wine and food was supplied as he was taken into a more private bath for Flacilla to care to his every whim.

Following his earlier bath most of the grime of his weeks on horseback had been washed off, it was for his new companion to gently cleanse and soothe his body of all its cares, following this they moved to the bed where having dried him she massaged fragrant oils into every part of his body that was long overdue female attention. She never expressed surprise or disgust when his reaction rose to the occasion; she continued to rub the oils concentrating on the growing issue cupping him in one hand while working full long strokes with the other. He was laid down and she had just straddled his legs across his knees gaining better access to her main focus. As she did so she pulled her toga off, over her head. Her breasts seemed tight and stretched as her arms were high above but as they came back down to return to their work they became things of beauty, round and full without being overly large. It didn't take long before Caratacus was approaching a point of no return so he gently sat up and moved her round so she was now in his vacated position and he commenced reciprocating the gentle but deep rubbing of the sweet smelling oil. He saved the attention to her sex till last and used copious amounts if oil to lubricate her inner sanctum. The small groans became louder as he penetrated her dark skin revealing the contrasting light pink folds which lay concealed within. With her growing excitement so his copied and the ache in his groin could take no more. He pressed himself against her oiled folds and pushed forward, spearing her to his full length. Both rived and moaned until his warmth was pumping into her and then they lay together for several minutes until he became ready to resume his attention.

The sex was followed by another bout in the bath before he ate and drank. She was good company as well as good sex and told him of her family story as well as her high status in the Lupanar as she was the one chosen by Mistress Cato to go to her villa and ensure her pleasure. She wore this achievement like a badge of honour which saddened Caratacus.

Their bouts of bathing and sex grew regular and he soon found out from Flacilla about when she visited the villa that he had called home for a short period. Aemilia still had the young officer as her consort and Flacilla would be expected to perform on the pair of them during these sessions many times some of the household slaves were forced to join in as the private session's descended into orgies of lust and wanton carnal desire.

News spread across the city like wild fire. Aleric and his Visigoths had entered Italy and were heading south. Having not received the agreed overdue payment, they had taken their opportunity when the northern army now lead by Sarus moved back into Gaul leaving their way clear. The city was in panic there was no army standing between the invaders and the centre of civilisation. Only the garrison force was left the defend them and that was not large enough to meet the barbarians in open combat. Caratacus and his men rode north back to Tuscany and met with the Goth leader before he reached Stilicho's estate. They were welcomed as friends and Aleric was appalled to hear of Stilicho's demise. Caratacus had no wish to join the Goths he still intended to return to his people in Britannia when he concluded his business in Rome but had rode out to plead for Aleric's protection of Serena and her two daughters, Maria and Thermantia which he got immediately with Aleric marrying his eldest son to Thermantia.

Caratacus returned to Rome with the whole Visigoth army close behind. He was to act as the envoy of Aleric who had no wish to lose a large part of his army laying siege to the city so they set to blockade and starve the city while negotiations took place. In the proceeding unrest that followed throughout the whole of Italy, the wives and children of the foederati, the barbarian mercenaries that fought for Rome were slain this resulted in thousands of men flocking to Alaric's camp, pleading to be led against this cowardly enemy from who they wished to extract their revenge.

Alaric was relying on hunger to work in place of his warriors might and it was a most powerful weapon. A massive city such as Rome had an equally vast population and needed provisions to be brought in through its gates constantly to feed the people. Literally within days of the Goths arrival the poorest residents started to feel the pinch by the time negotiations had commenced. In a short time the same people were starving and it was the turn of the wealthy to start to suffer. At first the senators and the very influential had wanted to tough it out and wait for the Northern Army to re-cross the Alps and march down the length of Italy to lift the blockade. Unfortunately it had taken a further month for word to arrive that the Army they were relying on were engaged with a combination of Jutes, Gaul's and Suebi who had once again rebelled. With another army tied up fighting in the Prefecture of Illyricum just across the Adriatic Sea against a combined force of Alans and Vandals they too could not assist. Honorius's nearest free army was in Numidia and it would take months for a fleet to be readied so that army could come to the aid of its capital. It finally became clear that the city could not rely on a reprieve from their predicament. Far too late for much of the population the high and mighty of Rome agreed to negotiate.

After much bargaining with Caratacus moving back and forth, the famine-stricken citizens agreed to pay a ransom of five thousand pounds of gold, thirty thousand pounds of silver, four thousand silken tunics, three thousand hides dyed scarlet, and three thousand pounds of pepper. Along with the treasure forty thousand Goth slaves were freed. It was at this point Alaric ended his first siege of Rome. But he would be back.

As the bartering approached its conclusion and under the protection of Aleric as nobody would risk imprisoning his envoy, Caratacus decided it was time for him to pay Aemilia a visit.

The whole of the city had been brought to the point of starvation. The poorer citizens had suffered the worst and emaciated body's lined the streets. Even the wealthy which Aemilia was one, suffered. It was only people in the very top bracket of Roman society who appeared not to suffer. But Caratacus and his men were able to move in and out of the city quite freely so when they returned to Alaric's camp they could eat their fill and take provisions back with them. It meant that their companions at the Lupanar were looked after. The night before the ransom was to be paid he and Flacilla paid Aemilia a visit.

Flacilla had been used to making the journey from the Lupanar to the villa in darkness; she also knew how to gain access through the servant's quarters. To his shame Caratacus realised he had no knowledge of this section of the villa and was surprised by the fact it was deserted. As they moved through into the main villa the lack of slaves revealed a once fine home in tatters. The large doors that opened up onto the huge balconies swung in the breeze the dust of the city causing the mosaic floors to resemble a desert dust and filth covered everything. It must have been weeks since anybody had bothered to clean the place. They had started to think that the villa was empty when they heard low voices coming from Aemilia's chambers. Flacilla knocked over a vase which crashed to the floor and smashed. Suddenly there was a moments silence followed by an urgent whispered voice.

"Go and see who it is, god knows we have nothing left for them to steal." It was the voice of Aemilia but not the voice Caratacus remembered.

The door to her chambers slowly opened, the point of a Gladius slowly came into vision preceding its owner. As the hand was exposed Caratacus brought down his weapon with the force of an executioners blow. The screams and the metallic clatter of the sword bouncing across the floor were almost simultaneous. Caratacus moved into the door way and used the sole of his foot to push the figure backwards as he was desperately trying to stem the bleeding from the resultant stump on the end of his arm.

"Please don't harm me, take anything, take her, look," the figure nodded his head towards the less than glamorous figure laid on the bed. He could not point as he was wrestling his wound into a dirty sheet. "She can be your high class whore and the Goths would pay a high price for her."

"You pathetic bastard!" Aemilia snapped at him in a strangely weakened but more familiar tone.

He was here to set the record straight with the person who had betrayed him but even so he was disgusted at the weak specimen that stood trembling before him. He kicked the man backwards so hard that he flew through the doors on to the outer balcony and then turned to Flacilla.

"So who is that?"

"Oh that is the brave Paulus Scaeva, officer of the imperial guard. The man who likes to have women tied up so he can force objects inside them while he makes them perform on his bitch," she flung her arm pointing at the dishevel Aemilia who had suddenly realise who had entered.

"You might want to have some revenge on him while I have a quiet talk to the not so lovely Aemilia," he said in a cold even voice.

"Caratacus, oh my love I have missed you so much I have worried for your safety every day we have been parted."

"So is that why you had that, that," he paused as if trying to recall what she had just called him. "Oh that's right...pathetic bastard, into your bed the minute I was gone. I have heard so many stories from so many different people especially Flacilla she has told me of all your seedy little exploits. I had come to take my revenge but it appears that fate as lent a hand.

There was a scream of excruciating pain and Flacilla entered, the freshly removed parts of Paulus Scaeva dripping blood from her hand. "He won't be using then on anybody ever again."

"It's really not been a good evening for him as it. But I doubt he will last till morning having lost his hand and his prick and balls. It will be a painful death." They could hear a pitiful whimpering coming from just outside.

"Aemilia, I was really considering killing you," he said as if he was just passing the time of day with pleasant chatter.

She shrieked in fear, only to be silenced by Caratacus raising his hand. "But I have changed my mind; you look like you have suffered and it must be so hard to find yourself in such a condition, no better than a slave girl."

"Oh Caratacus, I have suffered. It has been days since I have eaten and weeks since we had any slaves to keep the villa clean. I haven't had a bath in over a week. It has been horrible." She looked at him, puzzled at the smile that was widening across his face.

As he led the cart with Flacilla and her mother driving the single horse and lump underneath the pile of blankets started to stir. They were just a few hundred paces from the gates when Caratacus pulled back the covers and removed Aemila's gag. She did not stop screaming until she arrived at Aleric's camp as Caratacus had told her what her fate was to be just before he had knocked her unconscious.

"It is time for me to leave and travel back to my homeland to face my destiny," he said as Aleric greeted him. "Before I leave I would like to present to you a present. A slave for your pleasure. Of noble Roman birth she is used to plenty of fucking and is well versed in pleasuring. Do with her as you wish." Aemilia had fallen silent as Caratacus had addressed

Aleric but she now howled and hurled obscenities at her former saviour and lover.

Aleric took two strides towards her before hitting her with the back of his hand. "I will take great joy in trying her out and teaching her some manners. Now I have a small gift for you and your men as well as my best wishes. It is a shame you do not want to stay but I know the draw of returning to your homeland."

In the cart was five hundred pounds of silver when they headed north for Tuscany. They left Flacilla and her mother with Serena who promised to find them good work on the estate and arrange their future. That evening it was a bitter sweet night of love in the arms of Flacilla she was still asleep when the Brigante warriors moved off to find the army of the north and the Brigante Cohort.

Britannia.

Caratacus had a great respect for Sarus but he wanted his men so he had at least a small fighting force when he reached his homeland. He knew everyman, even a general of Rome had a price and for three hundred of the five hundred pounds of the silver the Brigante Cohort was released from service under the orders of Sarus.

He used some more of the silver to buy passage across the sea which set Britannia on its own. The small fleet sailed up the east coast well above the Humber, allowing its military cargo to disembark on a small island with a causeway that linked it to the mainland that the captain had used for other clandestine business. Not knowing the state of his tribal lands Caratacus did not want to land anywhere that was populated in case they met an unpleasant surprise.

The captain showed him where Lindisfarne sat in relation to his lands. He ship was kept back until the tides receded proving the man's word was trustworthy. As promised the causeway appeared with the fall of the tide so the fleet was allowed to sail away. This temporary strip on land was only the width of a couple of carts, therefore it would be easy to defend and with seals and sea birds in abundance food was not scarce. They made the best of the exposed island bringing wood from the mainland to build shelter from the raw north east weather while riders moved out to try to make contact with his people as well as gathering information from any local villages.

Ingarm was sent first as it should have been his land, he reported that the immediate mainland was still Votadini but the Picts almost had free reign over the land terrorising the villages. There was some dispute as to whether the Saxons or the Angles were the prominent force to the south of the area as they seemed to be so similar and appeared to live together as allies. It wasn't until Ruadan and Brelus returned with a familiar face that they got a more detailed picture. After their reunion Severus painted the current tribal scene.

Nearly the entire east of Britannia from as far south as they could ascertain up to the now totally defunct wall was under the control of the Saxons to the south and the Angles in the north. They had formed an alliance to fend off the attacks from the Cornovii and Corieltauvi who had joined together under the leadership of an ex Romano-Briton called Arturus and the Picts from the far north.

The news of his Brigante was good; with the exception of a few skirmishes they had largely managed to stay out of the fighting and had strengthened their defences around the old Roman site of Vinovia when all the invaders had finally lost interest in plundering it. Very little had remained but the walls and the high ground had encouraged them to move back into the area. News from the low lands of Brigante territory was not as good. It had been taken during a battle where the two Germanic invaders had first joined forces and had all but wiped the tribe out of their ancestral home. Severus spoke of hordes of Anglo-Saxon warriors pouring down on their Isurium Briganum capital before the defenders realising they were under attack. Their tribal king had been slaughtered and hundreds had fallen at his side. Those not taken as slaves had fled north and had joined them at Vinovia which the Brigante had taken to calling Oaklanius due to the forest of ancient oak trees that sat on the meandering banks of the river.

The Brigante Cohort set off the next day having sent out scouts led by Ingarm to find a safe route. They camped the first night under the cover of the familiar Caledonian forest north of the wall and during that night Caratacus led Severus, Venpasian, Caracalus Ruadan, Brelus and Ingarm to the site close to the sheer cliffs near Vindolanda to retrieve the silver coins and the eagle that had been buried after the defeat of the Roman legion so many years earlier.

"Silver seems to be something that will buy almost anything in this world and therefore we need this now," Caratacus had announced as he overturned a huge boulder and started to dig. He had buried it in solitude. Back in the day he would not have known why to preserve it, it had been the old druid who had told him to.

It was a further five days of riding before they reached Oaklanius. They passed through the wall and investigated what was left of the Roman fort. It had been ransacked and many of the buildings had been robbed of stone and tile as that sort of building material would be highly sort after but it left the whole place with a sense of ghostly futility. How something so impressive, useful and safe could be deserted for the few mud huts that Caratacus had seen since landing back in Britannia left him almost speechless.

It was the same when he finally rode up to the settlement he was to call home. His people had moved into the area that had been the fort and victus of Vinovia but they had built a new timber stockade instead of utilising what still stood. He would set to the very next day by incorporating the great engineering that existed from the Romans to create a stronghold that was fit to be called the home of the Brigante.

Over the next months the building work went on as well as scouting parties moving out to contact the neighbouring tribes and it soon became clear that everybody was talking about the leader to the south east, Arturus. It was time for Caratacus to meet this man.

After several days riding Caratacus and his men reached the familiar surroundings of Victrix (Chester). Arturus like he had resurrected some of the roman ruins. He was using the military commander's villa as a headquarters as well as his home, the bath house was also repaired, again like his counterpart he understood from his Roman tuition the benefits of staying healthy and that meant a level of cleanliness the ancient tribes had never considered. It was a meeting of like minds and during their many conversations Arturus admitted to seeing Caratacus fight in the Victrix arena. He also explained the complicated situation that had materialised in Britannia during his absence.

There had been a Vorigern crowned as high king of the Britons, the position was not recognised by the Brigante but gave the man elected power over the tribes of the south. This man had invited the two brothers who led the Anglo-Saxons, Hengest and Horsa to settle on the Isle of Thanet offering provisions and payment in return for their mercenary services against the Picts and Scotti. It was with great concern that the Saxon numbers had grown and they had spread on to the mainland effectively manipulating the Vortigern into granting more and more land until they commanded most of the south east corner of Britannia. They had previously fought many battles with the Army of Britannia under the Vortigern's command. In the first, one of the brothers, Horsa had been slain giving total rule of the Saxon forces to Hengest with his son Æsc. Enraged by his brother's death, it was followed by another battle where over four thousand Britons had been slaughtered and resulted in the entire army fleeing leaving the Saxons ruling the land south of the old Roman city of Londinium.

Caratacus listened as they prepared their mounts to attend a great parley on the ancient plains of Salisbury. The meeting was between the Vortigern and the tribal kings with the Saxon leader. Arturus had waited for Caratacus's arrival so they were late and needed to make good time if they were to reach the gathering in time to be heard.

As they rode a man wrapped in a dirty grey robe with an equally dirty and unruly mop of hair and matching beard came along side him.

"So you are the mighty Caratacus? The man who beat all comers in the Roman arena, finding great fame in its army, like my lord Arturus."

There was such a resemblance to Amergin Gluingel that he had to take and very careful look and made his curiosity plain to see.

"I am of the same people as your mentor Gluingel. I am known as Ambrosius Aurelianus to the Mercian's and amongst your people, but the tribes of the Britons call me Merlin Ambrosius."

"You know of Gluingel? Have you seen him recently?" he asked without waiting for his first question to be answered.

"So like you, some things have not changed Caratacus," was his strange answer before he continued. "Gluingel sends his regards; he is well and reminds you of your destiny. He then proceeded to use the exact wording that had been used all those years earlier by the old druid to remind him of the prophecy.

Over the next days they rode hard but the weather had closed in and their progress slowed. So many things about Ambrosius seemed to suggest that it was in fact Gluingel but then there would be just the odd thing that set the old men apart. They had been on the journey for over a week when the druid came up the column and alongside Arturus.

"We need to move with great care, I feel a great sadness and pain. There has been treachery on the ancient grounds, many fine men are dead." It was a sobering warning. One that Arturus wisely took heed of and set up camp away from the road and with just, Caratacus and Ambrosius they move forward.

They had only travelled for another two hours before they met the first of the battered soldiers of the Vortigern's troops. They had no mounts and few weapons but all had taken a terrible beating.

Taking refuge in a small but dense wood they gathered the stragglers in to hear what had befallen them. It was said with great pain that during the peace conference with all weapons left back in the individual camps that Hengest had called out to his men who produced knives from the underside of the soles of the shoes. They had attacked all the three hundred defenceless elders of all the tribes, slaughtering them like dogs as well as taking King Vortigern prisoner in chains intending to use him to ransom more land.

Suddenly a warning rang out as Saxons approached, trying to track down the escapee's. Ambrosius spread his arms and mouthed out a silent incantation and even before the spell was finished the lower branches on the outer trees started to thicken and interweave with each other creating an impenetrable wall. The Saxons saw how dense the forest was and with no signs of broken branches that would suggest anybody entering they moved on.

Understandably it took some coaxing to convince the survivors to lead them back to the scene of the crime, but eventually they did and what a scene it was. Three hundred elders taking part in such an important conference would have come dressed in their finery to pronounce their high status and right to take part. Each throat had been cut and the body stripped. The few troops who had accompanied the elders had also remained unarmed and had been easy prey for the deceitful Saxons hidden nearby with their bows. Death on such a scale was not unheard of, it was the fact that they had been piled high as a warning that made the blood run cold. After searching through the pile of corpses it was confirmed that Vortigern was not amongst the dead. They could only wait for the ransom to arrive. There was nothing to do but to return north and await the demands.

When the sole remaining living elder arrived at the camp of Arturus he was to demand on behalf of Hengest that two hundred pounds of silver be paid as well as huge tracks of southern lands. The land had already been seeded by Vortigern and witnessed by the elder. The new lands were to be known henceforth as Est Saxum, Sut Saxum and Middelseaxan. It was just the silver that had to be found.

Both Caratacus and Ambrosius advised against it but as far as Arturus was concerned he had little choice, he had to be seen by his people to do everything in his power to free the rightful king.

"I understand you have to try, but they have already demonstrated their treachery. They are very likely to take the silver and still kill the king," Caratacus argument was backed by the druid who could only see the death of Vortigern in his visions.

The old druid was to be proven correct as the king was killed apparently by his own archers immediately after his release as it was claimed by Hengest they had attacked the Saxon escort and in the ensuing fight all the Britons were also, very conveniently put to the sword.

With all the tribal kings dead it came to Arturus and Caratacus to defend the ancient lands. The Picts still plundered the east coast while the Scotti took advantage of the turmoil within the tribal lands of the Britons to pillage down the west coast. Fortunately for the Brigante the Picts were much more directly an issue for the Angles and their Saxon allies. This gave Caratacus the confidence to raise his army leaving his lands lightly defended when they headed back south to join the new King of the Britons to take the fight to the invaders finally facing the foe that Gluingel had predicted.

"It is not always as straight forward as it seems," was the confusing answer that Ambrosius gave to Caratacus when he confided in the druid that he had wanted this opportunity to arrive, when he finally got the opportunity to repay Gluingel for his tuition and guidance. "Remember that invaders come in many guises, some might do our lands well, others on the other hand have nothing but evil in their hearts. You need to read your foe closely today's enemy could be tomorrows ally. Look beyond the obvious."

Now Caratacus was certain that Ambrosius and Gluingel was one and the same person. Nobody but he could speak in such riddles!

They had been hunting in the forest that bordered the land of the Britons from those of the Mercian's although some of this land was now being claimed by the Angles. Arturus has been away when Caratacus had arrived with his force, going to aid the tribes in the far south that had come under attack from Æsc and his army. Once again the relief force had arrived too late to prevent another bloody defeat for the Britons and news of further defeats came in thick and fast. It was taking its toll on the Saxons but not enough to stop their relentless march. Arturus listened to the council of Caratacus and the druid who both urged him to take control of what was left of their wide spread army and not leave it splintered in small pockets under the control of local Thanes who only saw their own problems and not those of all the Britons.

"We need to call a war council where I will declare you king and leader of the Britons that is the only way we can unite everybody behind you," Ambrosius looked to Caratacus for support as he spoke.

"Aye and I will pledge the support of the Brigante only on the understanding that you are their leader. We need to make your Thanes understand that individually they will be beaten one at a time, only gathering as one mighty army will we defeat these bastards." The old druid was nodding his agreement beside Arturus as he listened to Caratacus.

The war council was held at one of the most iconic gathering places in all of Britannia. Although Caratacus had never visited the massive stone circle of Glastonbury, he had heard many tales of its powers and realised it being the centre of Druidism it was the perfect place for Ambrosius to wield maximum power over those attending.

It was expected to be a no contest as far as anybody challenging Arturus for the Kingship of the Britons. That was until a Thane called Gorlois stepped up and surprised everyone hurling abuse at both "Arturus and his pet druid".

"You dare to challenge me!" boomed, Arturus incensed, not at the insult towards him but to Ambrosius.

"If you would allow me my king," Ambrosius stepped forward emphasising the title he had used ensuring all heard him. "It is not for the King of the Britons to fight a mere Thane and especially in a place such as this. Gorlois insulted me in my most sacred place and if you please I will chose my champion to defend my honour."

Arturus could tell the old man had something in mind and having relied on his wisdom so often before he waved him forward to finish what he was saying.

"I call on Caratacus of the Brigante to act as my champion and settle this dispute. That way Briton will not fight Briton within the great circle thus not defiling the word of the Gods.

It came as a surprise to all present. Nobody really

understood what the druid had said but one thing was clear Gorlois was to fight the giant from the north.

Caratacus, on the other hand, had been warned by the druid that if anybody challenged Arturus's right to the throne that he would attempt to use him so he was expecting it as soon as the dissenting voice had been raised.

Caratacus walked forward, he weaved his war axe like it was a child's toy looping it alternatively forehand then backhand in his right hand. He then drew his Gladius in his left and simultaneously started the same exercise with that.

For Gorlois there was no going back even if he regretted his outburst. He had known he would be up against it if he fought Arturus as the man was a mighty warrior but from what they said about the man now facing him he was every bit as good but twice the size. If talking before he had thought things through was a particular trait of Gorlois, being a coward was not. He walked forward to the centre of the stones with shield held high and his sword tip pointing menacingly and directly at Caratacus's throat. Caratacus stopped the swinging of his weapons and with axe in hand gave his opponent the customary gladiator salute and took up his stance.

"Tarnis God of thunder give your favour to the man you want to prevail. If Gorlois of the Britons is to take the day then he will be King of the Britons. But if the Brigante known as Caratacus wins your favour then we take Arturus as King." With a drop of his arm he signalled for the combat to begin.

Gorlois was aware he was out of his depth but decided that attack was his best policy. He brought his sword back and hammered it forward from the enormous backswing. Caratacus had watched his body twist to allow the blow to coil up prior to the weapons release and with a simple block from the axe head a metallic clang burst out, the sparks flew as if a new log had been thrown of a fire. The failed attack continued with the stumbling assailant getting his entire body behind his shield and driving into his opponent. It was as if he had run into a wall and he bounced off to one side dropping to his knees. Caratacus was lightning quick in his follow up. Far quicker that anybody watching, who had not seen him before, had expected. Gorlois had put both hands down on the ground to help his recovery back to his feet, but that placed the shield flat with the rear facing upwards. Caratacus stamped on it and brought his foot up under the man's rib cage lifting him physically into the air. The cracking of ribs rang out making the forced exhalation more of a cry of pain and shower of spit, but it did enable him to regain his feet, albeit unsteadily. He was staggering with just his sword that was no longer pointing tip up, but was more in a loose hanging position as he waved it limply. Caratacus probed with two short jabs of his Gladius each parry slow and just managing to make contact. The third jab forward only reached half way to its target but it did get the reaction Caratacus was wanting. Gorlois desperately brought his sword over to parry the attempt that never came. Instead the war axe was prodded forwards, the metal spike which sat between the two blades catching the over committed defender in the face driving into his cheek and knocking him off his feet. A wave of blood and broken teeth gushed forth from the gasping open mouth. Once again Caratacus moved far too fast for any sort of reaction and he stamped down on the sword pushing his own Gladius on to the windpipe of the defeated man. Caratacus looked to Arturus, as he would have in the arena, for the decision of the editor of the games, there was to be no "missio" on this occasion. With a simple nod of Arturus's head Caratacus pushed hard on the hilt and severed the throat and spinal column in one move.

The fight had been very one sided and the whole gathering knew it. But as the druid had called out to the gods, surely they had spoken in the result and the few doubters had been given Tarnis's verdict. Arturus was to be their new king.

"All hail Arturus, King of the Britons!" Ambrosius cried so not a single man present missed the acclaim.

One at a time each man that stood within the sacred circle took to their knee and offered up their sword in homage to the new king and a staggered chorus of Arturus was drowned out by the tumultuous cheers as each man stood up and waved their weapons in celebration. Quietly almost unnoticed the lifeless body of Gorlois was dragged from view by some of Caratacus's men until he was left in the perimeter ditch around the great monument.

"Men we have to be united from this moment on." Arturus was starting to call to the gathering making sure they understood his wish for all the armies of the Britons to fight as one and not take on their enemy piecemeal as they had been doing until then. But until that moment they had never had that one person who had given them clear unquestionable leadership. It was a different Army of Britons that the Anglo-Saxons would be facing in their next battle.

Saxon.

Arturus liked the idea that Caratacus had suggested. He was impressed by the thinking as well as the power the warrior possessed. That was why he followed the big man's idea by sending out scouts to continually report back on any movements that the enemy might make. They set up a chain of watchers that could pass information back far quicker than any one person could travel left on their own and it also guaranteed that at no time were the eyes of the Britons blind to the actions of the Anglo-Saxon invaders. Not only could he rely on his men but also his people even those living behind the enemy could smuggle information back to the nearest watchers who would then get it back to Arturus almost within the day.

It was this local knowledge that enabled the separation of the Saxon forces to become known so quickly. It also explained why Hengest had split his force dividing it almost two thirds to one and leading the smaller band south to the coast of the area know known as Sut Saxum.

Another Saxon chieftain had landed on the shores of Britannia. Æsc had been left behind at a place called Mons Badonicus while his father went to meet the newcomer who the local spies said that he was called Ælle and had landed with many ships and his three sons, Cissa, Cymen and Wlencing. It was the perfect opportunity the Britons and Brigante had been waiting for. The force commanded by Æsc was far smaller than theirs and even though they had camped on the high ground Arturus and Caratacus with spiritual guidance from Ambrosius saw it as a winnable fight which would reduce the Saxon numbers considerably.

They also hoped that Hengest was moving south to take on the new Saxon Army but really they didn't hold much hope for that being true. If it were he would have taken the majority of his force, not the smaller band of warriors, but even if that force united it would still be only the size that they intended to defeat at the end of the march they were now on.

All journey long the two leaders discussed their plans and how best to overcome a force who held the high ground.

"I think I have the solution," smiled Caratacus. "But we should stop here and the main force needs to proceed under the cover of darkness. Only my Cohort of Brigantia in full gleaming Roman armour will travel in daylight in full view." He went on to explain.

A full show was put on for the Saxon scouting parties. Nearly eight hundred mounted cavalrymen with armour that flashed its presence in the bright sunlight. At its head was Caratacus with Ruadan who carried the eagle of the Ninth Legion. The proud golden raptor displayed itself; wings outstretched looking every bit the prize that any self respecting invader set of pillaging would never turn down. To add to the mouth watering temptation were two wagons laden with huge chests that looked mysteriously like they should be filled with loot. Only the close inspection of the dusty road after their passage, which had surprisingly light tracks, suggested anything different.

The hill itself was not particularly impressive, certainly not by the standard of the mountains and valleys Caratacus and his men were used to back in their homeland of Brigantia. But it was enough to give a major advantage to whoever held the ground. They approached from the road that came from the north as it had forest either side creating a corridor no more than three hundred paces wide. They timed their arrival carefully so it was nearing dusk so any negotiations or fighting would have to wait until the following day. They built huge fires and made the scene appear to be one of celebration with men drinking heavily from the ale barrels that were actually full of water. The demonstration of stupidity amused the young Saxon leader who had personally come out to view the magnificent shining eagle. Æsc also coveted the chests of treasure and all the fancy armour that had been on display, how his father would be proud of him when he saw what his son had won. With all eyes on the performance around the camp fires nobody was paying any interest to the hundreds of men that filled the forests on either side of the road, packing it down the entire length of the corridor.

In the morning the show continued with Roman cavalry staggering round as if still suffering the effects of a heavy night. The fact was that as the night grew even darker most men had managed to get some sleep before taking over their turn of the tomfoolery.

Caratacus, Ruadan and a few men who looked like his bodyguard rode halfway up the hill knowing they would be received by a similar entourage before they got close to the defences. The young man who spoke could hardly take is eyes of the eagle and Ruadan even managed to dazzle him by turning its wings to catch the sun. It amused Caratacus to see his friend playing tricks but resolutely continued to look hung-over.

"On behalf of his Imperial Emperor Honorius I command you to leave these shores or we will be required to take this hill by force." Was the stern warning Æsc heard from a man who appeared not to realise that the Roman legions had left the country years earlier. Could it be that these fools had been lost for all this time and only just finding their way towards the coast? All the better, it would be easy pickings.

"I suggest you give me all your treasures including the bird there," he nodded at the ninths eagle, "and all your armour and weapons and I will think about sparing your lives, Roman."

"Then you had better come and take it boy," Caratacus emphasised the word boy to dig his contempt for the youngster deeper into Æsc's head ensuring he would take the bait.

"Have no fear of that Roman, I will be drinking your ale and wearing your armour before this day it out." With that his party turned their horses and galloped up the hill.

When Caratacus got back to camp it was a very different and altogether more coordinated group of warriors that had mounted their chargers, not a thick head in sight. The Cohort of Brigantia lined up three deep filling the corridor and urged their mounts forward, slowly walking behind the one man who led them. Even before they had started to gain the slope the Saxon cavalry came spilling out of the camp followed by hundreds on foot. Under his breath so the attackers could not see him talking he kept encouraging his men.

"Let them come closer, a little closer, just a little more. Now!" With that command the entire three lines separated before turning and racing away from the oncoming horde of screaming Saxons sweeping down the hill as a tidal wave would engulf a shoreline.

The retreating Brigante were in full flight when they passed the end of the corridor and entering a much more open plain they split in opposite directions. Out of sight of the pursuers they doubled back round the tree line to return to the base of the hill where they had started. Their passing was the signal for hundreds of Britons to create a wall of freshly cut timber stakes twice the length of a man and behind their shield wall they formed an impenetrable wall that caused the frontline of Saxon cavalry to veer in any direction other than the one that spelt death for man and horse. With the first riders falling from their saddles and startled horses crashed into the next row behind the chaos continued to ripple backwards through the entire mounted army each row being affected greater than the one before. The loose horses scattered and crashed into the infantry that were coming up behind kicking and stamping felling men by the hand full. Suddenly the flanks of the forest came alive as thousands of men closed in on the frenzied scene. The Saxon foot soldiers at the back saw the plight of those ahead and slowed and turned only to see the Roman cavalry come into view behind them. Gone was their ale soaked revelry instead they wore the face of men who wished death upon them.

The thunder of heavy hoof on turf vibrated under foot and travelled up the stricken Saxon's legs turning them to jelly. They were warriors and had seen what a cavalry charge such as this did to an infantry in disarray as they were. Without time to construct the sturdy shield wall that their enemy had done so effectively they were mere sport of the horsemen. There was no one man in charge as their leader had been mobbed and pulled from his horse somewhere in the distance and instead of forming as cohesive defence each man tried to find his own way out of the trap they had been led into. So badly were the Saxon infantry splintered that there was not even one large crash as the cavalry hit the front of the prey. It was more of a series of individual smaller collisions so closely spaced it was like a rolling rumble of thunder, followed by the swoosh of sword and axe sweeping from lofty heights splitting skulls and cleaving shoulders. Caratacus was using his double handed attack with great efficiency. He had his reins tucked under one of his legs and used the giant limbs to steer his horse, knees pressing into Vulcan's neck, while he swept forward and backhand with the axe and jabbed with his Gladius.

It was not only the Britons foot soldiers who appeared from

the dense tree line. Arturus had brought his cavalry on foot through the forest and had them mount at the last minute. He led one of the flank attacks and moved forward with the ferocity of a man on a mission to save his people from a foreign foe. Like Caratacus he carved a path of destruction that his men did their best to emulate but although they tried they could not match their leader in his deadly skills.

By the time the three cavalry units closed on each other there were few Saxons left alive. The few that had stayed guarding the camp and the chests of war loot they had plundered over the previous years had started to realise that things had not gone well and as they started to form a shield wall they were assailed by a rear attack by the rest of the Brigante, the offensive foot soldiers who had circled round their victims as they had been drawn to watch the proceedings below.

Why in the name of the Gods had his son not sent his scouts back when they had announced his imminent arrival wondered Hengest as he rode with his ally Ælle and his three sons, Cissa, Cymen and Wlencing at his side. He had been in a good mood until he had started to think of his arrogant son. If only his lad was like any of the young men that his newly arrived friend from back in the old country had he would have had someone to be proud of, but instead he had an impetuous offspring who never seemed to learn regardless of all the mistakes he made. This time he failed to see the need to honour their guests by sending out a welcome party. He would kick his arse for this slur against his old friend.

On the other hand Ælle had less of a concern for any disrespect being evident. But it was the same lack of riders coming out towards them. They were now just within sight of the hilltop stronghold and even if the lad had forgotten his manners surely he would remember when his guard called the alert of approaching riders? Something was wrong; he could feel it in his bones. He could hear Hengest cursing his son.

"I will let you go forward and remind the lad of his duties my friend; there might be good reason for the oversight?"

Ælle turned to his three sons, "Cissa, Cymen shield wall on our flanks. I will sort out the front and rear wall, Wlencing ride with Hengest. Before Hengest had got the base of the hill of Badonicus Ælle and his men had formed up in a defensive square and watched across the plains to the nearby forest as well as the hill in the distance.

As Hengest started up the track toward his hill fort he had started to have the same misgivings as his ally. Even though the day was bright and warm he had a very cold shiver running down his back. There was no sign of activity other than a few guards standing on the small wooden turrets that the gates of the fort hung off. They waved their recognition with great enthusiasm and many more men gained the walled positions. The bright sun on his back was reflecting against highly polished objects almost blinding him. He could not think what could catch the sunlight with such power other than highly polished armour and his men did not have........

A shout came from the rear and he turned to see cavalry appear from the forest below him. His attention was then brought to his front as more riders galloped out of the fort and spread out forming a line of charge. Then it all made sense. His fort had fallen and what of his son? Now was not the time to concern himself with such questions he needed to get back to Ælle.

Hengest turned his cavalry downhill. It was the furthest direction to get back to the safety of his ally but it did give him momentum so he could hit the enemy in the lower position hard.

Arturus had waited until the Saxons had passed the edge of the forest before he once again had his men bring their horses forward and mount. He had realised that these Saxons were not as easy to fool as their previous opponent had been. But they still had over a hundred cavalry and the same number of men on foot to attack and defeating that number would further set back the Saxon ambitions so he was happy enough as Caratacus's men in the fort gave him the signal. The men on the gate firstly started waving to gain the Britons attention and then the blinding signal of shining armour gave Caratacus's cavalry time to file out of the fort and form up for a charge. As the dazzling reflective light turned away the line of horses outside the fort set off as did they. Once again the enemy proved to be no fool. Arturus saw that he had turned so as to gather his mounts speed and that meant it was his men that would take the brunt of the charge this time.

The Britons spurred on their chargers to gather as much speed as they could before the clash but the terrain was against them and even with the best horsemen at his disposal Arturus knew they were going to face a powerful charge so he slowed to ensure all his riders closed up to create a much more solid unit that would not separate, one that could punch at the point where the leader rode.

Hengest saw what his opponent was up to and it played into his hands. His infantry were lost but he wanted to save as many of his cavalry as possible and to get entwined in a fight with this band of warriors he was heading for would slow them down so the other jaw of their attack could snap down on them, hitting them with all the force a downhill charge would deliver.

A few spears were thrown as the two sides tried to manoeuvre. The Saxons tried to avoid any clash staying high and setting a course for the safety of the shield wall that was waiting for them across the plain.

Caratacus could see from his higher position what each

leader was trying to do and to try to cut off the fleeing Saxons he set a heading that would ensure he would converge on the cavalry's right flank. The Saxon charge was only slightly disrupted by a glancing blow by the Britons below. But it was all that was needed for disaster to befall both belligerents. Arturus had fixed his sights on the Saxon leader, but as the collision had nearer he had just been absorbed into the main body of his warriors by his bodyguard who had moved around him. Arturus riding up hill had reached forward keeping low and driven his sword into the armpit of the nearest man avoiding his chainmail. He, like the other Britons had turned his horse so it moved parallel with the Saxon direction of flight. He had hacked twice more at nearby riders successfully dislodging one and killing another who carried a cross blow hitting him squarely across the face with the blade of his mighty sword. His shield was on the downhill side of his horse and therefore useless and it was restricting his ability to wield his sword but he did not want to lose it in case the fighting became close quartered later. As he chopped one more time a gap opened up and he was at the side of the enemy leader that he had targeted, but the earlier chop had caught deep into the neck of the recipient and he needed to drag it free which twisted him in his saddle and left him exposed.

Hengest had realised that avoiding some form of contact with the cavalry below him was out of the question and just as he expected his loyal bodyguard had come to the same conclusion and had circled around him. He had heard of the two leaders of the enemy and new both worn the armour of the Roman army they both once served. Without knowing which one it was he saw with amazement the bravery and horsemanship of the man as he killed and injured several of his men at the gallop without losing control of his mount. His enemy had blasted his way right to Hengest's side and the

Saxon leader brought his sword across to fend off the expected assault when Woden, the Saxon God of War shone good fortune on him. Something had unsettled his attacker and it enabled him a moment's opportunity to jab his sword across to the other side of his horse. He was at full reach and the tip of his weapon caught the bottom of the Roman breastplate. The Saxon was not going to lose this chance to rid himself of at least one of these Roman pet barbarian warriors so he lunged to the side hoping his weapon would enable him to throw himself back up right. He felt the give as the blade penetrated the soft flesh below the armour and when it struck bone it did indeed allow him to push back upright. That was when Woden deserted him.

The sudden pain that shot through Arturus's body gave him a brief moment of monumental strength. He ripped the trapped sword free from the man behind him, as it freed he turned the blade through ninety degrees so as it scythed forward and struck Hengest across his neck as he was pushing himself back upright. The two opposing movements combined to severe the Saxons head and as his horse veered to the right it dropped onto Arturus's lap. Holding it up at arm's length he waved his trophy hoping the enemy would give up and surrender as he knew he too was done for. Two Saxon warriors tried to capture the bolting horse that still carried the decapitated body while another made an attempt to retrieve the head. Both acts ended unsuccessfully as Arturus had turned back to his men and the rogue horse was heading toward the closing Caratacus.

The King of the Britons slowed as he could no longer control his horse. It was his bodyguard who he had left behind in the moments leading up to the clash that eventually caught him that prevented him from falling. The Saxons having witnessed the skill, courage and ferocity of Arturus only had eyes for the safety of the nearing shield wall and fled as fast as they could.

Caratacus had misjudged his line. What he had not seen was a large stream that ran around the base flank of the hill and it meant slowing to negotiate it and that was all that was needed to see the Saxons reach Ælle whose men opened up the rear wall and allowed the riders into their safe haven closing up corralling both warrior and steed. Without the momentum and facing a solid well prepared shield wall he broke off the attack and went back to help the foot soldiers who now battled their opposite number. That task didn't take long and soon the ground was littered with more, dead Saxon's.

In the elation of the victory Caratacus looked round and saw Arturus's horse, rider less and a group of men gathered round a prone figure still holding the severed head of Hengest in his hand.

Caratacus looked at Ambrosius as he dismounted and approached the scene. The old druid just looked up at him, closed his eyes and slowly lowered his head back towards the dying king. Kneeling at the side of Arturus he took the man's hand.

"We have all but wiped that group out; all we have left to deal with is that shield wall with the few cavalry that managed to reach safety. That should not take long in the morning." Caratacus brought his other hand to clasp the hand that was hanging limply in his other and tapped it lightly.

Arturus just managed to open his eyes slightly and gave a weak smile. "You will have to do that little job without me my friend. I have taken my last Saxon life," he could only just manage to nod at the gory object now lying beside him.

The two warring factions called an end to the fighting for the night. That wasn't until Caratacus had delivered the severed head to the Saxons, sending them the message of what awaited them come the morning. With the two tribes of Britannia taking the high ground, the Saxons set up camp where they had stood firm with their shield wall defence. It was the turn of the Saxons to be over looked while they built their camp fires and licked their wounds.

It was a sombre camp as men awaited for news of their king. Rumours spread as was the nature of war camps after a battle, about Arturus having been seen walking around with his ribs bandaged. Then another swept the camp proclaiming the king dead. Neither at the time Caratacus had gone to see him were true but the later was the closest.

"Arturus it is Caratacus can you hear me?" He asked wondering if he was too late. The king lifted his hand offering it to him and Caratacus took it immediately hoping that it was a good sign of his growing strength. There was no grip and the arm fell back only stopped by Caratacus holding on to it. "Ambrosius says you wanted to see me, what is it that cannot wait until morning?" he wanted to sound encouraged and confident that all would be well by sun rise.

Arturus beckoned him close with his other hand. His voice was pathetically weak and without having his ear next to his mouth he would not have heard what was said. "You are a brave, powerful warrior, a great leader and a good thinker, but you are shit at bluffing," Arturus smiled weakly enjoying his own humour. "I am done for and will not see morning my friend, promise me you will help Ambrosius return my body back to my own land, he knows were that is."

"You have my word on it."

We have inflicted great hurt on the Saxons today but many more will come and we cannot keep fighting them as our numbers grow smaller theirs will only continue to increase. Now is the time to negotiate a peace while we sit in a position of strength. Listen to Ambrosius if we miss this opportunity we may never get another. You alone can assure the ancient tribes live on and rid this country of our true enemy to the north." He dropped back breathing heavy and started to cough as he coughed a small rivulet of bright red frothy blood escaped from his mouth. He coughed more violently and frothed up more red bubbles. Caratacus backed off looking at the old druid for help. The old man came forward with a goblet and eased a potion down Arturus's throat nearly causing the subsiding coughing fitting to gain strength but as soon as the liquid hit his stomach he went to sleep and for the first time since he had seen him after the battle Arturus looked at peace.

"What did he mean?" Caratacus asked the druid.

"Well it's quite simple he wants to be returned to his ancestral home of Tintagel."

"Not that! And you know only too well what I mean."

"I am the lone person that can assure the ancient tribes live on and rid this country of our true enemy to the north." Caratacus repeated the words although the druid had been their but may not have heard.

"That is surprisingly close to the prophecy that Gluingel spoke of and at the time I thought he meant the Romans, then I thought he must have meant the Saxons, now Arturus says it's the Picts. Who in the name of the Gods are our real enemy?"

"Well eerrr..."

"Just for once can you not speak in riddles and give me a straight answer?" Caratacus jumped in, having guessed that something almost incomprehensible was about to escape from the old man's mouth.

"Did I not say that it is not always as straight forward as it seems, that you should look beyond the obvious? When the time is right today's enemy could be tomorrows ally. Just because new people enter your land it does not make then enemies, newcomers come in many guises, some might do our lands good, others on the other hand have nothing but evil in their hearts, read your foe and you might see away of them becoming useful friends especially when they fear you," when Ambrosius had finished Caratacus was silent as if absorbing what he had said.

Finally he answered. "Thank fuck you kept it simple!" his words laced heavily with sarcasm, he shook his head trying the rid the conundrum of the druid from his brain.

"You have always had a habit of asking stupid questions. Always when I am beginning to be impressed by you, your stupidity spoils it."

That is so very like what Gluingel said to me when I was a boy. It is you isn't it?"

The druid ignored the question but appeared slightly annoyed at himself which pleased Caratacus. "Arturus said it clear enough for you did he not?" He waited a few moments before continuing, repeating Arturus's word verbatim, reminding him of negotiating from a position of strength.

I will talk with Arturus in the morning when he feels a little stronger and clarify what he meant said Caratacus, turning to leave when the old man stopped him gripping his arm with surprising strength.

"You will not be able to I'm afraid, you will never speak to him again on this earth." Caratacus spun round to look at the peaceful expression and then realised why his pain had left him. The king was dead.

Caratacus walked around the camp. A strange peace was in the air, the thought of the morning's battle far from his mind.

Ruadan came up to him his face drawn as if carrying grave news, "I hadn't wanted to burden you with bad news as the kings wound must be of great concern to you?"

"Not anymore it isn't, what is it that bothers you Ruadan?" Brelus had joined them as he replied.

"Both Caracalus and Venpasian fell today. Venpasian took a spear in his guts and died in the field. Caracalus overran the stream and was thrown. We found him just before dusk his neck broken."

Caratacus sat on a nearby log devastated by the news. "Caracalus and Venpasian," he whispered to no one particular. "After all we have been through," he looked at the pair of friends who stood by his side. "So we are the last of the Brigante Gladiators. It is time to bring an end to all this fighting and for us to grow old and fat telling tales of our deeds to the young men until they scream at us to shut up." At that moment his path forward had become clear and he knew exactly what Arturus and the druid had meant.

"There's one more thing, I don't know if you have been told but we took a couple of prisoners today and one is the son of that new Saxon lord that is down at the bottom of the hill. Brelus saw his chieftain's eye light up.

"It seems that the Gods are lighting the way for me." Neither Ruadan nor Brelus knew what he was talking about but he seemed very upbeat all of a sudden.

A commotion was stirring across the camp so the three followed the migration of whispering warriors as they gathered outside Arturus's hut where Ambrosius stood. "Our great king is dead. I was at his side and heard his last wishes." He paused looking at the faces willing him on.

"What was it?" shouted someone from the crowd who could not bear the suspense any longer.

It was exactly what Ambrosius wanted and was playing his audience like a fish on a line. "He has told me where he is to be laid to rest."

"And, and!" they were begging for more.

"He named his successor.... Caratacus of the Brigante is to unite all the ancient tribes under the banner of Britannia. He will lead us to peace and prosperity and victory against our foe from the north."

There was silence for a second until the druid cried out. "Hail King Caratacus of Britannia, champion of the arena, soldier of Rome, protector of our homeland. The cheer started from within the Brigante ranks but soon spread to all. Ambrosius held his arms out to Caratacus who had moved to the front of the men and the cheering reached fever pitch.

The Saxons could also be clever and during the night having built their fires up in certain areas of their camp they had retreated using the darkness as their screen. There was no knowing how many hours start they had on the Brigante Cohort but the tracks were easy enough to follow. As a funeral procession took the body of Arturus to its final resting place Ambrosius accompanied Caratacus to Sut Saxum and the Saxon camp where Ælle had first come ashore and where his ships were still moored.

As the cohort approached Saxon riders went out to scout to see if any hidden forces trailed in the shadows. Caratacus deliberately made slow progress so this could be completed and the news returned to Ælle. The only thing the camp had that resembled a longhouse was one of the ships which had extra sails that had been spread to create a roof from bow to stern. It was hear that the two kings met.

As Caratacus came aboard he brought with him Ælle youngest son and freed him immediately. "We have all lost many men and some that are very dear to us. There is no point in continuing this bloodshed, it will only sap both our peoples so the Picts in the north can trample my weakened force when I have defeated you," he was remembering the words of Arturus and Ambrosius. Negotiate from a position of strength and he needed to ensure that Ælle understood that he had no doubt that the Army of Britannia would prevail in war continued.

"I thank you for your mercy and kindness in returning my son. You and your men are my welcome guest and as such, what is mine is yours. I hear what you say and although I doubt the outcome of further battles would grant you your victory I do share your sentiments of needless bloodletting other than that of the blue face bastards to our north. Before the Romans our people traded and lived amongst one another without issue. I see no reason why that should not be the case once again if both people are willing and the terms are agreeable."

There started day of talks and the two men grew to know and admire each other.

Before the sixth night of their stay as they prepared for a celebration feast, Ælle made an announcement to all present:

"Men of Saxony, I give you Caratacus of the Brigante, leader of all the tribes of this land, a great warrior who became champion of Rome and leads the people of these rich and plentiful lands."

There was much banging of ale mugs on the tables so Ælle encouraged the applause to calm down by waving his hands and raised his mug towards his guest, who acknowledged the introduction with a courteous nod of his head.

"Our people from this day forward are at peace with each other and are free to travel these lands unhindered. There will be no animosity between Saxon and the ancient tribes of this land and we pledge to each other to rid ourselves of the northern threat once and for all."

The rapturous reception that the promise of fighting the Picts got told of the Saxon dislike from the men from above the wall. Caratacus was very happy with the situation as giving them something else to concentrate on would hopefully preoccupy then for a while and the next part of the announcement was to ensure by the time that task was completed the two people would be one.

"Further bonding our two people is my debt to Caratacus for the safe return of my son without any demand for ransom. It is also my pleasure to announce that Thea Nelda my only and much loved daughter is to marry Caratacus and in time will produce blood ties between our families."

The volume of the cheering was ramped up even more and adding to Ælle's very pleasing description of his daughter's appearance which Caratacus knew might be a little exaggerated he heard encouraging comments such as, "lucky bastard," and "I would like to be him for one night with her," as well as some less tasteful but in their own way were also very positive. The only negative as far as Caratacus could see was the unknown wife he was getting as part of the deal. It sounded by the men's comments that she was as their leader had indicated, a fine looking woman but he had mentioned a couple of kids she had. This was slightly unsettling but remembering how his father took on his step mother and her son, he knew it was his duty and a small price to pay for the safety of Britannia.

It was time to leave for Tintagel. The body of Arturus had lain in the deep caves below the fortress where low temperatures would slow the decaying process down, but not for long. Ambrosius had to treat the dead king's corpse with special ointments and prepare it for its journey to the afterlife but he had followed Arturus's dying wishes by helping guide Caratacus in the negotiations that had just been completed.

Understandably it was a solemn ceremony where the enshrined body was placed on a long boat and sent out to sea. A row of fifty archers shot flaming arrows at the craft as the tides dragged it outwards. The timbers laced with a secret combination of oils and liquor caught readily and soon engulfed the vessel, quickest of all to be enveloped was the sail that carried the sign of the Britons. So he left the place of his birth for his final journey to meet up with his father Uther Pendragon and the Gods of the ancients: Teutates the God who protected the Tribes, Esus the provider and Taranis the God of Thunder.

Ambrosius once again acclaimed that Caratacus was the new King that united all the tribes and that he had announced it within the great circle of Glastonbury where the Gods had accepted the succession.

It was then time to return to meet his wife to be, who had been sent for by Ælle even before the trip to Tintagel. In the short time he had been away the Saxons had built up a respectable fortified village having had the foundations of a Roman settlement as a good start. It was with a little trepidation that the great warrior waited to see his wife for the first time. He sat at the right of Ælle and the gathering went silent as the father called his daughter in to the hall to meet her husband to be.

The hall was full of battle hardened warriors who had been drinking for sometime but the huge room hushed as the slender figure dressed in a delicate, white gown with green and red embroidery around the neck and wrists topped with a headdress of twisted Mistletoe, Alder twigs and Oaks leaves seemed to float into the room.

Her head was bowed in respect to her father and the man she was betrothed to.

Come my girl, lift your head and let Caratacus cast his eyes on the jewel of my life and you on him. Slowly her head lifted. Her hair had changed; it was blonde but her face familiar. His heart skipped and his smile broadened to such an extent that Ælle did not have to ask if what he saw pleased him. It did, it was Becuille.

"Do I please my lord?" she asked when their eyes met. The sparkle within her blue pools shone mischief and amusement, it also told him she knew the answer to that and her gently growing smile told everybody in the room that she was more than pleased with her chosen man. Not a person in the hall had any doubt it was meant to be, but only two knew it had already been and that fire had never died. Now Caratacus knew who the father of the two children that Ælle spoke about was and he would soon meet his son and daughter but not until he had reunited himself passionately with the beauty that was Becuille.

As the village was still under construction one of the ships had been converted into the bridal suite with the rear cabin having been extended and filled with furs. The noise of the cheering crowds diminished as they closed the cabin door behind them. Her nearest arm had been around his neck as he carried her across the deck, her outer arm hung down allowing her hand to brush his increasing eagerness with a regularity that caused Caratacus to almost run to find the privacy he craved. As soon as the door closed, she like he was in a frantic rush to discard the clothing that separated both sets of hands touching each other's nakedness and tease and reacquaint themselves and that they did with the pent up passion of years of longing. Her body was just the same perfection he had remembered and her inner warmth welcomed his hardness as he could not hold out against the building climax which resulted in him pumping his seed deep inside her willing sex. She took his wet manhood and worked it in her hands, while using her tongue to draw lines down its length. It did not take long before he was back inside her and this time it was a steady powerful rhythm that had the pair reaching a reciprocated pleasure locked in a lovers clench that wild horses would not part.

Food and ale had been placed in the room so after fortifying themselves they returned to their love making that lasted well into the night. Early the next morning they finished off the food and it was then that Caratacus asked for an explanation as to how he had found such a perfect solution.

"It was ordained that you should deliver the ancient tribes to freedom and save them from being wiped from the memory of men. Amergin Gluingel foretold of your destiny when we first became lovers and I carried our first child. Our second child is the girl we wanted and both will marry into the royal blood line of the Saxons and therefore our people will live on through them as the combined tribes and Saxons."

"But how did you become, well err..... Thea Nelda, daughter of Ælle?"

Do you forget that my mother is Flidas, Goddess of the Woodland? She can play many tricks with earthly men. In the Saxon tongue Thea means Goddess and Nelda, from the Alder trees when we first met where did you discover me?" she quizzed him.

"I will never forget the hanging mistletoe draped off the branches of the Oak and Alder trees."

She smiled that he could remember so vividly and continued. "Remember the Gods play a long game and look beyond just a single life time that is just a moment in a God's existence. Many people worship the Gods but have different names for them in their native tongue. Eostre is the name that the Saxons have for the one who brings spring and rebirth; she is Flidas in just another guise. I have been part of Ælle's family since being a child but with my real mothers help I could visit you when I was needed." She could see his confusion and smiled drawing herself close to him once again. "Do not worry about it my darling, we are together and we have our children who are our future and the future of our people." With that she pulled him back to the warmth of the furs.

When they finally made their reappearance the consummation of the union obviously pleased Ælle who along with his wife and sons gathered round the couple ensuring a warm and intimate welcome into the royal fold as they ate and drank to their health and it was them that Caratacus got to meet his two children who had been under the protection and supervision of Ælle's wife, Afton. With her three sons not having any children as yet these were her only grandchildren and it was clear that the pair doted over them.

It was a few days after meeting his children that Ælle called him to the newly finished longhouse. "Caratacus I cannot tell you the joy I have to see how you have taken to my grandchildren and the glowing pleasure that Thea Nelda radiates with whenever you are by her side." He slapped his son in law on the shoulder and whispered. "Hopefully it won't be too long before we have more little ones? At least you can as my son's only seem to like whoring and show no signs of settling down as yet. I swear I will be in my grave before they produce me an heir." He laughed at his own joke and then turned seriously to Caratacus. "How many men can you put in the field, it is time to head north?"

Revenge.

It took several days to gather his men and move the entire army north and set up camp outside Vinovia. He had persuaded Ælle to allow him time to set up his patrols so he could get a good picture of the whereabouts of the Picts. With the end of the winter weather it was the season for the raiders to go about their business of plundering the east coast so it did not take long for the reports of the northern invaders to arrive.

Ingarm of the Votadini had been away from his tribe since he had been used as a guide by Caratacus on their rescue mission into his lands. It was understandable that he would want to travel back to his people and to see his family once again. When he returned he had been fortunate not to have been taken captive. It was only the fact that he had taken the precaution to enter his village on foot under the cover of darkness that ensured it was only his family that knew of his visit. The Picts now lived alongside the Votadini across the lands he had once called home. Not all of his kinsmen were happy about the arrangement and it was those who wanted their regain their independence that had vowed to move south to join Caratacus. It was these men who were to bring the Pict raiding plans with them and would give Caratacus his chance to snare the one man he had never managed to better, Alvor.

It was Eboracum that once again was to be the first target of the season's attacks. Alvor had become more ambitious in Caratacus's absence. Half his army was to sweep down over the wall and assault Epiacum (Alston) a Roman earth work fort that had been re-colonised by some Votadini that had fled the Picts. It would not be much of a prize they probably just wanted to send a message to others who defied the new alliance where Alvor was by far the major partner. From there they planned to move south and hit the Brigante stronghold where they currently stood before carrying on to launch a landward attack on their main objective. This was to be coordinated with a seaward assault by the rest of the army and it was to be this one that Alvor led.

Although the whole area was under the combined rule of the Anglo-Saxons alliance it was the Angles that predominated Eboracum. So it was for Ælle to move his army up to join the Angles by ship and await the arrival of Caratacus so they could discuss the strategy.

"The people of Epiacum and Vinovia can hide in the hills and a small band of warriors with a cart that carries tempting but empty chests will retreat south ensuring a hard pursuit by the Picts who will think they are closing down on fine plunder." Caratacus was explaining his plan to Ælle and his sons before they meet the Angle war lord of Eboracum. If we hit them hard while they are still on the high moors and we stop them from warning their fleet we can take the land army before we turn our attention on the sea raiders."

Ælle was nodding his head in agreement. "I like it; we will outnumber them and have the element of surprise. We are at full strength and they only have half their force we just need to wipe them out so they can't warn the fleet."

Exactly and I have a special surprise I would like to welcome Alvor along the Ouse with. He went on to explain further.

They went to see the Warlord of the Angles. Acwellan did not command an army anywhere near as large as Ælle and was by far the junior member of the coalition. But it was common courtesy to have his blessing as the fighting would be around his fortress. Even Caratacus led more fighting men than the

Angle if you included the regular villagers who carried bows, a weapon that few Anglo Saxons bothered with other than for hunting. But it was these men that Caratacus hoped would make an impact out on the open moors.

As they came away from the war council Ælle placed his arm around Caratacus's shoulders. He could barely reach but it was done so as he could talk to his son in law quietly. "Hopefully we will make men of my boys in this battle and they too will get a head for thinking and balls for screwing like you." It was a rather strange comment but when he looked puzzled the grin he was greeted with somehow allowed Caratacus to understand what he was telling him.

"Is Thea Nelda in good health?"

The grin broadened even wider, "She's never been better, she as one mighty appetite but what would you expect when she eats for two!" Ælle had set off trying to remain calm about the news but the joy of having another grandchild on the way had got the better of him and he had babbled the last few words in excitement and now was shaking Caratacus's shoulder.

That night the family of warriors drank to the health of both mother and her unborn child before toasting each other for a successful battle with Ælle offering a drink up to Tiw the Saxon God of War.

Ruadan and Ingarm with the small Votadini force had been chosen to remain in the north to bring the Picts into the trap so before they arrived, the hills surrounding Eboracum was to be searched for Pict spies. Everyone was aware of the importance of keeping the seaborne army ignorant of what was happening on land. The odds of success were much better if they fought two battles where they greatly outnumbered the opposition as opposed to fighting one on even strength. Therefore Caratacus went with Brelus and Ælle's three sons to check the regular haunts.

Just as they had done all those years ago Caratacus and Brelus moved out of the town disguised as travelling merchants on heavy ponies with a cart carrying what looked like goods for sale. What was under the hessian cover was Cissa, Cymen and Wlencing who dropped out of the back of the cart when they had passed the rocky, overlooking cliffs that had been for so long the seat from which the ancient tribes had kept an eye on Roman daily business. Knowing the area well Caratacus and Brelus found a little used track that took them to the opposite end of the rocky scar where they started to make their way back towards the brothers.

The men from north of the wall were consistent if nothing else. They had taken up their position in exactly the same place as the men that had been killed and captured following Caratacus's last visit into the cliff tops. Firstly, just as before they located the horses and this pointed to three men that needed eliminating. Closing in on the position they had to beware that the three brothers was doing the same and care needed to be taken that they did not spring a surprise on each other. That was why Caratacus was ensuring that he and Brelus moved slow and precisely making sure of every step and checking for any signs of movement each time they rounded a rock or bush. A voice from over to their left gave away their targets hiding place, they dropped even lower into a near crawl, readying themselves for action at any moment. Every slight crack of a broken twig or an overturned stone seemed to be amplified a hundred fold to the pair, but they knew in reality that the wind whistling through the high ground would drown out such small disturbances. It was the heavy crash beyond where they suspected their prey to be that did earn a reaction. Calls of alarm were barked out in the guttural accent of the northern tribesmen and a sudden cry of pain. The fight was on and there was no further need for stealth. They had just gained their feet to push on through the bush that had hidden them when it was swept to one side and two blue painted faces appeared calling to some unseen comrade. Caratacus was just about upright and regaining his full balance when the two men move around the opposite side of the small stand of Hawthorne. It rammed the bush over to him and jabbed its thorns into his face unsettling his stance, just for them to run head long into Brelus, knocking him to one side before making their hasty way towards their mounts. The man at the back seemed to be injured as he was carrying his right shoulder awkwardly while still holding his spear in his opposite hand. The front man seemed to be without a weapon and had no intension of waiting for his fellow warrior. Caratacus spun to face the fleeing men while at the same time pulling his war axe from his belt. It flew in the lopsided end over end fashion that such an unbalance weapon would, striking the rear Pict on the back of the head. It did not hit cleanly but struck with sufficient force to cause a huge chunk of scalp to fly into the air surrounded by a spray of red. He wasn't dead until Caratacus had covered the few paces and plunged his Gladius between his shoulder blades. He looked to see why Brelus was not moving past him in pursuit of the front escapee realising in an instant where the lead Pict spear was. Brelus had a shocked, almost unbelieving expression on his face. He had tried to turn to follow their path and see what was going on behind him but the long shaft of the spear that protruded from his gut prevented his movement causing him to fall backwards into the adjacent bush. Caratacus looked on and saw Cissa come into view.

"See to Brelus. I will deal with this one," he called setting off and retrieving his axe as he did so.

The man in the distance had just a slight start but it kept

sufficient tall vegetation and rocks between the pair so he could not get a clear opportunity the hurl his axe. He was closing, but not fast enough to stop him reaching the horses but that did not concern Caratacus who knew that they had hobbled the mounts so they would take time to free. He had just transferred his Gladius into his left so his preferred hand carried his war axe when from nowhere the third Pict appeared from the left still doing up his breeches and calling out to get clarification as to the alarm. The spike on the head of the axe shaft ripped through his eye socket, penetrating deep enough to puncture the confused brain. As Caratacus ran past the hapless man the spike turned into a lever sending the dead man spinning to the floor. In doing so it pulled the weapon out of his hand and twisted him so he fell, head first into another Hawthorn bush. He felt each of the hundreds of thorns tear his skin, each individual barb leaving bleeding gashes across his face and hands. He stumbled back to his feet shaking his head to clear the fog of pain and taking his only weapon back into his right hand before recommencing his chase. When he got to the horses he was not surprised to find all three still hobbled and tethered to their original trees. One of the round shields had gone from one horse and for all Caratacus knew the man in front of him was now armed with a weapon. A crash away in the distance told him that the man was not intending to stand and fight but was in full flight, he took off after the noise and trail of trampled undergrowth.

They had been running for what seemed like an age and they were now on the open moors. The Pictish warrior seemed to know his ground as he had started to veer off to the east heading towards where the flotilla of war vessels would be arriving over the next few days. It was also taking his towards a small outcrop of large boulders that sat impressively in an otherwise flat landscape. The smaller man could move quickly but he was breaking fresh ground so Caratacus followed the trampled track and this made up for his disadvantage. It was obvious to the pursuer that the prey would head for the rocks and try to make a stand on the high ground so it was of no surprise that the man moved tightly round to the rear of the grit stone boulders and out of view.

Caratacus had been thinking of the different scenarios that might present themselves when they reached the rocks. One was that the man would just carry on running using the feature to give him temporary invisibility and with Caratacus being forced to show caution and slow it would increase the gap. But looking at the body language of the man in the distance he was sure that he was running out of energy, the thick heather and gorse having taken its toll. Also being in front he had no chance to see how well his chaser was doing so as was human nature he would assume the worst. No, he was going to have to make a stand and having the benefit of the rocks this seemed to be the logical place to do it.

Caratacus had lost sight of his adversary so slowed and moved round the ambush site in the opposite direction to the one that the other warrior had. It wasn't a huge feature but did dominate the barren terrain but it did allow Caratacus to quickly ascertain his assumption was correct. There was no sign of the man running beyond the rocks. Knowing that the man had been at the prominent grit stone feature for a while before his arrival he expected that he would gain height and look to use it to achieve the upper hand in the fight that was to come. He also knew the Pict would most probably be hiding expecting to see him follow the same route and therefore he might be more vulnerable by the approach he had adopted. His selected route brought him round so he faced into the wind. He was heaving trying to gulp down sufficient air to feed his greedy lungs, his heart was beating at the same speed as he had been running and would not be settling down any time soon. He needed to blank his bodily reactions out of his senses and focus on finding his prey; he might have been out of the forest, his most natural habitat but he still had that connection with the earth that the druid and Bechuille had taught him.

He sniffed the air as an animal would. It was faint but it was something out of place in a surrounding such as this. It was piss. Wherever the man was he had relieved himself while waiting. He was just below the base of the rocks and the human smell was growing stronger. One step at a time he moved then waited straining for another sign, and then he would move again. He was beyond the very back of the rocks from their direction of approach when the hairs on the back of his neck started to bristle. Out of the corner of his eye he saw a thin wet trail running down the course surface of the geology above and within an instant he brought his Gladius up above his head. A dark shadow momentarily hovered above him and that was the Picts downfall. The diving man led with his long knife, attempting to slash at his quarry below, but the short sword was still twice the length of the knife and held at arm's length above Caratacus's head the tip was piercing the man in midair before his blade came close to the Brigante warrior. Caratacus let the falling body's own momentum plunge onto the tip before rolling out from under the plummeting torso and directing the corpse on to the floor. He withdrew the blade and plunged it deeply through the man's throat, as he had done so many times in the arena. It was a long way back to the others and he was not intending carrying a dying prisoner.

His energy levels were depleted so it took time to return to the place he had last seen Brelus with the spear sticking out of his gut. During the long walk he had plenty of time to think of the sight he had left behind and as much as he hoped for the best he knew in his heart that such a wound if it did not kill instantly the victim was facing a much slower more painful death. He tried but failed not to think about it.

Two men lie prone next to the Pict camp fire. Cissa and Cymen tendered to their wounds and only responded to the noise in the bushed when Caratacus burst through brandishing his sword and recently recovered war axe. For all he knew more enemy warriors had been present and had retaken the camp. For all the two brothers knew Caratacus had been defeated and the Pict had brought others to help him retake the camp. His look of disapproval told the two young men of their mistake but that expression soon left him as he saw both Brelus and Wlencing.

"What happened to your brother?" he asked bending over his old friend and slowly pulling away the ripped cloth that had been packed against to large round gut wound.

"We had just got to the side of the Pict camp when one of them turned quickly. Wlencing thought he had seen us and charged catching him on the shoulder but took a blade in a groin."

Hearing his leaders voice Brelus managed to open his eyes and lifted his hand up trying to reach out as if those clouded eyes were unseeing. "Caratacus is that you?"

"I'm here my old friend."

"Did you get them?"

"Both dead, they won't be telling anybody about our plans."

"Good, so we were victorious once more?"

"As we always have been Brelus, now rest before we return to the fort."

"Caratacus!" he swallowed and partially choked on a dry throat grabbing at his arm as a bolt of fiery pain shot through his body. "I am done for you can see it, don't let me suffer, give me my weapon and let me face death as a warrior, despatch me cleanly my friend."

Caratacus stood, fighting back the anguish. It was how he would want to die, not overcome by an ever ravaging fever that stripped him of his dignity, but armed ready to fight to the death. He had seen the injury and his friend was right. It was a death wound. He placed Brelus's hands around the hilt of his sword that he had laid lengthways down from his chest and used his Gladius as he had done on the Pict warrior just a short time earlier.

Ironically the vantage point where they were was one that, years earlier when Caratacus had first become chief of his people, Brelus had often frequented when observing the Romans. It was where he would now rest for eternity.

The two brothers seemed concerned that the same lay in store for Wlencing and Caratacus saw it in their eyes. "Relax lads, only if he wishes it," and with that he placed his Gladius back in his scabbard.

More horses than men returned to Eboracum and the cart had just the one passenger. Like Caratacus, Ælle knew his youngest boy would not survive his wound.

A rider charged into the fortress with news. Ruadan and Ingarm had left Vinovia with the Pictish Army not far behind them. They had sent out raiding parties to try to bring the small retreating force to battle hoping they would fancy their chances against a smaller force, which would give the main invading force time to envelope the Brigante and Votadini band and take the cart that carried the treasure that was so tantalisingly close to the plunderers. Twice the Picts had been so desperate to slow down the retreat that they had over committed their patrols and paid the price, losing most of their men but managing to take a couple with them. Most importantly it had not slowed the withdrawal that to the Picts was seen as a head long retreat in a vain attempt to find safety.

The road that had been known as Dere Street was still an in

good state of repair and running through the high moors it provided the only speedy route to travel. It was why the ambush was set in the confidence that the prey would march into it without much fear of them taking a different route. Ælle had gone along with Caratacus's plan but had been surprised by his choice of site. On the high moors he was sure that there was very little change in the terrain and therefore needed to be reassured about its suitability for a trap.

"That's what is so perfect about the place," Caratacus explained going on to specify how he wanted things to work. It was his attention to detail that impressed Ælle the fact that he seemed to consider all aspects even the fact that with the Picts pushing hard would stay on the road and not slow their pursuit by trying to send anybody over the heather clad moors, not even riders. It was imperative to the overall plan. They needed this army to arrive days earlier than the war ships so each unit could be dealt with separately.

From a distance the northern approach to Eboracum was barren and featureless. To men unfamiliar to the area there wouldn't appear to be anywhere to hide a single person let alone an army. But to those who had travelled the route and hid from the Romans on many occasions they knew that by lying down amongst the heather the vegetation would spring back up and cover them if they took care. At the point where the attack was to take place the road was slightly sunken with the ground on either side rising gently for fifty paces when it dropped away in a very steady gradient. The two features allowed riders on horseback to remain unobserved by travellers negotiating the road.

Ruadan had noticed that the ponies pulling the cart had started to labour and he had got a couple of the Votadini to hitch their mounts to the sides to help pull. They only had the reach the next rise and they would have completed their mission. It would be down to the reception committee to deal the fatal blow. His heart was pounding as they crested the slope and looked across a plain open track of land that seemed to go on forever. Somewhere out there was an army in hiding; he hoped.

It was now or never as far as the Pictish leader was concerned. Away in the distance was the forest where his scouts would be watching, high up on the rocky scar that overlooked the fort of the Anglo-Saxon invaders. Once the cart reached there it was lost as they ran the risk of running into the enemy army and without the other half of the two pronged attack they would be very vulnerable.

Caratacus was lying on the crest of the eastern rise that paralleled Dere Street. Behind him was his cavalry but just in front of them and who was to commence the attack was his village warriors armed with their hunting bows. With a one armed signal they moved forward and eyed their targets letting fly with arrow after arrow. Until then in Britannia the bow was mainly a hunting tool but Caratacus had heard his old general, Stilicho talk of the killing power of banks of arrows fired at distance, killing so many without putting your own force in any danger. The old general would be proud of him he was sure. In the distance he could see the mayhem it was causing. Man or horse it didn't matter, the metallic tipped arrow did not distinguish between equine or human flesh it pierced either with impunity. The noble steeds if not killed outright, kicked out in agony smashing into the foot soldiers and unseating their riders. With the same number of archers on the opposite side of the road mirroring their counterparts to the east the Picts were caught with nowhere to go apart from back. As they tried to turn round to flee the arrows stopped and the whole ground spewed men armed with spear and sword. The chaos that had ensued following the hail of deadly projectiles meant that there was nobody to organise a shield wall or to take charge and try to counter the onrushing men. For some of the warriors from above the wall the first they knew of the attacking infantry was when they were struck down from behind.

As the noose tightened Caratacus made his final play. He led his cavalry moving them out of the low ground which positioned them to cover both front and rear; they then started to slowly move forward, with the infantry down each flank it reduced the perimeter width that held the doomed enemy. He was to lead the charge from the south and had Cymen at his side. With a long loud horn blast the infantry withdrew breaking off contact but holding position and without giving the defenders time to organise themselves. The spears of the cavalry was lowered and the trot became a canter which increased into a gallop just a few paces before plunging into what remained of the once confident hunters. Spears flew from the battered ranks of the besieged blue faced warriors but after that initial flurry they had nothing left but their disorganised swords and shields. That was no defence against what faced them. As the horse warriors withdrew the men on foot moved in with specific orders to kill every man so nobody would be left to warn the armada which as the battle died had entered the estuary of the mighty Humber unaware what had befallen their kin. Caratacus looked around trying to get a glimpse of Cymen, but only saw his black and white mount standing alongside a pile of bodies kicking its hoof into the reddened heather covered turf. Cymen had taken one of the Pictish spears square in the chest. The horse seemed to lament the death of its young master as it nosed the prone man's head trying to wake him up from a sleep that there was not escape.

Along with the customary looting of the dead Caratacus had his men carry the corpses off the road and out of sight, down the reverse side of the slope that the cavalry had used as their screen. It was not to enable other roads users' easy travel but the mountain of cadavers did created a substantial barrier to navigate, it was again to prevent however unlikely the scene being discovered by scouts and word reaching Alvor.

A large group of Angles had gathered and seemed intensely interested in something in the middle of the ranks. Caratacus went to investigate as their non participation was slowing the mopping and cleaning up, so hampering there march to the Ouse where he finally intended to pay back a long standing debt.

"It is Acwellan, he was dragged from his mount in the first charge," said Ruadan who had been at his side, on the opposite side of the two flanked attack to Caratacus and had seen the man's demise.

The Angles lifted their leader up on two of their round battle shields and carried the lifeless body over to the cart that had been the temptation that had drawn the Pict to their destruction.

Acwellan had lost his only son a year earlier in a battle with the Britons, his wife, the lad's mother had been taken by the fever years earlier. He had recently taken a new wife but had not produced an heir to take over the role of King of the Angles. With the now rich blend of Angle and Saxon mixed by a generation of allegiance it was Ælle that was immediately named the first king and recognised as overlord of all their peoples and the term Anglo-Saxon was permanently taken.

It was a very subdued army that prepared for their final battle. On returning to the fortress with their dead they had learnt that Wlencing had succumbed to his earlier wounds. Great plans to honour the dead leader as well as Ælle's two sons was to be arranged but before that there was the small matter of a showdown with the remaining enemy who had been reported as having set up camp close to the mouth of the great estuary of the Humber and were likely to be moving up into the Ouse over the next day or two where they would be sending out scouts to try to make contact with their vanquished land army. They needed to find this floating army and deal with it before they found that they were the sole remaining Picts south of the wall.

Ælle, understandably was a shadow of his former exuberant self. Of his three young brave sons who he had great plans for, he had just Cissa left alive. He allowed Caratacus to arrange the army for the coming battle, therefore several patrols were sent out to watch for the progress of the flotilla as well as to intercept any scouts, while the allied armies of the Anglo-Saxons and the ancient tribes re-stocked with weapons. The rest of Ælle's forces had arrived over land and brought with them the royal seat with all its accoutrements which included his remaining family. It meant that before they moved out Caratacus had just a few hours with Thea Nelda, his Becuille and their children.

She seemed totally unaffected by the loss of her brothers. "It is the will of the Gods and part of the greater plan that they have for us my love." Was all she said in acknowledging their passing. She saw his usual surprised expression. It was the expression of a naive mortal man, for all his great size, strength and intelligence, he still did not appear to grasp how the Gods worked their magic, full of mystery and intrigue, but always with a long term objective of protecting their people.

The few hours they had together was far too short, but he had enough time to make gentle love to his Becuille who encouraged him with her tantalising hands, massaging him into erectness, insisting that she was not some fragile little flower just because she was with child.

He looked back to the longhouse as he rode at the head of

the army, Becuille and their two children Brigid and Cerdic stood there waving at their father.

Two small scouting parties had been intercepted and from each one a single prisoner had been brought to Caratacus. He faced what he hoped was his final battle and thinking of what Becuille had said he wanted the Gods to grant him success, so both men would be questioned and regardless of the willingness to cooperate they would face the three deaths of blade, fire and water and where better to fulfil the final deadly chapter of the sacrifice but the very river that his enemy was sailing upon. That night he witnessed the Gods appreciation of his gesture as a shower of falling lights fell from the sky and as they did for the first time since he had been reacquainted with Becuille, Ambrosius walked into the camp as if he had been only missing for a few minutes. As the grey dishevelled druid approached Caratacus heard him call, "you performed that very well Caratacus, my brother taught you well."

Caratacus turned to see the old man slapping someone who looked almost identical to him on the shoulder in praise. It was Amergin Gluingel. So there had been two of them after all and he could tell by their dirty facial creases that they found their secret highly amusing.

"You old pair of......er... old rascals, it's good to have you with us," he was about to use a much stronger profanity but for some reason though better of it and instead dropped one great arm across each of the old men's shoulders with sufficient force to cause their bandy legs to give slightly. Realising his overexuberence he quickly dropping his arm down their backs to ensure they did not fall under his friendly blow.

They had managed to get plenty of information out of the pair of doomed warriors before they had met their fate. Both gave the same answers confirming its authenticity so a patrol was despatched to report back to Ælle. Not long after

Caratacus finally got the word he had waited for so long to hear. Alvor was indeed present and the small army seemed to be readying for battle and awaiting news of the other half of his army. They had camped on the side of the Ouse just a morning's march from Eboracum their ships anchored in a small inlet which kept them together and easy to control in the tidal waters. But it did make them an easy target.

Caratacus moved up with another patrol keeping his army well back and hidden deep within the nearby forest. He crossed the river, fording it up stream taking Cissa with him.

After watching the enemy for a short while and listening to what his men reported he was happy with his original plan of attack. "Cissa I need you to carry out probably the most important part of the battle," he lied to the only surviving son of Ælle as the king had asked for his son not to be placed in too greater danger. With the men on the opposite bank understanding their role Caratacus returned on his own to the king and the rest of the army.

Caratacus had wished that Ælle had stayed back at the fort but at the last minute the old king who had visibly faded since his recent losses had mustered his strength and seemingly reinvigorated his passion for war. He had insisted on coming along but had agreed to stay on the high ground with his bodyguard watching the proceedings. It was he who Caratacus came back to, confirming that his son was safe on the opposite side of the river to where he intended the fighting to take place.

"He wasn't happy but he is a good soldier and will carry out his orders, you should be proud of the lad," Caratacus complemented the old man.

His response was a slight nod of the head appreciating his remark. "So he will be the one who starts it with our surprise signal?" asked the king who was trying hard to remember something that had been explained just a few hours earlier.

It saddened Caratacus that a great leader and warrior should deteriorate so quickly, so he just nodded his confirmation before moving to join the troops.

It was unusual for armies of the time to fight at night, but that was what Caratacus liked to relying upon; doing the unsuspected. He didn't really expect Alvor to be off guard as it was to be a similar assault to the rescue of Aemilia just a short distance up the east coast, but it would be to his men and it was that element of hesitation and confusion amongst the ranks upon which he intended to capitalise upon.

Cissa was anger with Caratacus, but more so with his father. He knew that it was the king's hand behind why he had been moved out of the main battle. He would do his duty and carryout his instructions just as he had been given them but in fairness that was where his orders had ceased and after that point he was free to do as he saw fit. He would make the blue faced bastards pay for the death of his brothers.

It was a black sky with heavy clouds skipping along on a stiff breeze. It took the men on the opposite bank of the River Ouse some time to row their small craft across as they had the fight the strong cross wind that wanted to push the light animal skinned crafts downstream and away from the moored war ships. The river was not wide so after a little more effort than they had expected to use the circular vessels that carried one man and several pots of animal fat managed to work their way into the centre of the fleet and started to look for the ever vulnerable fire risk, the sails. As with all ships of their time, the sail was one large piece of material, slung beneath a single beam which was hoisted up a sturdy mast. When not in use it was lowered and turned through ninety degrees so it ran down the length of the vessel and the furls of the sail would spread across the deck close to the sides of the ship. The arsonists climbed using the oar holes and poured the treacle like coagulated fat down the inner side of these apertures watching it slowly spread across so as to near the vulnerable cloth. It could not be coordinated too closely as it depended how long the smouldering embers took to catch to the dry moss they carried.

It was always a tense time and Caratacus had been as still as a Roman statue, his eyes closed thinking how he wanted the battle to go, imagining, over and over the impending events and any possible last minute concerns. To his men he looked a picture of composure and that filtered down the ranks. The army were ready and confident that their leader would bring them victory once again.

"There can you see it?" asked Ruadan. It brought the instant reaction of his leader opening his eyes and looking down from the cliff top that overlooked the dark beach cove.

One by one small flickers of yellow light started to dance and as soon as they reached the height of the side of the craft they caught the wind and raced along the length of the sails climbing the masts. Soon there was a small forest of blazing masts, the flames being torn in the direction of the wind and sending brands like death sentences to the ships down wind.

"You know your orders?" It was a question Caratacus knew he needn't ask but did as a way of signalling he was moving to the low ground to lead the horse attack from the eastern end of the beach while Ruadan moved to take the western assault.

With the old king watching on Caratacus's archers moved forward on Ingarm's word. Once again there was a delay while they waited for the fire to take hold but this time the fat was readily warmed by men's body heat and the pre-prepared fire burst into to life. Each man in turn lit the flaming arrow and launched it at the men who had just started to stir as the alarm had sounded.

In the blackness, with the dark sea beyond the conflagrating hulls loomed large, a dense black object surrounded by violently cavorting oranges and yellows burnt the Picts eyes as they tried to focus on what was happening. Screams from behind had them turn to see hundreds of streaking bolts of lightning thunder down on them, it was as if the sky had dropped all its stars and everyone was earmarked for them. As soon as Caratacus and Ruadan had got to their men the stealthily placed assassins had moved forward and taken the sentries who had been identified by the observations of the previous hours. It took just a few minutes for the thousands of arrows to be spent and as the last star fell to earth the cavalry spurred into action followed by the men on foot.

Alvor had been wary of his position. But with the wind strengthening he had not been prepared to stay out on his ships in the mid channel of the river and wait for morning, when his march to victory would start. He had walked round the perimeter and had checked with his guards. The place he had chosen to land had both good and bad feature about it. It was hidden from being overlooked to the north by the high cliffs and gave good access along the sweeping beach to lower ground which led onto the flat approached to his target, but it did leave them open to a surprise attack. That was why he had posted so many lookouts and besides it would be unusual for his enemy to attack in the night. There was only one man he could remember who liked to attack during the night, when the slain would not be found by their Gods. His mind had gone back to that time on the east coast when he had experience the feeling of fear as he had seen the giant Brigante bearing down on him. The thought of his brother's death and his resultant survival crossed his mind as a cold shiver ran down his back. How like that night it was.

When the call went out that the ships were ablaze his

internal alarm bells had started to ring immediately. Too many ships were burning at the same time for it to be an accident. His men were racing to fight the fires when he called.

"Form a defensive semi-circle, backs to the sea, shield wall...." He had not finished his command when the sky over the cliffs lit up with a thousand dancing starbursts taking his men by the dozen. With flames at their backs and it raining down on them it was as if they had been swallowed by the fiery depths of the underworld.

"Shield wall, now. Prepare for an attack!" he called once again gathering his troops and getting some shields above their heads just as the hail had started to lessen. Peering out of the slits from beneath the overlapping shields Alvor saw the last of the arrows fall slightly short thudding into the sand and extinguishing itself.

The Picts had formed up well into a strong defensive unit, when the sand began to dance around there feet. They knew a cavalry charge had started and braced themselves.

Caratacus led his men down the sandy beach each hoof plant deadened by the softness of the ground. Looking at the defenders who were illuminated by the maritime furnace at their backs he could see dead bodies littering the area but was impressed by the discipline of the enemy. The first men in the charge carried newly cut timber staffs that had been sharpened at one end. They were nearly twice as long as the standard spears they expected the Picts to be carrying so he hoped to punch holes in the wall before the warriors behind could follow through.

The canter gathered pace and culminated into the gallop, Caratacus watched in amazement as the Gods granted him the sort of good luck that spells victory for one side a defeat for another. As the ships burnt, the masts had become unstable and crashed to the decks sending huge chucks of burning timber flying, some into the rear of the shield wall that started to disintegrate as men tried to avoid being burnt. The surge forward by the rear ranks pushed unevenly against the front just as the lances hammered home. The second wave of riders set about the broken wall disrupting it further still until it fell apart with men looking to flee either way down the beach. It was exactly what men on foot should not do when faced with cavalry, but the heart sometimes does not do what the head tells them when under such a threat. They had not gone far in their flight when horsemen caught up and slain them from behind. The now disorganised rabble had stopped to try individually to fight of the horsemen when the troops on foot arrived. The men from north of the wall were spent, their energy long gone and the adrenaline that had carried them thus far had started to wane. This last rush of fresh fighters was just too much and the first swords were thrown to the ground in surrender that soon became an epidemic.

Alvor had kept his bodyguard close to him. He knew who was behind this and for all the heat that was still radiating from the flame engulfed hulls he was cold with dread. He had seen the first rider appear from the darkness carrying the spear that seemed to be the size of a tree. It was carried with such ease it could only be one man. The man he had thought about earlier that evening. The one warrior he knew he could not beat in combat. Caratacus of the Brigante.

Alvor waited for the inevitable splintering of the defensive wall and the race for survival and had used that confusion to lead the guard into the waters to swim to the far side of the river.

Caratacus had hammered his lance into the wall just where two shields overlapped. Each man in the charge had cut the largest staff he could manage, so it was no surprise that his was by far the biggest, thus enabling the blow to break the arms of the men behind the shields, rendering them useless in the fight to come and therefore easy prey. His momentum had carried him beyond the line of shields having struck in at a shallow angle. Even as he brought Vulcan back round to charge again the Picts were in disarray and beginning to flee. He had brought out his war axe and Gladius and gone about his bloody business chopping with axe, stabbing with sword. He kicked with his armour covered legs. He was a one man demolition team and the Picts wanted no part of him and rather faced the other, slightly less deadly horse warriors.

As the infantry arrived Caratacus had looked back towards the collapsed hulks as the flames receded into the black water. He had now one objective. Alvor.

Caratacus hoped he hadn't been killed by the charge or the flaming arrows; he wanted him so he could fulfil his vow of revenge that he had uttered when the Romans had taken him prisoner under the towering cliffs and the great wall all those years earlier.

He smiled as he saw a group of men slinking off down the far side of the last wreck.

"You men," he called to a group on foot. "You take my horse and take good care of him, the rest of you come with me, and I hope you can all swim?"

With the last of the battle taking place at the western end of the beach Ælle and his personal guard had made his way down to the opposite end and were moving across the flat shoreline as Caratacus set off in pursuit of the head of the snake. He had got a good start and once again it appeared that luck had favoured him as Caratacus was sure that it was going to be impossible to track him if he was out of sight. He looked across to see the king pointing very animated to the rear of the end ship that was still burning, albeit a much less impressive sight as it once was. Gentle flickering orange flames wafted in the wind and gave a dull illumination to the scene that Caratacus heard before he saw.

Cissa had sworn over his brother's dead bodies that he would avenge their deaths and spending the final battle on the wrong side of the river was not his idea of keeping his vow. He and the other men who had paddled their little circular craft over to start the fires had stayed just off the back of the end of the last ship waiting to be sure it was safe to join the fight. By the time they heard the shields clatter under the cavalry onslaught and paddled the ungainly crafts ashore the fighting had moved up the beach and well out of view. They were just stepping on to the shore when a group of men with blue painted faced charged round into view. Cissa knew they were it trouble immediately, they had only just put down their oars so had no weapons in their hand something the enemy definitely did. They were also in the process of gingerly stepping on to terra firma so had no momentum and again the enemy did.

The fight was frantic. The Picts wanted to make good their escape and had no time for a fight that would slow them down. Even the slightest delay could spell the death for their leader and all were sworn to defend him to the last man. The guards were big men for Picts, they were some of the best warriors in the army and charged head long into the stumbling men who had surprised them having appeared from nowhere. Cissa had just managed recovered his sword but none of his men had shields available when the two sides clashed. The first Saxon was run through with his sword only half way out of the scabbard but the deep thrust of the killers weapon slid between his ribs separating two and jamming, as the body fell it ripped the sword from the attackers hand and it was his turn to be sliced open with a cross cut from Cissa who gaining a little forward speed brought the broad blade up and down across the side of another's head. The fight was taking place in knee deep water and the small light craft were scattered in the melee. The guards formed a wall and moved to one side to allow Alvor time to enter the water, but as he did he could not help himself, he turned and drove his blade into the back of the nearest man.

It was in full sight of Ælle. The old king watched his last son die, stabbed in the back by a fleeing Pict. At the same time Caratacus had just arrived and saw the young man drop to his knees in the water and fall face down with a fatal slash.

"Nooooo!" The kings cry was heard by all and Alvor looked round to see who had made it. He saw Ælle and his guard turn and move towards him. They were fifty to sixty paces away so he knew he would be able to lose them; it was the giant apparition of death that had just loomed into his vision, lit by the ghostly almost haunting orange, burning glow like a beast being released by the Gods of the underworld. In one arcing sweep of his mighty arm a war axe was sent thudding end over end towards the Pictish leader. In a flash Alvor grabbed one of his men and pulled him back from his ensuing fight. The man looked perplexed at his leader for the briefest of moments until his head was driven sideways by the force of the heavy broad axe blade as it crashed into his head smashing his helmet which gave sufficient resistance to bring the bottom half of the cutting edge round and carve his jaw away from his face. The men who were with Caratacus moved in, the tables were now turned. It was the Picts who had been stopped in their tracks and the new arrivals joined the fray at pace. The men from north were, as usual as brave as any warriors Caratacus had experienced as they protected their leaders flight. With Ælle's guard now closing in they were as good as dead but it was their duty to buy Alvor as much time as possible and Caratacus knew it. Running forward he first retrieved his axe and then almost simultaneously picked up the shield of the man that had been slain by Cissa. Holding the shield at arm's length he ran at the hastily constructed protective wall of Picts and like a human battering ram crashing through them sending men flying and marking them as easy targets for the men behind. He pushed his war axe down the strap across his back and plunged into the water following the light grey disturbance in the water some twenty paces ahead of him. He did not require to start to swimming until he was nearly a quarter of the way across the river instead he just waded making up a good distance on the panicking Alvor who had not realised how shallow the water was until he had committed to the swim. When he did dive forward he got a further boost in speed and almost grabbed the foot that struggled ahead of him. After the first few strokes Caratacus felt his armour pull him under, he kicked and jostled hitting the bottom of the silty riverbed and pushing forward and upwards launching himself in a series of explosive leaps, gasping air each time he broke surface before being taken back under. He managed to find a rhythm that allowed him to propel himself forward in this unorthodox manner until suddenly he was hitting the bottom and his head was still above the surface. He reached to his side and tore at the straps that held his chest and back plate, with that gone he felt the amazing difference. It was a strange time to curse his own stupidity but he did. What on earth was he thinking about entering water in full armour? He was now waist deep and wading looking from side to side for any sign of the fugitive. He was going to need to be free of his leg armour so he reached down and wrenched the two off.

Alvor had been lying in the shallows gasping for breath, hoping that the phantom of his demise had himself been dragged to the bottom when to his dreaded, amazement he had resurfaced like a whale breeching the water splashing down and dropping below the surface once again. He did not count how many times this marine manoeuvre happened but each time it brought his nemesis closer. The final time he was free of his armour and the push had allowed the crazed giant to stand just a few paces from him. He saw Caratacus look one way then the other, he had not seen him. Then his chance arrived, Caratacus was reaching down his legs and was concentrating on something other than finding him.

He rose from the dark waters dragging his sword free and charged. The water was just below his opponent's knees, but that made it well over his and his charge was more of a watery, swirling shuffle and gave the big man ample warning of the attack.

Caratacus looked up as the disturbance in the water was not hard to hear. He had been working to remove the second shin guard when the assault took place, his attacker being far too close to allow him the reach for his weapon. Everything seemed to slow down and played out in his head mapping out the assaulting moves. He looked at the twisted screaming face of the man he had wanted to kill for so long and then at his body angles. He was dropping his none sword arm and shoulder back which warned him that Alvor was about to lunge with the weapon. He was going to strike at Caratacus's left so he counted the move by twisting to his right while bringing his metal shin guard across and catching Alvor on the temple.

The side step and blow had the effect of speeding the charge up and past the defender. The Pict had thrown his metal helmet off before he had entered the water so the solid shin protection struck the unprotected temple sending the clang and subsequent ringing filling the skull of the assailant. He managed to stop before the combination of the head blow, the water and exhaustion caused him to lose his footing. Alvor spun round leading with his sword blindly waving it menacingly to where he expected to see his adversary. Once again Caratacus had seen the balance of his foe change signalling his intended move and had already moved further round behind him almost following the move that kept him on the blind side of this antagonist. He had transferred the shin guard to his left hand the brought it smashing down onto the hand holding the sword breaking several fingers that released the pressure that enabled the weapon to be wielded.

Alvor firstly was surprised that his opponent had seemingly disappeared, but as he continued his turn he saw a peripheral movement momentarily before feeling the pain in his hand. Secondly and more concerning to the Pictish leader was the involuntary opening of his shattered hand and the slowness of his cherished sword falling with a plop into the light grey waters below. He never really realised what the blunt object was that hit him square in the face. But the result was total darkness and more buzzing in his head before a semi-unconscious feeling of drowning.

The sound and taste of bursting bubbles and cascading, saltwater filled his mouth and head; he was screaming in anger and panic but was unable to gain his feet and his heels slipped on the riverbed. Water was rushing up his nose clogging the back of his throat and he started to choke. Suddenly he felt a force grab him by his chest and lift him free from his watery grave; the resonance of running water was the deadly aquatic world pouring from him and a slight lightness on the other side of his closed eyelids gave a little hope. He was just risking opening his eyes when he saw a massive black object rush his face and the crunch of crushed cartilage replaced the marine sound effects.

At the same time as the shin armour had struck its target there was a satisfying crunch of bones splintering. Caratacus had almost simultaneously thrown his right elbow out catching

Alvor squarely across the bridge of his nose with such force that his challenger had been thrown backwards, his feet actually coming free of the water before following the bloody mess of his head back under. It could have been the end of the battle. All he needed to do was hold the little bastard under for a while until the pathetically thrashing figure was drown but that would have been too easy. He reached down and grabbed at his enemy's chest dragging him free of the water with his left hand. He just saw the eyes flicker he smashed his fist into the painted face, further reducing the similarity of the features to that of a human face.

Ælle was still standing over the prone, figure of his dead son and heir. They had pulled him from the shallow waters the damp matted hair and wet clothes made him look all the more pitiful. He was leader of the Anglo-Saxons and in front of his men he should not show the weakness of being heartbroken but he could not help it. In a matter of just a few days he had lost all three of his sons. Each one would have made a fine king in the fullness of time but that was not to be. The kingship would now have to jump a generation to his grandson and with him approaching his later years he would need Caratacus, young Cerdic's step father to guide the youngster in his formative years if he was to die. That was if Caratacus was to survive the night? It was a question that now filled the king's head; he had last seen his daughter's husband disappear into the inky dark waters chasing the little bastard who had killed his son.

The prisoners had been gathered and they were used to carry the injured and dead. The few provisions that had been brought by the Picts had been gathered and the victors took their spoils and drank around the pyre where the dead Picts were thrown. The dawn was struggling to break the night's grip, when Ruadan called to one of the men who had been on

246

the far bank with Cissa.

"Did you leave anybody over there?" he was pointing to the far river bank where a large fire had suddenly broken into life.

"No we all came over on Cissa's orders; he did not want to miss the fight." Was the reply laced with a hint of regret.

"So who as lit that?"

The river was not too large that you would not be able to clearly see who or what was on the opposite bank when morning fully lit up the gloom. The fire was being kept well fed and a large figure was seen moving in front of the dancing flames. They continued to watch as things became clearer. Even before the light allowed a true recognition they knew it was Caratacus. The size alone gave that much away. He was standing next to a large tree that was at the top of the river bank, almost over hanging the water. A man was tethered to the trunk, his arms tied so they were held pulled up over his head exposing his bare torso. Caratacus was sharpening his axe blade on a stone, very deliberately so the man could see what was happening.

It was Amergin Gluingel who answered the question on everyone's lips.

"Caratacus has completed the will of the Gods and is about to deliver on the pledge he made many years ago. Ambrosius Aurelanus nodded his agreement as every man present line the northern bank of the Ouse and watched.

"I live with the moon," Boomed the voice from across the water.

"I live with the stars," as this was said a shower of embers from the fire crackled into the sky.

"I cherish the earth as she cherishes me," he bent down and touched the ground.

"I am the trees, I am the waterfall, and I am the air that you breathe."

A swift move of the axe sliced the prisoner from one side of the abdomen to the other. The prisoner was still alive even with his guts reaching down to the floor. He ripped at the liver raising it up to offer it to the sky and the forest in the background then took a bite out of it.

"I am the wolf, I am the bear, I am the eagle," he reached up into the chest cavity and tore free the beating heart and once again showed it to the sky and forest. Another shower of embers burst from the fire which had without help had regained its earlier life. Another bite was taken and the organ cast onto the flames. With the improved light, all could now see that the unfortunate prisoner was the Pict, leader Alvor. He was still very slightly moving as Caratacus took some embers and placed them into the bloody aperture of the hanging torso. The sizzling smell and steam seared the bleeding and filled the air, the final cry of defeat left the sacrificial body as he was chopped down with one heavy thud of the mighty war axe and the carcass tumbled down the bank into the water.

"Accept this sacrifice, killed threefold as the ancients would have it. Blade, fire and water. I am your servant, the appointed one who as defeated the tides."

Caratacus waded into the water and cut of the head of the corpse and showed it to the men on the far bank. He took it with him as he crossed the river and presented the trophy to Ælle as a tribute to his fallen sons.

"Had you foreseen this?" Caratacus asked Becuille. He was referring to the news that he had just been given by her father.

"Foreseen what?" she answered with a slight trace of the theatrical to her voice trying almost too much to sound shocked that her man should think such a thing.

"You know all too well what I am getting at," he grabbed her and pulled her to him. For the moment the question was dropped they had better things to be doing and it started by her pressing her thigh against the front of his breeches and gently gyrating taking his mind entirely off the questioning.

In the early hours she looked at her husband he was awake looking at the moon that shone through the window opening. "Remember the prophecy spoke of you "defeating the coming tides"?

He turned his head to look at the beauty that lay beside him, she continued without him answering. "The land has faced the Romans and the Gods removed that tide as it had run its course. The Angles joined the Saxons neutralising both those tides. You led the Anglo-Saxons to victory in battle over the Picts, that tide is now gone and we have started the process of ensuring that the ancient's blood runs within the veins of the Saxons. There are more ways than giving battle to turn the tide of invasion, sometimes a little cunning and stealth can do as much as the largest army. Our son Cerdic will lead the Anglo-Saxons and within his chest beats the heart of a pure bred ancient of Britannia. He will take a Saxon wife of my choosing and strengthen his place as the first Saxon king to settle this land but his roots will remain those of the ancients. With you at his side nobody will dare challenge. The Gods are happy my husband.

Historical Note.

The period following the withdrawal of Roman rule over Britain has been dubbed the dark ages for the lack of documented evidence of what truly happened. With the Romans gone so were the chroniclers and most of the men who would first write of the period would not actually walk the lands or if they did it would not be for many years. It is said that the "Chronica Gallica" tells about the provinces of Britannia, suffering various defeats and setbacks and being reduced to Saxon rule. This documentation was done from a great distance from these shores. The work of Gildas called the "*De Excidio et Conquestu Britanniae*", was of the sixth century and was possibly written by a man who saw the Christian moral qualities degrading by the Saxon pagans, so could be biased? Venerable Bede takes side with some work of the two previously mentioned chroniclers agreeing and also offering up his alternatives, but this is from a man who lived from 672 AD to 735 AD. More contemporary documents from the likes of Geoffrey of Monmouth started to include the rather grand the glorious Arthurian legend along with Merlin and the round table, thus adding disputably fictional characters that surely discredit the accuracy of the work as this dates from the twelfth century. As time goes on hopefully the archaeologists will discover more concrete evidence that will give a truer picture of these events, but in the meantime it leaves the door wide open for the imagination of the author of this book.

In the following few paragraphs the author will try to set out fact from fiction as far as his limited knowledge of the subject allows as well as pointing out some of the disputed events. He will also separate the fictional characters from those which are evidenced as true. It is not always possible to follow the chronological order of events when a storyteller is trying to weave fact and fiction together so please excuse the slight inaccuracies remembering that the academics cannot agree on many of the dates and outcomes. But the author tries to cover each area he views as needing clarification in the order in which they appear in the text:

Caratacus, the hero of the tale was a real character and as is suggested in the story the name of an early Brigante resistance fighter who would not bow to the wishes of Rome. His queen and king who had embraced the invaders and for his insolence towards them. Handed him over to the Romans where he was taken to Rome and put on show.

At the time of the Roman invasion Britannia was divided into several separate warring kingdoms which made the land easy to take as no allegiances meant no one army could stand up to the might of the Roman war machine.

The boy who was named after the real Caratacus and his father are fictional figures as are his tribal comrades. His people, the Brigante was a British Celtic tribe who are thought to have held territory which now forms Northern England and was the largest Brythonic Kingdom in ancient Britain. Isurium was the capital of this kingdom standing on the present day Aldborough, North Yorkshire. Spiritually they worshipped Brigantia who was the Goddess of the Brigante. Their lands, as suggested would have mainly consisted of moorland, marshes and forests which would be populated with beasts such as the Eurasian brown bear, wild boar, bison, wolf, deer and eagle. It was truly a wild place.

One of the other tribes of ancient Britannia who were feared by the Romans and therefore heavily persecuted and suppressed was the Druids. Arguably the greatest of these mythological druids was Amergin Gluingel and that was the reason for including him as Caratacus's mentor, the man who possessed the magical powers to transform a normal young man into a super being in just a short time. Written records of the druid's existence seem to tell of them disappearing around the second century but that does not mean they had all been wiped out; after all was not Merlin of the Arthurian Legend not a druid? His existence has been linked to a Romano-British war leader called Ambrosius Aurelianus the name twisted by some to become a figure called Merlin Ambrosius, this is possibly where Geoffrey of Monmouth came upon the name? In any case the author chose to portray the two old men as having more in common with the shamans of tribal societies than with the classical philosophers that some might argue the druids were. Late accounts in the tenth century chronicle, Commenta Bernensia does claim they made human sacrifices to the three deities, Teutates, Esus and Taranis and as in the author's story this was by, blade, burning and drowning, respectively while Oak and Mistletoe seems to have played hugely in their ritualistic events. The author added the presence of the use of Alder as he attempted to tie the Gods of the druids to the Saxons to establish the connection between the two using Becuille, daughter of the woodland Goddess Flidais and the daughter of the Saxon chieftain Thea Nelda whose name is explained in the book as Saxon meaning "Goddess" and "From the Alder trees".

The end of the Roman occupation of Britannia was similar in many of the ways to that told in the storyline without the individual fictional actions that the author portrayed. But with pressures from the tribes across the rest of Europe as well as Pict, Scotti, Saxons, Angles and Jutes all wanting stakes in the occupied homelands the Roman Empire was creaking and had to shrink to enable it to defend its borders.

One of the great mysteries of the Roman age in Britain was the disappearance of the Ninth Legion which has been the centre of many theories, films and books. The last attestation of their existence is an inscription in Eboracum or York as it is known today in 108 AD but it is widely accepted that the Legion Hispania as they were also known was lost from the Imperial records between 120–197 AD. There has been a theory that suggested it was as a result of a Brigante revolt, translated records have been interpreted as saying that *"Under Hadrian there was a terrible catastrophe"*. This could be the reason that the Emperor Hadrian had the wall built in the first place? But it is clear that the calamity happened several hundred years before the evacuation of Britannia as the author suggests, but he wanted to give the young leader of the northern Brigante a great victory and have him meet the fictitious Pictish leader who would betray him and drive him so hard to seek his revenge.

It was not only external strife that hindered the Roman Empire. Internally it was equally as hard to know who was friend or foe and emperors had to fight to keep the empires. But the relationships between Emperors Theodosius, Honorius, the usurper Constantinus and General Stilicho, himself are generally correct as are those of the lesser generals Iustinianus, Nebiogastes, Edobichus and Gerontius. The roles that Sarus and Aleric play in this story are also not far from the popular facts. The great general who at one time could have taken the throne while leading and protecting the young Honorius (as many would have) was responsible for the victories that brought the two parts of the empire together and was rewarded by Honorius's father Theodsius by marriage into the imperial family. All his military success did not protect him when others eventually won the ear of the ungrateful Honorius who eventually had him executed. Not only did the young emperor oversee the general's execution but his son Eucherius was to meet the same fate, presumably being too much of a risk to be spared. This lack of appreciation for his top general was all the more hard to understand as Honorius had been married to Stilicho's eldest daughter, Maria until her death in 407 AD when he then married the second daughter Thermantia. Clearly in imperial Rome blood was not thicker than water!

Without Stilicho to run the armies, Aleric the once Roman ally and his Goths became the first army in generations to sack Rome. Aleric got an unsuspected boost in numbers when the families of the barbarian *Foederati*, the foreign mercenaries that fought for Rome were slain throughout Italy by the local Romans. It resulted in an estimated thirty thousand fighters joining the Goths. The empire survived for many years after this disaster but it had passed the zenith of its powers and a steady decline would set in.

The gladiatorial events that had been such a central part of Roman life had started to fade with the introduction of Christianity but the Author used the followers of Mithraism, a very warrior based and bloodthirsty religion that remained popular in the army as the reason the emperor kept the games alive. No emperor however stupid wanted to upset the army. This allowed Caratacus to win his freedom and show his prowess as a warrior.

Cheshire was home to the largest Roman amphitheatre in Britain, used for entertainment and military training by the Twentieth Legion, they were based at the fortress of 'Deva' (Chester). It is one of the few sites where evidence of gladiator combat has been found, York being the other where a burial site of decapitated would be gladiators have been used as proof they existed in Eboracum. It was why the two sites appear in the story for the novice gladiator to start making a name that would lead him to the Coliseum

The gladiatrix is a modern term for the female equivalent of the gladiator. Like their male counterparts, female gladiators fought each other, or wild animals, to entertain audiences. Very little is known about them. They were considered an exotic rarity by their audiences. Their existence is known only through a few accounts written by members of Rome's elite, and a very small number of inscriptions were female gladiators, where they regularly were described as Amazonians.

King Vortigern is thought to have been a fifth century warlord but once again several interpretations of the period differ and some suggest it actually referred to the position and not the person. But accounts by Gildas talk of the Saxons being invited to the shores of Britannia to help defend against the Picts and Scoti. The small group grew to a large group and soon they had carved themselves a small kingdom in the south of the country. More warlords' arrived and new kingdoms stolen. Bede, two hundred years later near paraphrases this but says in addition that the *"proud tyrant"* Vertigernus (a variation on the spelling of Vortigern?) negotiated with the Saxon brothers, Hengist and Horsa.

The Anglo-Saxons under Hengist took the fight to the Britons to reinforce their claims of greater lands, defeating them at The Battle of Wippedesfleot (Ebbsfleet). Following the death in battle of Horsa, Hengist turned to his son Æsc, together they delivered even more bad tidings over the coming months. The betrayal of Vortigern by Hengist at the "Treachery of the Long Knives" is said to have taken place on Salisbury Plain as the author suggests but once again the chroniclers have their own spin on the event. The Anglo-

Saxon chronicle fails to mention any such treachery while the Briton Nennius states that Hengist had his men attend the banquet with concealed knives and massacred the unsuspecting Britons.

It is at this point the author introduced a little of the Arthurian Legend that still today grips the imagination and through this the beguiling Becuille brings forth Cerdic who will eventually take over the leadership of the Anglo-Saxons following the death of King Ælle's three sons Cissa, Cymen and Wlenching. Bede has claimed Ælle to be the first king to be overlord of the Anglo-Saxon kingdoms. It is thought that instead of Cissa being killed he did in actual fact inherit the throne from his father. It is hard to see how this lineage saw a certain Cerdic of Wessex being cited in the Anglo-Saxon Chronicle as a leader of the Anglo-Saxon settlement of Britain but when the author saw that the name Cerdic might be derived from the much older Briton name of Caratacus he saw an opportunity to ensure that the ancient tribes maintained their bloodline albeit mixed with that of the Anglo-Saxon. Many academics suggest that this is exactly what did happened. The old tribes of Britannia could not have been wiped from the face of the earth but instead would have been absorbed into the predominant race as new and old peoples joined as one over a period of time.

It is a very complicated period of history and the frustrating lack of credible evidence is on one hand annoying. But for a writer this maze of unknowns allow for boundaries to merge and time to fly or even go backwards. But on the whole the author as maintained something close to what he believes to have happened with the exception of our intrepid hero who at the end of this tale is still a young and powerful warrior with his son and a kingdom to protect.

37418167R00155

Printed in Great Britain
by Amazon